Murder Served Neat

Also available by Michelle Hillen Klump

The Cocktails and Catering mysteries

A Dash of Death

Murder Served Neat

A COCKTAILS AND CATERING MYSTERY

Michelle Hillen Klump

CROOKED LANE

NEW YORK

This is a work of fiction. All of the names, characters, organizations, places and events portrayed in this novel are either products of the author's imagination or are used fictitiously. Any resemblance to real or actual events, locales, or persons, living or dead, is entirely coincidental.

PUBLISHER'S NOTE: The recipes contained in this book are to be followed exactly as written. The publisher is not responsible for your specific health or allergy needs that may require medical supervision. The publisher is not responsible for any adverse reaction to the recipes contained in this book.

Published in the United States by Crooked Lane Books, an imprint of The Quick Brown Fox & Company LLC.

Crooked Lane Books and its logo are trademarks of The Quick Brown Fox & Company LLC.

Library of Congress Catalog-in-Publication data available upon request.

ISBN (hardcover): 978-1-63910-234-1
ISBN (ebook): 978-1-63910-235-8

Cover design by Brandon Dorman

Printed in the United States.

www.crookedlanebooks.com

Crooked Lane Books
34 West 27th St., 10th Floor
New York, NY 10001

First Edition: February 2023

10 9 8 7 6 5 4 3 2 1

To Edward and Evaline, with all my love.

Chapter One

Samantha Warren served what felt like her thousandth Sparkler—a red, white, and blue layered cocktail she'd created in honor of the Fourth of July. She topped it off with several dashes of bitters and a sprig of mint before handing it to the customer in front of her. With the flavors of rum, mint, and orange from the blue curaçao, the drink was refreshing enough for a beach vacation but patriotic enough for the holiday revelers at the Highlands' inaugural Independence Day festival.

Business had been so brisk at her booth that Samantha had barely had time to breathe, much less notice the commotion by the gazebo. But a loud shriek and the crowd's gasp drew her attention to a fight near the picnic tables, where festival organizer Patty Davis appeared to be ready to throttle the regal figure staring her down.

"You witch!" Patty's coppery curls flapped as she launched herself toward Highlands society matron Angela Clawson, who stood rigid and unyielding as she faced her attacker. With one hard shove, Patty pushed Angela to the ground. Patty's mouth flopped open for half a second, as if she was shocked by her own strength, before her hands clenched at her sides. "You're ruining everything!" Spittle flew through the air as Patty glared at the woman at her feet.

Angela clutched at a bench and clawed her way back up to a standing position. Not a silvery strand of hair out of place in her elegant wedge bob, a stoic Angela dusted off her Diane Von Furstenberg wrap dress, readjusted the chunky necklace around her neck, and drew up to her full height so that she towered over Patty. With one bejeweled finger outstretched, she stabbed Patty in the shoulder, punctuating her words. "This festival would be nothing without me!"

Patty's face flushed scarlet as Angela turned and pushed her way through a cluster of Highlands High Marching Band students, stalking toward the VIP tent.

Festivalgoers appeared to hold their collective breath for a moment as they waited to witness further fireworks. With none forthcoming, the crowds returned to their hotdogs and snow cones, ready to move on to the next-best entertainment option—a German brass band performing on center stage.

"What was that about?" Marisa Lopez, Samantha's best friend, dropped off a platter of food at the cart, motioning for Samantha to sample one of the glistening German-style sausages on the plate.

"I don't know. I've never seen Patty lose it like that." Samantha pushed her blonde waves behind her ears, getting her hair out of the way before she bit into the sausage, puncturing the crispy skin and releasing its flavorful juices. "Anyway, you'd better not leave my mom alone for too long. She's liable to get lost, and we'll have to call up a search party."

Samantha's mom, Lillian, had zero sense of direction. Even with the navigational tools on her phone, she was prone to getting turned around.

Marisa rolled her eyes. "She's not that bad, Sam. She's waiting with Beth over by the stage. Come find us when your relief arrives."

Samantha waved at her friend and again turned her attention to a line snaking toward her booth. Hustling into overdrive, Samantha poured drinks and chatted with customers, enjoying herself and smiling appreciatively at the tickets that filled her till.

The day was going well. When her mother, an old friend of Patty's, had suggested that Samantha work the event, Samantha had initially resisted. She'd been unconvinced that custom cocktails would draw much interest at an outdoor festival where hotdogs, sausage, and brisket were the chief attractions. But she'd happily admit she'd been wrong, and made a mental note to thank her mom for the recommendation.

I hope everything is okay with Patty, she thought, replaying in her head the earlier scene in which Patty shoved Angela to the ground. Samantha suspected the fight stemmed from a long-simmering feud between the two women about the tennis club.

In the week of planning meetings prior to the festival, Samantha had heard more than her fair share of griping about the controversial tennis club project that had threatened to divide the Highlands' German Lodge a few months before its one-hundred-and-twenty-year anniversary.

The controversy had played out on local television news and neighborhood blogs for months. A group of well-heeled Highlands residents searching for land to build a new country club–style tennis complex found the perfect location on the grounds of the Highlands' German Lodge, a social club dedicated to preserving the rich German Texas heritage in the region.

The lodge sat on nearly fifteen acres of undeveloped land on the outskirts of the Highlands, deeded to the organization by one of its founding members in the early 1900s. Originally intended to accommodate a school, a banquet hall, and housing for German families, most of the land remained undeveloped. Local scout troops rented it out for summer camps, along with yoga studios for the occasional yoga or spiritual retreat.

Tennis-center backers originally offered to buy the land to build their club, but when lodge members refused to sell, the tennis club organizers proposed an alternative plan, described as a win–win for both organizations. Under the proposal, the tennis club members would join the lodge and form a separate club within a club. Their members would get access to the land to build their tennis center, and the lodge would get access to a steady stream of income.

Half of the original lodge members appreciated the infusion of new life and cash into their aging organization, while the other half, led by Patty, believed the central mission of the lodge—to preserve and celebrate German heritage in Texas—would be lost. Lodge president Adam Muller had championed the tennis club project as a way to help fund needed repairs to lodge buildings, and Patty's side suffered defeat. The tennis club project was underway.

The Independence Day Festival, the resurrection of an old community tradition, was meant to be a public kumbaya occasion, showing that the lodge's rift had healed. But obviously, judging by the scene between Patty and Angela, there was still work to be done.

If nothing else, the controversy had been good for business, with the publicity drawing a large crowd to the festival. Customers flocked to Samantha's cocktail booth. She glanced at her watch, counting the minutes until Mila, the college student she'd hired to work the next shift, would show.

"Mila!" She waved to the girl walking toward her, corkscrew curls bouncing with each step. "Over here."

Samantha had met Mila during her first unofficial cocktail catering job earlier that summer—the job that had ultimately led to her joining in with her friend Beth to start the cocktails and catering business. Mila had helped her out during that earlier job, and Samantha wanted to repay her. Not to mention, Mila was a great worker.

"Hey, Sam." The girl pulled her bouncy hair back into a ponytail and pushed up her sleeves. "The crowd is nuts."

"I know—it hasn't slowed down since I opened." Though they had run through the steps earlier in the week, Samantha again showed Mila how to make the drinks, watching to confirm her proficiency before leaving her in charge of the booth.

Samantha was due at the VIP tent, summoned there by Angela Clawson, to make fresh Sparklers for around a hundred guests. The request came with a nice tip plus the opportunity to meet potential new clients among the well-to-do members of Highlands society, so Samantha readily agreed.

Lugging her supplies with her, Samantha plodded to the air-conditioned tent filled with a crowd of well-coiffed ladies in designer sundresses and men clad in khaki shorts and loafers. Much of the crowd was already drinking wine and grazing from tables laden with fancy hors d'oeuvres, with nary a hotdog or snow cone in sight.

As soon as Samantha rolled her supplies into the tent, Angela waved her over to an empty table. "Samantha, I've been telling everyone they must taste your delicious cocktails. Set up over here, and you can pass them around when you're ready."

Samantha busied herself assembling trays full of the drinks, ready to be delivered by black-clad servers. As she garnished the next set of cocktails, Samantha gazed up to find Angela back at the table, dragging along a pleasant-faced, auburn-haired woman.

"Olivia, you've got to meet Samantha. She runs a darling little cocktail and catering service and makes the best drinks. You absolutely must hire her for Matthew's fiftieth birthday soiree. The club will be finished by then, and it will be the perfect place to celebrate." Angela held the woman under the elbow, as if to keep her from running away.

Olivia's smile tightened. "I've told you, Angela, Matt and I haven't finalized plans yet. We aren't even sure there will be a party, much less at a particular location."

Angela huffed. "Nonsense. Of course, Matthew wants a party. I think I ought to know my son."

Olivia's blue eyes turned steely as she practically bored holes into her mother-in-law's forehead. "Angela, we've discussed this. I will let you know when I want your input."

Angela raised one eyebrow in warning. Samantha noticed a slight flinch from Olivia as she turned toward Samantha and offered a more welcoming smile. "I loved your drink. It's so festive and refreshing."

"Thank you." Samantha smiled back and turned her attention back to her drinks as Olivia broke free from her mother-in-law's grasp.

Angela remained standing in front of Samantha, unruffled by her daughter-in-law's hasty retreat. "Samantha, let me have a handful of your cards. Even if Olivia won't accept it now, I'll pass it on to her later. I'll hand them out around here too. I'm sure there are dozens of potential customers in this tent alone." She held out her hand expectantly toward Samantha.

Samantha reached into her jeans pocket and handed Angela a stack of the business cards she kept on hand, just in case. "I appreciate it, Ms. Clawson."

"Nonsense. Your drinks are delicious." She flounced away and joined a cluster of women congregated nearby.

"Are you ladies having a good time?" Angela puffed out her chest like a peacock showing off its feathers. "Can you believe that by next year, we'll be able to enjoy drinks at our own clubhouse after a game of tennis? I'm so looking forward to it."

"I saw the pictures of that handsome tennis pro from California you are trying to hire. He can help me with my backswing any day of the week." A brunette with a pear-shaped figure grinned lasciviously at Angela, who choked on her drink.

Samantha giggled to herself as she kept her eyes on the group, amused at their birdlike tittering. One woman in the flock, however, did not appear amused. The woman, fashionably dressed in a red, white, and blue wrap dress, and with what Samantha could only describe as big Texas hair—blonde, curled and teased within an inch of its life—had a major scowl on her face.

I wonder what's up with her. She doesn't seem to be in the party spirit. Samantha turned her attention back to her last tray of cocktails. When she'd finished garnishing them and passed the tray along to the nearest server, she gathered her supplies for the return trip to her booth.

She spotted Angela across the tent, engaged in what appeared to be an intense discussion with the scowling blonde woman. As Samantha passed by on her way to the exit, Angela caught her eye and her expression abruptly shifted. "We'll discuss this later, Calista." Angela turned from the blonde woman to face Samantha; the wide smile of a beneficent queen stretched across her face. "Thank you for stopping by, Samantha."

As if I had a choice. Samantha smiled a little stiffly. Though she was grateful for Angela's help, she was annoyed by how much appreciation Angela seemed to want her to show. "Thank you for the opportunity."

After a nod from Angela signified that she'd paid the proper homage, Samantha rolled her cart out of the tent.

Back at her booth, she checked in on Mila and made up a last, smaller tray of cocktails before crossing the grassy lot in search of her mom and friends. She found them in front of the main stage, all three heads bopping in time to music from a bluegrass band. Beth chuckled at something Lillian said, and Samantha admired their easy banter as she waited for the song to end before walking up to her mom.

"Hey, Mom. Are you tiring Marisa and Beth out?"

Her mom grinned. "Oh, honey, we're having the best time . . . But I have worked up a thirst and could use one of those fancy drinks!"

Samantha passed cocktails out to her mom; Marisa; and Beth, Marisa's girlfriend. She saved one drink for herself.

"Samantha, this is delicious!" Lillian sampled her cocktail. "You know, I hate to admit it, but when you said you were giving up journalism to start a catering business, I was a little worried. But if your food is as good as this drink, you and Beth will make a name for yourselves in no time."

Samantha glanced at Beth, hoping she hadn't taken offense to Lillian's comments. "Thanks, Mom."

The band announced it was taking a quick break, and the women sat down at a table off to the side of the stage to wait them out.

As they chatted about the festival, Samantha noticed a large crowd form in front of the stage, where Angela stood with a middle-aged man clad in khaki shorts and a white festival volunteer T-shirt. After a screech of feedback, the man coughed into a microphone. "Hi there. I'm Adam Muller, president of the Highlands German Lodge." The man droned on for a minute or two, welcoming the crowd and promising them a wonderful time at what he hoped would be a new annual Highlands tradition.

The man paused, beaming as he surveyed the surrounding festival, before Angela nudged him. "Oh yes. And with me here is Angela Clawson, head of the Tennis Club Committee, to say a few words."

Angela snatched the microphone from the man, her loud voice booming out over the crowd. "As Adam said, we are so glad you could make it out as we celebrate our venerable Highlands institution and create another one by opening the Highland's Tennis Club. I hope you will join us tomorrow for the groundbreaking for our brand-new stadium court!"

Adam retrieved the microphone from Angela and smiled again at the crowd. "And now, ladies and gentlemen, it's time to dance."

The crowd gathered near the front of the stage roared its approval, as the band launched into a rendition of "This Land is Your Land."

Marisa pointed at Angela as she walked off the stage. "That's the woman from the fight earlier."

"That's Angela Clawson in the flesh. She's been fighting with mom's friend Patty for weeks about the tennis club. Patty is one of the old guard at the German Lodge who thinks Angela is cramming the tennis club idea down everyone's throat."

Marisa raised her eyebrows. "Well, that lodge president didn't seem to mind sharing the stage with her."

Samantha took a long sip of her drink as she watched Angela disappear into the crowd behind the stage. "She hasn't made many other friends among the lodge members, but I have to give her credit: much of the success of this festival is because of Angela's organizing. You know, she used to chair one of those big foundation benefits for the Med Center. Not to mention, she's been nice to me. She offered to pass our cards around to her wealthy friends."

Marisa grinned. "It never hurts to have friends in high places."

Lillian, who had been listening, frowned. "I'm glad she's helping you, but if Patty doesn't like her, I'm sure she has a good reason."

Her frown disappeared as a banjo sounded the first notes of a popular bluegrass number. "The music is starting again!" Lillian jumped to her feet and moved toward the stage.

Samantha shrugged as she grinned at her friends. "Thanks for hanging out with her, but I'm free for a bit. You guys should go have fun."

Marisa and Beth finished their drinks and headed toward the carnival booths, with Marisa challenging Beth to a ring toss game. Samantha strained her eyes to pick out her mom from among the whirling dancers. In the middle of the crowd, she spotted Lillian twirling around the dance floor with a man whose only discernible features were his bushy gray beard and the orthopedic shoes that did not appear to slow him down in the slightest.

With her mom occupied for the time being, Samantha pulled out her phone and took a minute to call David. Butterflies fluttered in her stomach as she recalled her last evening with the handsome lawyer who had helped her out of trouble a month ago. They'd met up at The Continental Club to hear a local blues band. Samantha felt a flush of pleasure as she remembered the sensation of David's warm hand pulling her toward him as they danced, and the sparkle in his green eyes as he sang along to the music. At the end of the evening, he'd kissed her, leaving no doubt that, contrary to the song's lyrics, the thrill was most definitely not gone. Samantha, feeling overwhelmed by a rush of emotion, had pulled away, telling David she wanted to take their developing relationship slowly. Now, missing him, she wondered whether that had been a mistake.

David had flown to New York City on behalf of a client on Thursday and was staying in the city for a gallery showing of the paintings he sold as a side business to his law career. He wouldn't be home for a few days, and Samantha wanted to wish him luck. She dialed his number and felt her pulse quicken at the sound of his voice on the voicemail. "Hi David. It's Sam. I'm working a festival tonight, so I only have a minute, but I wanted to wish you luck at the show tonight. Take care."

I hope that wasn't awkward.

Her thoughts returned to the present when the song ended, and Lillian led her dance partner over to meet Samantha.

Now that the dancing had stopped, Samantha could get a better look at him. She grinned as she noticed the red, white, and blue birthday hat, sitting askew on the top of Thomas Jefferson's head on the front of the man's shirt. She took in his khaki shorts and pale legs, clad only in the white athletic socks and black shoes, which seemed to serve as the de facto uniform for men of a certain age.

"Oh, Sam! You've got to meet my new friend!" Lillian bubbled over with exuberance, her brown hair damp with sweat from the dance.

The man smiled and extended a beefy hand. "Karl Brandt. Nice to meet you. Your mom is the real deal—she can dance better than most of the women out there!"

Samantha shook his hand as she gave her mom a quizzical expression. "You two were quite the pair. I never knew you could dance like that!"

Lillian laughed. "Oh, honey, there's a lot about me you don't know! Anyway, we were just having fun. Karl's a longtime lodge member. When I mentioned my daughter made the cocktails for the festival, he said he had to meet you."

The man nodded his head and grinned. "I'm an old-timer—been a member here for over forty years. I told your mama I had to meet you because that was the best cocktail I've tasted in years. What's your secret?"

Samantha smiled, basking in the praise and enjoying the chance to talk technique for a minute. "You have to pour slowly to keep the layers from blending. Of course, the drink inevitably ends up a shade of purple, but it's festive for a little while, at least."

Karl nodded his head. "A woman after my own heart—someone who takes the time to do things right and to honor something important." His face hardened into a grimace as he shifted his gaze toward the VIP tent.

There was no doubt in Samantha's mind as to the object of his disdain. "I take it you're not a fan of Angela Clawson? She doesn't seem to be winning too many popularity contests around here today."

He scoffed. "That woman doesn't belong here. She only joined us because we've got something she wants—land for her silly tennis club."

Samantha had heard a dozen versions of the same complaint from Patty and a few others she'd met at the lodge, and she had no interest in listening as Karl relitigated the whole sordid story. "Well, hopefully everyone can bury the hatchet and come together—it's quite a milestone to hit one hundred and twenty years!"

Karl's eyes flashed for a moment. "It is a major milestone, and Angela acts like she can lay claim to all of that history. I've had enough of her." He took a breath, as if he were counting to ten, and smiled. "Forgive this crotchety old man. You two gals enjoy the rest of the festival." He gave each of their hands a last meaty shake and headed back into the crowd of dancers near the stage.

Samantha and her mom sipped their cocktails and wandered around the grounds, taking in the sights. They meandered over to the auction tent to check out the assortment of handmade crafts. While browsing a display of embroidered napkins and handmade candles, the pair ran into Patty, who had just arrived at the tent to check on volunteers.

"Patty!" Lillian called out to her friend. "You look like you haven't stopped to take a breath in hours. Come chat with us a minute."

Patty indeed seemed harried, her tight copper curls frizzing from the humidity, as she used a lace handkerchief to wipe her brow. "I can't stop for long. The other volunteers mean well, but you know the saying: 'If you want something done right,' and all that. Anyway, it's been worth it to see everyone enjoying the festival."

"It's been so much fun. You volunteers really outdid yourself. It was such a great idea to relaunch the Independence Day Festival." Lillian beamed at her friend. "We were going to indulge in a couple of funnel cakes. Can you join us?"

Before Patty could answer, her walkie-talkie squawked, "Code red emergency. The police are en route to the construction site."

Patty's face turned ashen. Samantha steadied the woman with her hands for a few seconds, before Patty regained her composure and raced for the exit. "I've got to go."

Samantha and her mom exchanged worried looks. "What could that have been about?"

"Let's find out." Lillian dashed after her friend.

By the time they caught up with Patty, half of the festival had joined them, drawn to the flashing police and ambulance lights over by the dig site for the tennis stadium. When Samantha peered through the crowd, she noticed the cops had roped off the perimeter around the construction site and were attempting to fashion a makeshift curtain to hide a covered form from view. They weren't quick enough to block access to a teenager who was snapping photos over the curtain with his cell phone. "It's a body!"

Chapter Two

Samantha gasped as she felt a familiar sinking sensation in the pit of her stomach. *I don't want any part of this.* She rubbed the raised scar on her left arm, almost as an afterthought.

Only a month ago, a different body had turned her entire world upside down, and she'd been forced to solve a murder or risk her reputation being ruined. She'd landed on her feet since then, partnering with Beth to start their own business. But Samantha was not eager to relive the experience.

She grasped her mom by the arm and steered her away from the scene. "Come on, Mom. Let's get away from here."

Lillian yanked her arm back from her daughter and pushed her way through the crowd. "No, Samantha. I want to find Patty."

As Samantha followed her mom, the police pushed the crowd back away from the construction site and into the main festival grounds. She caught up with her mom and shepherded her to a nearby table set up by the food booths. "We'll find Patty later. I'm sure she's all right."

Lillian's shoulders drooped. "I hate for something like this to happen and ruin all of her hard work."

Samantha gazed around at a crowd of hundreds, still chowing down on hotdogs, listening to music, and browsing the craft booths. Most people seemed completely unaware of the situation on the other side of the grounds. "Nothing appears ruined so far. We don't even know what happened. Maybe someone had a heart attack."

Even as she said the words, Samantha didn't truly believe them. With the number of police swarming the grounds, whatever had happened didn't strike her as an accident.

As they sat waiting, Samantha's phone buzzed. It was Marisa. "What's going on? Beth and I were trying to find you guys, and we noticed cops everywhere. I even spotted your old buddy Detective Sanders. If he's around, it can't be good news."

Samantha's eyes widened at the news. Jason Sanders was a homicide detective. Samantha had had a few run-ins with him during the earlier murder investigation. Though they had parted on good terms, she had hoped never to run into him again in a professional capacity.

Samantha told Marisa to meet her and Lillian by the food booths. As she hung up the phone, she noticed her mother staring at her.

"What is it?" Lillian clutched her daughter's arm. "I saw that face you made. What does it mean?"

"Marisa recognized a homicide detective. He's the same one we met during the last . . . situation." Samantha saw no reason to hide anything from her mom. News of a murder would spread soon enough.

Lillian clasped her hand over her mouth. "Murder? Another one? I've always defended your decision to live here whenever my friends talk about the dangerous big city, but now I'm beginning to consider their point."

Samantha rolled her eyes at the familiar topic as she spotted Marisa and Beth in the crowd. "Come on, Mom. Murders can happen anywhere, even in quiet Corpus Christi. But don't worry—I plan to steer clear of whatever is happening on the other side of that crime scene tape." She waved her friends over.

Marisa and Beth drew closer, Beth awkwardly clutching an oversized plush eagle. "Word is filtering through to the crowd." Marisa gestured her arm toward the exits, where the police had erected a perimeter and appeared to be collecting people's contact information before allowing them to file out into the parking lot.

Samantha pulled out her phone and scrolled through her Twitter feed, confirming her suspicions that the dead body had become a local trending topic. Already she'd seen several retweets of the photo of the covered body taken by the teenage boy at the construction site. "You guys should head home too. Can you drop Mom off? I need to go check on Mila and help her close the booth."

Lillian protested, "I want to find Patty."

"Mom, it's already chaotic out here. We'll never find her. Not to mention, I'm sure she's going to have her hands full. We can connect with her later, I promise."

Lillian pushed her shoulders back, as if girding for a fight, but grimaced as the crowd jostled forward. She lost her balance and reached out to hold on to the edge of the table. "You know what? You're probably right. We should leave before we get trampled. But promise me you'll hurry back to your apartment."

"I will, Mom." Samantha gave her mom a quick hug and thanked her friends before setting off for her booth on the other side of the food tents.

When she reached the booth, Samantha found a long line still stretching around the next tent, full of people waiting for one of her cocktails. Despite her anxiety about the likely murder, Samantha flushed with pleasure at the sight of so many people willing to wait for one of her creations. At times, she still couldn't fathom that this was her life. It was so different from the fumbling, directionless existence she'd led only a few short months ago. As she contemplated her change in fortune, a shout broke her reverie.

"Sam! A little help here?" Mila waved, her curls drooping under the weight of the sweat that poured off the girl's forehead. "It's crazy. I can't keep up!"

Samantha climbed into the booth and carefully prepared the tricolored drinks, passing them to Mila with each order. They developed a rhythm and made fast work of the line until they served their last customer.

"I wanted to try one of your drinks before the police shut the festival down." A young woman exchanged a ticket for a cocktail and took a taste, dabbing her forehead with a handkerchief.

"Why do you think they'll close it down? The police haven't closed it so far." Samantha held a cup of ice against her forehead to cool herself as she spoke.

"My cousin's been working in the grill tent closest to the construction site. He said the dead lady is one of the festival organizers, and from what he heard, the police seem to think it's an inside job. If that's the case, I doubt they'll let the festival continue . . . unless, of course, they can quickly arrest the murderer." The woman drained the last of her drink and threw the clear plexiglass cup into the recycle bin. "Thanks. This was delicious."

Samantha waved goodbye, troubled by the woman's words. Of course, it might be idle gossip, but if the woman was right, the police might force the festival to shut down early. She surveyed the grounds, which were rapidly clearing out. In her mad rush to serve all the customers in the line, she hadn't noticed how quickly the festive atmosphere had faded.

"Well, I hope for our sakes, she's wrong. Otherwise, we'll lose out on a lot of money, and I'll be stuck with more blue curaçao than I will ever know what to do with." Samantha helped Mila clean up the booth. "I guess we're done for today. Let's leave everything for now. I'll let you know when I hear something about whether I'll need help running things tomorrow."

"Can I walk out with you? To be honest, I'm too creeped out to go by myself." Mila waited while Samantha secured the booth for the night.

The two women walked toward the exit, joining the last few stragglers on their way to the parking lot. Once she'd walked Mila to her car and turned toward her own, she noticed two police officers escorting someone from the exit closest to the construction zone. Curious, she inched closer to see if she could identify the person being led to the back seat of a police unit. The white T-shirt was the same worn by all the festival volunteers. When the officer stepped away from the back door, Samantha had a clear view of the back seat. She clapped her palm toward her mouth as she recognized the copper curls. The police had Patty!

Chapter Three

Samantha's stomach sank as she watched her mom's oldest friend being driven away in the back of a police cruiser. She tried to convince herself there was a less foreboding explanation. Maybe the police needed Patty's help identifying the body. But that hardly seemed likely. The rumor from her customer about the dead person being a festival organizer left her with a bad feeling. What if it was Angela Clawson? Samantha closed her eyes, recalling the fight half of the festival had witnessed earlier between Angela and Patty.

Patty, what did you get yourself into?

Samantha didn't relish the idea of telling her mom about Patty, but she realized it would be better for Lillian to hear it from her than from the evening news. She considered calling David again, hoping a chat with him might steady her nerves. But the impulse to call him at the first sign of trouble was the exact reason she had wanted to take their relationship slowly. She didn't want David to regard her as a perpetual damsel in distress.

Her ruminations took her to the steps leading up to her garage apartment. She felt a warm glow as she peered inside her kitchen window at her mom and her friends laughing together around her table, sharing a sleeve of Oreos. She hated to ruin the moment, but the news couldn't wait, so she opened the door and strode inside.

Lillian's face fell as she caught a glimpse of Samantha.

"Honey, what's wrong? Is everything okay?" Lillian jumped up from her chair and stepped toward her daughter.

Samantha hated to share the news. "Mom—the police put Patty in the back of a patrol car."

Lillian dropped her arms, which had been reaching toward her daughter. "Patty, with the police? Why?"

Samantha reached her mom and pulled her in for a hug. "I don't know, Mom."

Lillian gasped, clenching Samantha's arm in a vise-like grip. "Patty would never hurt anyone."

Samantha caught Marisa's eye, and they exchanged a knowing look.

But Lillian, attuned to her daughter's every move, noticed. "What is it? What are you two thinking?"

Samantha described the scene they had witnessed between Patty and Angela Clawson and explained to her mom the drama between the two factions at the lodge: the traditionalists, who didn't want the tennis club; and the others, who had thrown their lot in with Angela's crowd.

Lillian listened but shook her head. "That means nothing. Honey, I've known Patty for over fifty years. I can assure you, she might argue or call a person names, but she is incapable of murder." She grabbed her purse and began rifling through it before she pulled out her cell phone. "I'm calling Martin."

As Lillian dialed the number and walked into the living room for more privacy, Samantha gritted her teeth. Though she couldn't stop her mother from calling Patty's son under these circumstances, the irritation she felt at hearing his name was hard to hide.

Beth, always perceptive, was the first to notice Samantha's grimace, tilting her head with a questioning look.

Samantha rolled her eyes. "Martin is Patty's son. Let's just say he's not my favorite person."

Beth pursed her lips. "Why?"

Samantha shrugged, feeling foolish about the long-standing grudge. "It's nothing, really. We've known each other since we were kids, and in college he turned into a massive jerk after I went out with his roommate. I haven't seen him much since then, so clearly I should get over it."

"It depends on what he did." This time, Marisa raised her eyebrows.

"He was generally a jerk, which I could handle. But he crossed the line when he tanked an interview I had lined up with one of his fraternity brothers for an investigative story I was going to write involving a hazing scandal at the university. I'd been working on that piece for months—it was going to be my ticket to internships at a major newspaper—and he ruined it with a few words. I know it doesn't matter anymore in the grand scheme of things, but I couldn't believe that someone who was supposed to be a friend of mine would attack me in such a personal way. Anyway, listen to me . . . poor guy's mom is being questioned by police, and here I am dwelling on a grudge from college." Samantha turned toward her mother, who had just ended her call.

"Martin hadn't heard anything yet. He'll call the police and see what he can learn." Lillian's shoulders sagged as she collapsed onto the couch. "Poor Patty. I can't imagine what she's going through right now. She believes she's invincible, but this could break her."

Samantha flopped down beside her mom and patted her hand. "Hopefully, it's no big deal, and the police will let her go soon. If we're lucky, they'll find evidence that will lead to the killer."

Even as she said the words, she didn't believe them. She chewed on her lower lip as a growing sense of unease caused her muscles to tense. If it had been a simple ID of a body, or a few quick questions, the police would have released Patty hours ago.

Beth and Marisa began straightening up the kitchen.

"The festival was fun until now. Hopefully, the police will clear up this mess quickly." Marisa picked up her purse and nodded at Beth, signaling her desire to leave. "It was lovely to see you, Lillian."

"I hope everything works out with your friend." Beth smiled at Lillian before turning to Samantha. "Sam, I've got the Clarks' baby shower in the morning. Before I go, do you have the syrup and bitters ready for the mimosas?"

Samantha opened her refrigerator and pulled out two bottles of homemade mint syrup. She put them into a bag along with a bottle of her special aromatic bitters. While she worked the second day of the festival, Beth was catering a baby shower. Their little business needed to earn as much as possible in these early days, to pay off their investments and to provide a cushion against slow times. "Here you go. This should be more than enough. For the mocktail version for the mom-to-be, skip the bubbly."

"Got it. Good luck at the festival tomorrow. The shower should end by three PM. I'll be around after that, if you need anything. But for now, we'll leave you two to rest."

"Bye, girls." Lillian offered a half-hearted wave before picking up her phone again and staring at it, as if willing it to ring.

Samantha headed into the kitchen to make them each a cup of tea. “Mom, it’s going to take Martin a little while to reach someone who knows something. Let’s talk about something else for now.”

Her mother popped up from the couch and paced in the living room. “What else is there to talk about? My oldest friend is being questioned by police. What if they charge her with something?”

Samantha handed her mother a mug of chamomile tea and led her back to the couch. “Let’s not jump to conclusions yet. We don’t know what’s happening.”

They sipped their tea in silence for a minute before Lillian’s phone rang. “Oh, it’s Martin. I’d better get this.” She answered the phone and stood up, pacing around the living room again while she listened to Patty’s son.

Watching Lillian pace made Samantha antsy. At least now she knew where she’d learned her own pacing habit.

“Okay, I’ll pick her up and wait with her until you get there.” Lillian ended the call.

“Pick her up where, Mom? What’s going on?”

“The police haven’t arrested Patty yet, but they suggested she get a lawyer. Martin is driving down from Austin tonight, but he wants somebody to pick her up from the police station and wait with her until he gets here.”

Samantha seized her purse. “You’re not going alone, Mom. I’m coming with you. I’ll drive.”

* * *

At the police station, Samantha and Lillian waited in the lobby for Patty to come out. When she did, her shoulders hunched and her entire body sagged with exhaustion. She seemed nothing like the self-assured woman Samantha had known since childhood. When Patty saw Lillian, she straightened up and appeared to steel herself, even as Lillian enfolded her in an enormous hug. "Oh, honey. Are you okay?"

"Let's get out of here." Patty's eyes darted around the room, as if searching for a familiar face. At the sight of the dull-gray institutional walls, she quickened her pace and slipped out the door.

On the car ride home, Patty confirmed that Angela Clawson was the victim, and from what she could gather, Patty herself was the number-one suspect. "There's no hard evidence to tie me to the crime other than gossip about our fight, so they released me for now. But it won't take them long to pin it on me. And before you ask, I had nothing to do with it."

"Of course you didn't, Patty. We know that." Lillian sat in the back seat with her friend. Samantha watched in the rearview mirror as Lillian patted her friend's knee. "But Patty, what caused the fight?"

Patty sighed. "I let that horrible woman get under my skin when I shouldn't have."

Samantha caught Patty's gaze in the mirror. "It must have been something serious. I've never seen you that upset."

Patty's lips pinched together, as if she'd tasted something sour. "It was serious to me. She insisted on bestowing the volunteer award on one of those tennis club ladies who had raised the most money for that blasted tennis club rather than Edna Welch who has been with the lodge for twenty years and made ten cherry pies for the pie sale." Patty sighed. "It's such a stupid thing, but the award included a weekend trip to Fredericksburg, and Edna had been eagerly anticipating it. That other woman could pay for fifteen trips to Fredericksburg without batting an eye. She probably won't even go. She just wanted the title."

"Do the police have any evidence? Other than that fight?" Lillian was using her soothing librarian's voice, but Samantha observed more fire than fear in Patty's eyes.

"It's no secret I hated the woman, and I publicly tried to get the board to kick the new tennis club members out of the lodge. There's no way they won't blame me."

Samantha parked in the driveway in front of Patty's small bungalow on the northern edge of the Highlands. A row of three-story townhomes across the street dwarfed the bungalow, but the exterior of the home appeared as well cared for as any on the block. As Samantha led her mother and Patty out of the car and up the sidewalk to the front door, she smiled at the small birdhouse that hung from the lowest branch of Patty's oak tree.

Patty's hands trembled as she tried and failed to fit the largest key into the lock. Lillian leaned over to help, but Patty pushed her friend's hands aside and forced the key into the lock herself. Once inside, she flipped a switch to bring light to the living room. She briefly sank onto a mound of decorative pillows in the center of her antique couch. Lillian and Samantha sat on either side of her. "What am I going to do?" Patty mumbled to herself. "This is the last thing Martin needs."

She jumped up from the couch and straightened a throw blanket and pillow on an easy chair and tidied the already straight magazines and books on the coffee table. Patty spoke during her unnecessary tidying binge. "Will they cancel the rest of the festival? The lodge needs that money!"

"Let's not worry about it now." Samantha stood up and walked toward the kitchen. "I'm going to go make us some tea."

Lillian stood up and directed her friend back to the couch, where she sat beside her. "Oh, Samantha, no more tea, please.

Patty's had a shock. Bring brandy." She turned to her friend. "No arguing, Patty. You need to relax and try to remember what you can, to help us."

"Remember? What do you mean? There's nothing to remember. I had nothing to do with Angela's death." The pitch of Patty's voice rose, and the pace of her words quickened.

"Of course you didn't, Patty. I only mean it would be good to record your movements today. Walk us through your whole day—everything you can remember and everyone you can remember seeing you at a particular time. The more we can corroborate your story, the better off you'll be."

Samantha, who had been listening in the kitchen, walked back to the room, with three brandy snifters. "Mom's right, Patty. We should jot your story down while details are fresh in your mind. We don't want to miss anything important."

"But I've been over everything with the police already." Patty sniffed the brandy and shuddered as she took a taste.

"Even more reason to tell us what you told them. Any lawyer you hire will ask you to recount your movements, and it's good to get it out while your memory is fresh." Lillian patted her friend on the back in the soothing manner of a mother encouraging a child to take her medicine.

Patty took a deep breath. "It's such a blur. I was so busy all day, running around to the different booths, making sure that everyone had the tickets they needed, and helping them to stock up on items when they ran low. I'd say practically everybody who was working the festival saw me at least four times."

Samantha pressed the record function on her iPhone, not wanting to distract Patty from her story by taking written notes. It was a tactic she often used during interviews when she was a reporter. People often forgot that a recorder was running, but it was much harder to ignore a person jotting down their every word. "That's great. Were you ever alone?"

Patty pressed the brandy snifter to her chest, as if hoping to transfer the warmth of the brandy into her bones. "That's what the police kept harping on. Once an hour, I had to swap out the money from the ticket booths to make sure everyone had enough change for customers using large bills. I did the swapping in the lodge office. During the festival, I had the only key to the office, to control security."

Samantha groaned. "How long did it take to make change?"

"Around twenty-five minutes, which the police seem to believe is a sufficient amount of time for me to have murdered Angela before making my rounds again." Patty took a large sip of the brandy. "It's hopeless. I've got no alibi, and I clearly hated the woman."

The three women sat in silence. Samantha contemplated Patty's predicament. "Okay, so your alibi isn't great. But surely there are other suspects? Since you didn't do it, someone else did. Who else might have wanted Angela dead?"

Patty played with the tassels on a nearby throw pillow, rolling the silky threads between her thumb and index finger. "I hate to sound flippant, because the woman is dead, but it would almost be easier to name people who liked her. She was not a popular woman. Even members on her side of the tennis club fight found her abrasive."

Lillian chimed in. "Well, that's promising, right, Samantha? It sounds like there are endless potential suspects for the police to consider."

"It would be helpful if we could point them to one or two great ones." Samantha played with her glass. "Can you think of anyone else in particular who recently fought with her or really disliked her?"

Patty crossed her arms. "No—I could name a dozen people who disliked her. But those people are my friends. I don't want to put them through what the police are putting me through. I won't do it."

Samantha exchanged glances with her mother, who nodded her head slightly, signifying she should let it go. Samantha ended the recording and put her phone back into her purse.

Patty stood up resolutely, collecting empty glasses as she strode into the kitchen. "There's no sense in you two sticking around here. Martin will arrive shortly. You may as well head home."

"I'm not leaving you here alone." Lillian followed her friend into the kitchen and grabbed a towel to dry the brandy snifters Patty was already rinsing off.

Samantha set her glass near the sink and stood awkwardly in the corner, not sure what to do with herself now that the only two tasks in the neat-as-a-pin house were being completed by Patty and her mother. "Martin probably won't be here for another hour at least. Let us keep you company."

Patty took the towel from Lillian, dried her hands, and hung it perfectly straight over the towel bar on the oven. "Oh, for heaven's sake. I've been on my own—well, all except for Martin—most of my adult life. I can take care of myself."

"Patty, we know you can take care of yourself, but today has been exhausting for all of us. Let's go into the next room and chat." Lillian put her arm behind Patty's back and tried to steer her back into the living room, but Patty walked in the opposite direction toward a little office in the back of her house.

"You two are welcome to stay, but I've got work to do." She fired up a small laptop on her rolltop desk and punched a series of keys, bringing the screen to life.

Lillian followed her into the office and glanced over her shoulder. "Are you trying to find a lawyer? That's not a bad idea. You should definitely have someone in mind before those police officers question you again."

Patty's resolute expression deflated for an instant before firming up again. "Not now. I need to deal with the festival. If it's going to open again tomorrow, so much needs to be done. We've got to cancel the groundbreaking for the stadium tennis court and someone's got to set up the stages for the speeches."

Lillian rested her fingertips lightly on the back of Patty's shoulders. "Come on, Patty. Surely someone else can deal with that now."

Patty rubbed her arms. "There's nobody else. Only I know the procedures. I just need to send a couple of emails." She shooed the women away as she typed furiously on her computer.

Lillian led Samantha back into the living room to await Martin. "I'm so worried about her. She's always been like this. Ever since Rick died when Martin was a toddler, she won't accept help from anyone. She tries to do everything herself. But this is too much pressure. She looks like she's going to crack."

"Maybe having something else to focus on for a few minutes isn't the worst thing in the world for her. Come on, let's give her space."

"I guess you're right. When Martin gets here, we'll get everything sorted out."

Samantha clenched her jaw at the reference to Martin. She knew she should have long since gotten over his treatment of her in college, but her mind turned to their last confrontation every time she heard his name. "When Martin gets here, we should leave him to sort things out with Patty. He can get through to her easier on his own than with us hanging around."

Lillian studied her daughter and nodded. "You're probably right. I'll just make him promise to call me with an update when he knows something."

The women waited in the living room, flipping through magazines on the coffee table until, a half an hour later, they heard a key twist in the lock. A tall, blond man burst through the door, calling out, "Mom!"

Chapter Four

The man stopped in his tracks when he saw Lillian and Samantha. "Mrs. Warren! Samantha?" He took a step backward, his eyes widening as he ran his fingers through a longish crew cut, trying to smooth down his wavy fringe.

"Martin!" Lillian rushed forward to hug him.

Samantha stood glued to her spot. She hadn't seen Martin in nearly twenty years, and her distaste at the mere mention of his name hadn't prepared her for the chiseled, athletic man who had replaced the lanky young man she remembered. She crossed her arms in front of her, not willing to let his improved appearance override her feelings about him.

Before she could give him another thought, Patty rushed into the room and wrapped her son in a bear hug. "I'm so sorry to drag you to town like this. This is the last thing you need now. Lillian shouldn't have called you."

"Mom, honestly! It's my turn to take care of you." Martin hugged his mother fiercely back.

Samantha tapped her mother on her shoulder. "I think that's our cue to leave."

"Okay, Patty, you're in excellent hands now. We're going to head home. But I want an update as soon as you have one."

Lillian leaned in for a side hug, offering Patty one last reassuring pat on the back.

"Thank you, Lillian. And you too, Samantha. But don't worry about me. I'll be fine."

The two women waved and walked out the door as Patty led Martin toward the kitchen, no doubt to offer him something to eat.

* * *

Back in her apartment, Samantha made up her bed with fresh sheets for her mother and got a blanket for herself for the couch. After saying goodnight to Lillian, Samantha tossed and turned, unable to sleep. In less than a month, she had stumbled into a second murder, and now her mom's oldest friend topped the suspect list. She'd promised David and her friends that she would stay out of danger after her last brush with death, and the idea of becoming embroiled in another case caused goose bumps to rise on her arms. But she couldn't leave Patty, or her mother, to handle this on her own. She needed to help, and unfortunately that meant more encounters with Martin.

Ugh. Samantha had mostly avoided Martin for the past decade, which had been a challenge given how close their mothers were. Lillian and Patty had grown up together in the same South Texas town. Inseparable as children, they still talked at least once a week.

Rolling over on the couch in search of a comfortable spot, Samantha dislodged her cat, Ruby. Offering the kitty an apologetic pat, Samantha's mind flew back to her sophomore year in college and the fraternity party that had been the beginning of the end of her friendship with Martin. They'd been hanging out fairly regularly after winding up by chance in the same geology class. At first they just studied, but soon they started getting together on the weekends too. So, when he invited her to his fraternity's fall mixer, Samantha had been looking forward to meeting more of his friends. Unfortunately, it all turned sour that night at the party when, slightly buzzed from the trash can punch, she found herself in a lip-lock with his roommate, Eric.

Even now, Samantha's stomach tightened at the memory. She'd known how Martin had felt about his roommate—his insecurity and his belief that Eric had everything handed to him. But in that instance, when Eric had kissed her for the first time, she'd put all of that out of her head, basking in the glow of the attention from the most popular boy in the room. She still felt a twinge of regret when she pictured Martin's face, full of hurt and sorrow, when he'd spotted the two of them. But it didn't excuse the complete betrayal that came a few months later when he had ruined her investigative piece for the school paper.

She punched her pillow, feeling a fresh burst of anger over Martin's disloyalty. Samantha had never told her mother about Martin's actions, knowing that she would find a way to make an excuse for him. Instead, she'd cut off contact with Martin, leaving her parents to think they'd simply grown apart.

* * *

Whenever their families planned to get together, Samantha made other plans. She'd largely avoided Martin. Until tonight.

While she recognized that she should be able to move past the hurt, she couldn't help but feel that Martin had broken a sacred trust between them, forged during summers chasing fireflies and picking dewberries as children. She hoped their interactions remained limited.

Samantha's phone flashed with a text message. It was David: *Thanks for the call. Show was great. Sold two paintings. Miss you.* She smiled as warmth spread from her chest to her extremities. It felt nice to be missed.

* * *

In the morning, Samantha awoke to the scent of her mother's coffee. Despite being a tea drinker, Samantha's senses tingled with the bitter, nutty aroma wafting from her kitchen.

"Did you sleep well, dear?" Lillian nursed black coffee from a mug at Samantha's kitchen table while scanning the headlines of the *Gazette*.

Samantha stretched, letting her thin blanket fall to the floor, as she wandered into the kitchen and warmed her teakettle on the stove. "I slept okay. How about you, Mom? Any news in the *Gazette* about yesterday?"

"There's a story about the incident, which fortunately does not name Patty as a suspect, and then a feature on Angela, who seems to have been rather prominent in the Houston community." Lillian passed her daughter the newspaper. "I'm going to hop in the shower now. The festival is on today, so I'll go with you this afternoon."

Samantha was relieved, but not surprised, that police hadn't canceled the festival. So many plans were already in place, including fireworks, so a cancellation would have been difficult. With July 4th on a Saturday, everyone would be in the mood to celebrate. Today should be her busiest and most profitable day, as long as news of the murder didn't scare customers away. And with her and Beth splitting time between the baby shower and the festival, they'd hopefully keep their business account in the black.

She checked the clock on her microwave: seven thirty AM. Plenty of time to dress before the festival opened at ten AM. "It's early, but any word from Patty this morning?"

Lillian washed her coffee cup in the sink and left it to dry on the counter. "Martin texted. He and Patty are meeting a lawyer this morning. He said he'd check back in with me after that."

As her mother headed to the bathroom for her shower, Samantha poured the water from the now whistling teakettle into a mug with her favorite brand of chai tea and sat down in the still warm seat vacated by her mother to read the paper.

The story about the murder contained a few added details. Angela Clawson had been found at the bottom of a pit that would eventually become the club's tournament court stadium. She'd been the victim of blunt force trauma to the skull. The murder weapon was, as yet, unknown. The story said a festival attendee had found Clawson around eight PM and that, for now, police were still pursuing all leads. The police requested anyone with potential information, no matter how big or small, to call a special tip line published at the end of the story.

That suggests that the police don't have much evidence. Hopefully it will be good news for Patty. New information could lead to more suspects.

Her tea now ready, Samantha inhaled the aroma of allspice and cloves as she took a sip and turned to the sidebar, a feature story on Angela Clawson and her influence in the city of Houston.

Society Maven Murdered Amid Final Fundraising Push

Angela Clawson, 72, a prominent philanthropic fundraiser, was found dead Friday night, at the bottom of a tennis stadium construction site. When completed, it would have been the fulfillment of her latest fundraising effort.

Clawson spearheaded the controversial tennis club project to build what she had envisioned as an exclusive country club–style tennis club on the grounds of the Highlands German Lodge's expansive property. Despite resistance from several of the lodge's longest-standing members, a few of whom had threatened to sue her, Clawson found backing for her plan, which supporters described as a labor of love for her community.

"The project was her gift to the children of the Highlands," said Christina Clawson, Angela Clawson's daughter. "She wanted children to have access to nearby tennis facilities, and the opportunity to compete in tennis leagues."

Clawson pointed out that her mother had been very firm on a desire to create a scholarship fund, allowing admittance to at least ten underprivileged children from the Highlands who might otherwise not have the chance to participate in competitive tennis.

The tennis club was the latest in a long line of fundraising accomplishments for Clawson. She'd also chaired the Med Center gala for two years in honor of her late husband, Dr. Jack Clawson, who worked there until his retirement as a heart surgeon.

Clawson was most active in fundraising that benefited children, said Calista Beech, who volunteered on several committees with Clawson. "She wanted to improve the lives of all young people," Beech said, describing Clawson as "a force to be reckoned with" on the fundraising scene. "She was a leader who knew how to make things happen."

Police are seeking information in connection with Clawson's death, which took place during the first day of the two-day Highland's Independence Day Festival. Money raised at the festival will help support the club's efforts, including the tennis scholarship fund.

Even before construction is completed, membership to the tennis club is in high demand, with the club selling out its membership cap within two hours of opening to applications, despite a hefty membership fee.

"That just proves the need out there," Christina Clawson said. "My mama wanted to do something about it. We are horrified and heartbroken that someone took her from us at the prime of her life. We desperately want justice."

Samantha rolled her eyes at the effort by the paper's society writer to make the tennis club project out to be a grand civic achievement that would benefit at-risk youth rather than Clawson's own grandchildren and their friends.

By the time Samantha had finished the story, Lillian was out of the shower, and Samantha jumped in for her turn. When she was dressed, she wandered back into her kitchen to find her mother pulling out a perfectly browned batch of cinnamon toast from the oven.

"I thought we should eat breakfast before we head out for the festival. You didn't have the ingredients for much else. Besides, you always did like this, didn't you?" Lillian placed the crusty brown slices on two plates and poured them each a glass of orange juice.

Samantha took a big bite out of her toast and washed it down with a slug of juice. "Thanks, Mom. I haven't had cinnamon toast in ages. Are you sure you want to come back with me to the festival? If it's as busy as I think it is going to be, what with the rubberneckers and the usual Saturday crowd, I won't have much time to spare and can't guide you around like last night."

Lillian took a dainty bite of her toast. "Sam, you always think I'm going to get lost, but I'm an adult. I'll be fine. I can find my way around and occupy myself."

Samantha eyed her mother, certain of what she had in mind. "Are you planning to snoop?"

Lillian opened her mouth in mock outrage. "Me, snoop? Never. I'm just going to wander around and keep my eyes and ears open."

"Mom, you have to be careful. You may think it's no big deal, but snooping can be dangerous." Though it was hypocritical of Samantha to chastise her mother after Samantha's own record of snooping, she wanted to make sure Lillian stayed on her guard. Samantha's eyes drifted again to the scar on her arm from her prior encounter with a murderer.

Lillian caught the expression and covered her daughter's hand with her own. "I know it's serious. But I also know how important this is. I can't sit by and watch Patty be railroaded for a crime she didn't commit."

Samantha nodded. If Marisa or Beth faced a murder charge, Samantha would be the first to jump in to clear either of their names. Still, she wanted her mom to be safe. "Okay, Mom, but I want you to visit the booth and speak to me at least once an hour." She grinned, enjoying the opportunity to use one of her mother's favorite tricks on her.

"Fine, Samantha. And I promise I'll be home by curfew as well." Lillian swatted her daughter on the shoulder as she headed to the bedroom to gather her things.

Samantha's laughter at their shared joked faded. She rubbed her skin to abate the shivers, recognizing their jokes wouldn't protect them from a murderer on the loose.

Chapter Five

The first thing Samantha noticed when she and her mother walked onto the festival grounds was the increased police presence. Officers were stationed near both the entrance and the exit, and questioned them about why they were on-site before the festival opened. Samantha brandished her festival badge, and the officers waved her through.

On the way to her booth, she spotted more officers guarding the tennis club construction site. Samantha picked up a revised program, in which any mention of the groundbreaking for the tennis court had been removed. The rest of the schedule appeared unchanged: musical entertainment on the main stage, historical reenactments on a secondary stage, craft activities for kids, an apple pie contest, a pet parade, and the grand finale—a selection of Sousa marches performed by the Highlands High School Band, culminating in a small fireworks display.

Lillian followed Samantha to her booth, and for twenty minutes they worked to set up for the afternoon. After filling up two coolers with ice, they prepared garnishes, ready to be plopped into the red-white-and-blue-hued concoctions as Samantha made them.

"Seems like you're all set here. I doubt you'll be too busy this early in the morning, so I'm going to wander around." Lillian headed toward a secondary stage where a group of costumed ladies were preparing for a folk-dance demonstration.

Samantha wiped down her booth one more time before setting out her tip and ticket jars and sitting on a stool to await her first customers. The hipster brunch set who liked to attend festivals "ironically" usually enjoyed morning booze, so Samantha figured she wouldn't have too long to wait for her first clientele.

When officers opened the entrance gates, an enormous crowd dispersed across the festival grounds, resembling a red, white, and blue confetti explosion. A few festival goers waved mini-American flags, while others sported Uncle Sam hats. It didn't take long for the festival to hit its stride. The crowd dwarfed the previous day's, and within twenty minutes Samantha had served a dozen customers. As predicted, the hipsters had paired her cocktails with slices of apple pie for a serviceable brunch.

By noon, the line at Samantha's cart was the longest it had been, stretching across the grounds to the entertainment tent, where a band performed modern country to a crowd of two-stepping fans. She was relieved when Mila showed up, allowing Samantha to speed up her drink-making process.

"Geez, this is crazy." Mila made trays of drinks and passed them to Samantha to garnish. "I'm surprised at how many people showed up after the incident yesterday. Have you heard anything more about the murder?"

Samantha continued to take tickets and hand out drinks. "Nothing more than what I read in the paper."

"I overheard two officers at the gate as I came in." Mila paused her mixing. "It sounds like they've recovered the weapon, and there might even be fingerprints on it."

Samantha stopped midway in garnishing and turned to stare at Mila. "Really? What is it? Did they say?"

Mila shrugged her shoulders. "I didn't hear anything further. But hopefully that means they can clear up the case soon."

Samantha went silent, wondering whether this latest development might be good news for Patty.

Mila, oblivious to Samantha's introspection, continued to chatter. "I wonder when they'll be able to restart construction. They haven't made much progress yet beyond digging the hole for the stadium court." Mila gave an involuntary shiver. "Ugh, just picturing that woman's body in that hole gives me the heebie-jeebies!"

The women worked steadily for another hour before the line finally slowed enough for Samantha to take a break and search for her mother. She ambled by the entertainment stage and back through the craft booths but found no sign of Lillian. Samantha fought back her panic and quickened her pace as she headed to the food booths.

Just as she turned to call the nearest police officer, Samantha spotted a familiar brown frosted bob and her mother's red-checkered shirt in the distance. She raced over to join Lillian, slowing her pace when she realized her mother was talking to Karl, her dancing buddy from the previous evening. Samantha held back to give them a chance to finish up their conversation, when her mom spotted her.

"Samantha! I was searching for you over at your booth. I got nervous when I couldn't find you!"

Samantha laughed. "Me too. But we've found each other now." She turned to Karl. "It's nice to see you again. Has my mom been showing off more of her dance skills?"

The large man grinned, his dimples hidden by his thick, bushy beard. The light moment didn't last, and a minute later his expression turned stony. "No, your mom's been telling me about Patty and her trip to the police station last night. It's not right for them to pin this on her. She didn't do it."

Lillian looked aghast. "Of course she didn't do it. We just have to prove it."

"What do you have in mind?" Samantha eyed her mother warily.

"We are at the literal scene of the crime, with many of the same attendees from yesterday. We need to ask people what they remember." Lillian's exuberance had returned.

Samantha had known her mother would try to rope her into investigating. She shivered as she noted the construction zone with the crime scene tape still looped around it. Still, it wouldn't do much harm to ask a few questions. "The crime scene is a good distance from the rest of the festival grounds, but the people working the grill tent might have seen something. Karl, you worked over there yesterday. I don't suppose you saw anything?"

Karl lowered his head, appearing defeated. "I wish I had."

"Talk to anyone who worked there last night. Ask if they noticed anything suspicious. The body was found around eight PM, so the murder likely occurred just before then."

Samantha searched the festival grounds for easy vantage points of the construction site. She spotted a booth with a potential line of sight next to the grill stand. A few women stood at the booth, but Samantha couldn't make out what they were doing. "What's that over there?"

Karl's gaze followed her finger. "Oh, that's where they held the first round of the pie bake-off last night. They'll hold the finals there later this afternoon."

Samantha indicated to her mother that they should head in that direction. "Mom, let's go question the bakers. We'll split up and talk to as many people as we can."

When they arrived at the booth, Samantha spotted the blonde woman with the big hair who'd been engaged in the tense discussion with Angela in the VIP tent on Friday. She was organizing pies for sale next to the stand where the contest judging would take place later that day. *May as well start with her.*

Samantha walked up to the woman and began perusing the pies. "Oh, hi there. I'm Samantha, from the cocktail booth. I saw you yesterday in the VIP tent with Angela. I'm so sorry for your loss."

The woman looked up, slightly startled. "Oh yes. Calista Beech." The woman offered her hand to shake. "It's all so awful. I didn't want to come back today, but I knew Angela would have wanted everything to run according to her exacting standards. Plus, someone needed to fill in for her daughter, Christina, who was supposed to be working the pie booth again today."

"That's good of you. It must have been a shock for her daughter. Did you see anything yesterday? I was on the other side of the festival, so I didn't know what was happening until the police showed up." Samantha tried to keep her questioning as casual as possible.

"I was here at the pie booth, watching the preliminaries when it happened." Calista continued stacking pies, organizing them by type.

"This is so close to where they found her . . . did you notice anything strange over by the stadium court?" Samantha picked up a cherry pie, deciding to buy it to extend the conversation.

"Unfortunately, no. I'm so clumsy, I bumped into the table and managed to knock a peach pie off and onto my dress. I was trying to clean everything up when I heard the alarm and saw the police head that way." Calista rang up Samantha's pie and took her money. "But you know what? I did hear another volunteer say they saw someone creeping around Angela's car in the parking lot last night."

Calista appeared to shudder. "I don't know if it's connected or not, but it's a little unnerving given what happened. I sure hope the police solve this case soon because it's got everyone on edge."

That detail about the parking lot is interesting. Samantha glanced at her phone and realized she needed to get back to her booth. She thanked Calista and walked off to find her mother, whom she spotted talking to an elderly woman in an apron. Not wanting to interrupt, she mimed tapping on her wrist as if she had a watch, hoping her mother understood her signal that she was headed out.

* * *

Back at her booth, Samantha set the pie she'd bought next to the cooler and apologized to Mila for being away so long.

Quickly, she got back into the rhythm of making drinks while Mila took a turn preparing garnishes. "The gossip mill is in full force today. The murder is the topic du jour."

Samantha's ears perked up, wondering what Mila might have heard. "I guess that's not shocking given how many people had such strong feelings about the victim."

Mila snorted. "Strong feelings. That's the diplomatic way of putting it, I guess. From what I heard, there were strong feelings about the whole tennis club business too. I overheard one woman in the hotdog line joke that whoever killed that woman probably wanted her spot in the club."

Samantha raised her eyebrows as she watched a stilt-walking Statue of Liberty pass in front of the booth. "The membership is pretty exclusive. I think the minimum to join is a twenty-thousand-dollar fee, with monthly dues of four hundred dollars, and still they sold out within a week of opening up to members."

Mila whistled. "That's enough to pay my tuition for a year! But a tennis club membership hardly seems worth killing over."

Samantha shrugged. "You'd be surprised what will drive some people to murder." She shivered, remembering her last encounter with a murderer.

The crowds ebbed and flowed over the next few hours as the temperature climbed. A kite-flying Benjamin Franklin dragged his red, white, and blue kite behind him, with no wind available to help it take flight.

The temperature reached its boiling point when an announcement came over the loudspeaker about the start of the pet parade. Samantha's shirt stuck to her back, and the small, battery powered fan she'd been running was now only moving hot air around the booth. The crowd grew suddenly frantic, everyone wanting to get hold of a snow cone or cocktail in time to watch the action. Fortunately, Samantha's booth was on the parade route, so she could monitor the participants while she continued to sell drinks.

"Yankee Doodle Dandy" played over the loudspeaker, and Samantha craned her neck to look over the crowd at the parade's grand marshal, a tiny wiener dog wearing a hotdog costume and led by a young boy dressed as a bottle of ketchup. Following close behind was a fluffy white poodle in a red, white, and blue skirt, and a golden retriever dressed like Uncle Sam. A little girl in a red and blue jumpsuit rode her scooter with red, white, and blue streamers hanging from the handles, holding her pet bunny in a carrier between her legs.

"They're adorable, aren't they?" A woman wearing a volunteer T-shirt turned back toward Samantha and smiled. "I'm so glad they went through with the festival today, even after what happened yesterday. I think we all can use the distraction."

"Absolutely. It was horrible, wasn't it? Did you see anything yesterday?" If she couldn't go out to snoop, Samantha took the opportunity to interrogate whomever fate brought to her booth.

The woman lowered her voice conspiratorially. "Well, of course, there was that fight between Angela and Patty Davis yesterday. Practically the entire world saw that. But later last evening, I spotted Angela having words with a man over by the VIP tent. His back was to mine, so I couldn't make out the face, but I have no doubt they were arguing. Angela looked furious!"

A little boy rode down the parade route on his bicycle, bearing a bowtie-wearing iguana in a basket.

"Did you hear what they fought about?" Samantha tried to get the woman to focus before she got distracted by more cute children and pets.

"No. I'm surprised I noticed them, because they weren't being loud. But Angela's face was pinched like it gets right before she's about to give someone a piece of her mind. When I glanced away for a minute, they were gone."

Samantha fished for more information. "Do you know what time it was?"

"Probably around 7:10. It was right between the two bands who played last night." The woman cooed as a pug with a cheerleading outfit ran past, chased by a girl in pigtails.

This woman may have seen Angela with the murderer. "You sure you couldn't recognize the man? Did you notice what he was wearing?" Samantha tried bribery to recapture the woman's attention. "Here, have you tried one of my drinks? It's on the house. It's so hot out, and you're a volunteer. But don't tell your friends!"

The woman slurped the cool drink. "Thank you. Yum! Your secret is safe with me. I don't remember much about the man or what he was wearing. He seemed sort of preppy, I guess. On the young end—younger than Angela anyway. I was mostly focusing on her because she appeared so angry. Of course, that's not so unusual with Angela these days—plenty of people wanting to pick a fight with her."

The woman suddenly squealed. "Oh, there's my neighbor's little girl carrying her guinea pig. Isn't she the cutest? I've got to go say hi. Thanks for the drink!" The woman bounded after the little girl, waving goodbye with her free hand.

Well, I guess that was worth a free drink. The woman hadn't been able to identify the person Angela was arguing with, but she had offered proof of another confrontation besides the fight between Angela and Patty. One that took place much closer to Angela's death.

Following the parade, the cocktail booth experienced another rush of people lining up for drinks before the music started. Festival organizers had booked several acts, including another bluegrass band and a few rock bands, hoping to appeal to all tastes. The Highlands High Marching Band would end the evening with patriotic music and fireworks.

In the half hour before the concert, Samantha and Mila served close to a hundred cocktails. The booth was firmly in the profit zone. When the first twangs of the country singer's guitar floated across the festival grounds, the activity at the booth had slowed, and Samantha felt comfortable leaving it in Mila's hands while she went to search for her mom and Karl.

She spotted her mother first, tapping her toes in front of the music tent while balancing what appeared to be a pie in one hand and a bratwurst in the other. "Hey, Mom. Looks like we're going to be eating a lot of pie! I bought one too." Samantha eased the pie from Lillian's hand, allowing her mom to take a bite out of the juicy sausage without dripping grease down the front of her shirt. "Did you find out anything good?"

Lillian took another bite of the sausage, clearly enjoying herself, before fixing her attention on the pie. "The baker chatted me up for nearly half an hour after I bought that thing."

"And what did you learn, exactly?" Samantha tried to keep the exasperation out of her voice. Her mother's desire to build tension in her stories was often at odds with Samantha's desire for quick facts.

"I learned what the other tennis club ladies think of Angela." Lillian launched into her tale of the tennis club ladies who admired Angela for her exacting standards. "Even after they'd signed up for the club, she kept promising the highest-end furnishings and the most state-of-the-art equipment, and even a new hotshot tennis pro from California, after initially promising the job to a less well-known guy from Texas."

Samantha didn't want to dampen her mother's enthusiasm, but she wasn't sure how any of that could be relevant to the murder case. "Okay, that's nice, I guess."

Lillian pursed her lips, appearing annoyed at her daughter's dismissiveness. "No, the point is, they didn't know how she made the finances work. The woman I talked to said she thought the upgrades were expensive and wouldn't likely be covered, even by the high membership fees the club charged."

"Well, that is interesting. I'm still not sure how it relates to Angela's murder, but we'll file it away as potentially useful." Samantha filled her mother in on her conversations with Calista Beech at the pie booth, and told her about the chatty lodge woman. "Let's find Karl. I hope he did better than we did."

Not wanting to push their way through the concert goers, the women circled the outskirts of the stage, searching for the large, bearded man. They eventually spotted him backstage at the concert tent, helping to move speakers around for the next performers. Lillian waved at him, and he indicated he'd join her in a minute.

The country band ended their set, and the backstage crew got to work unloading equipment for the next band. Karl helped to connect speakers for the bluegrass band that was performing next, before joining Lillian and Samantha.

"How are you ladies doing? Did you learn anything good?" Karl used a handkerchief to wipe sweat from his brow.

Samantha caught him up to speed and noted his grimace as Lillian described overspending, as noted by the tennis club ladies. Clearly, the blown budget was a sore point with Karl, but Samantha didn't want him to dwell on it. She was more interested in learning what he had picked up over the course of the afternoon.

"I talked to one guy who thought he saw somebody skulking around in the parking lot near the construction site around seven fifteen last night. He heard a car alarm go off, but when he raced over to investigate, the person ran away." Karl lifted his palms up, signaling he didn't know anything else.

That matches what Calista heard. Samantha pressed further. "Could he describe the person?"

"Nope, he couldn't tell if it was a man or a woman." Karl hung his head, as if ashamed of the meager information he had to offer.

"Did the person run toward the construction site?" Samantha continued prodding, knowing from her reporting days that sometimes people knew more than they thought they did.

He turned his palms up. "He didn't see where they went, but he was sure that the person had been lurking near Angela's car. It was a white Cadillac. Anyone who's ever seen her drive up to a lodge meeting knew her car."

Samantha raised her eyebrows. "You are the second person who's told me that story. He should tell the police. He can call it in on the tip line."

Karl nodded. "Not a bad idea. I'll mention it to him. I've got to go back over to the grill tent. I'll talk to you ladies later."

Samantha watched him go and realized she needed to head back to her own booth. The band change would mean more customers.

A quick glance at her mother convinced Samantha that Lillian was wilting in the heat. "Mom, I need to head back. Do you want to stick around for the music and the fireworks or head home? I can call Marisa to come get you."

Lillian surveyed the crowds and grimaced. "I'm not sure there's any more for me to learn here today. I may as well go back to your place."

Samantha dialed Marisa and asked if she could ferry Lillian home. "Mom, Marisa will be here in twenty minutes, okay? I told her you'd wait with me at my booth. Come on."

Samantha led her mother back to the booth and settled her into the folding chair she kept stashed in the back for times when she couldn't handle being on her feet any longer. She sent

Mila off on a break, realizing that the booth wasn't big enough to hold all three of them comfortably.

As Samantha prepared another tray of drinks, Lillian reached for one, putting the straw to her lips. "You don't mind, do you, dear?"

"Of course not, Mom. It's been a long day. Listen, when you get back to my place, just take it easy. Order dinner, take a nap, or try to relax. You should be able to watch the fireworks from my balcony."

"Samantha, I may qualify for a senior discount, but I can still take care of myself." Lillian rolled her eyes.

"I know you can." Samantha garnished the drinks she'd just made. With the next band set to start in ten minutes, she expected a slew of customers seeking something cold and festive.

After serving another stream of nonstop customers, Samantha leaned against the wall of her booth, relieved to see Marisa's long legs striding across the grounds toward her. "You made it! Thanks for coming. I know Mom wants to get home, and I'm slammed here."

Marisa grabbed a cocktail off the tray, offering a grin. "I assume I can accept a cocktail as payment?"

"Of course!" Samantha smiled. "I'd say take two, but you are driving my mother home."

"It's no trouble. I was studying at home while Beth worked that baby shower. I needed a break anyway. Lillian, are you ready to go?"

Lillian stood up and gave her daughter's hand a squeeze. "I'll see you back at your place, honey."

The hectic pace continued with every band change. During calm periods, Samantha enjoyed the community spirit on display as the crowd swayed to music, kids played carnival games, and the smell of grilled sausage permeated the air. It felt wonderful, if exhausting, to be a part of it, but Samantha was grateful when the Highlands High Band took seats on stage and started piping out Sousa melodies. Fireworks would follow, signaling the festival's end. She'd return to clean up tomorrow, but for now, she longed for the comforts of home.

When the last firework exploded, leaving the sky filled with smoke and smelling of gunpowder, Samantha locked up the booth for the night and dropped off her tickets at the lodge office. The lodge's finance committee would spend the next morning completing a thorough accounting of the vendors' tickets, to calculate how much they'd earned so that checks would be ready by the afternoon.

That chore done, she trudged to her car on exhausted feet and finally took the time to check her voicemail messages. Her pulse pounded as she pressed "Play" for a voicemail from a phone number she didn't recognize.

Chapter Six

The voicemail was brief. "Hello, Samantha. This is Olivia Clawson, Angela's daughter-in-law. We met yesterday, before . . . well, everything. Can you do me a favor and call me as soon as possible? There's something I'd like to discuss with you."

Samantha raised her eyebrows in surprise as she neared her car. *What could she want with me?*

Samantha glanced at her watch. It was after ten thirty PM. Normally, she wouldn't call anyone back that late, but Olivia's voicemail had sounded urgent. *No time like the present, I guess.* She opened her car door, took a seat behind the wheel, and pressed the button to return the call. The phone rang a few times before a woman answered.

"This is Olivia." The woman's voice sounded tired.

"Hi, this is Samantha Warren. I'm sorry to be calling so late, particularly after what you and your family are going through, but I just got your message. I've been working again at the festival today."

"Oh, Samantha. Don't apologize. Thank you for calling me back. This may sound strange, but do you cater funerals?"

Samantha fumbled for the right words. "I . . . uh . . . can't say that's ever come up . . . but I'm happy to discuss it."

She cringed as she played the words back in her head. *You're happy to discuss it? Way to show compassion to the grieving family member.*

But Olivia didn't seem fazed or, frankly, grieving. "Wonderful. Listen, we are still trying to finalize the details, but Angela enjoyed your drinks, and Matt, my husband, thought it would be a fitting tribute to have you serve at the memorial service. You cater food too, right? I realize this is last minute, but could you come by Angela's house tomorrow morning to discuss further? I'd prefer to meet early—around eight, if that's alright."

Samantha took down the details, promising to see Olivia the next morning. Shaking her head at the oddity of the situation, she drove home, wondering if her mother had spoken with Patty.

Ten minutes later, she walked up the outdoor staircase to her garage apartment and opened the door, stepping into her living room. "Mom?" She threw her bag onto the sofa and flipped on a light, illuminating the dark apartment. "Mom?" Still hearing no answer, Samantha turned to the bedroom, wondering if her mother had fallen asleep.

At the sight of a freshly made bed and an open bathroom door, her chest tightened. There was no sign of her mother. "Mom?"

Where could she have gone? Samantha ran to her purse and pulled out her cell phone to dial her mother. But the call went straight to voicemail. Samantha groaned. Her mom never answered her phone and often let the battery die, rendering her unreachable. *I can't believe she didn't even leave me a message.* She glanced at the time again. It was now after eleven, and too late to call her dad at home in Corpus Christi without causing a major panic.

She took the stairs two at a time and ran down her landlord's long driveway to the street, to search for her mother's red Ford Taurus. The gloss from the car's finish shone under the streetlamp.

Samantha's heart beat faster. *Where can she be?*

She dialed Marisa.

"Hey, Sam, what's up?"

"Did you drop my mom off this afternoon? I came home, and she's not here."

"Yeah, I dropped her off about fifteen minutes after we left your booth. She planned to order delivery and wait for news from her friend."

Realization dawned in Samantha's mind. "Patty. She's got to be with Patty. But how did she get there? Never mind—I'll head over to Patty's place and see if I can find her."

"Want me to come with you?"

"No, it's fine. I'm sure she's there. When I see her, I'll give her a nice lecture about keeping her phone charged." Samantha wished she felt the confidence of her words.

"Well, let me know when you do. You've got me worried now."

"Thanks, Marisa."

Samantha briefly searched for Patty's phone number but couldn't find it in her call log. She ran back upstairs to get her purse before hopping back into her Sentra. The ten-minute drive felt like an hour as she cursed poorly timed traffic lights on her way to Patty's.

She parked in the driveway and raced to the front door, pounding until it opened.

"What is it?" Martin's blue eyes flashed as he opened the door, but he took a step back when he saw Samantha. "Oh, it's you. I thought it was a reporter. They've been calling all day, and I thought one had decided to ambush us at home. You, of all people, know how pushy reporters can be." Martin opened the door wider, allowing Samantha to enter.

Samantha ignored the dig, her heart still pounding as she searched for traces of her mother. "My mom—is she here?"

"In the kitchen, with my mom." Martin's words came out in a huff as he stared pointedly at Samantha, but Samantha breezed past him, preferring to avoid further confrontation.

She breathed a sigh of relief to find her mom carefully drying china teacups as Patty passed them to her. "Mom! I was so worried! How did you get here? Your car is still at my place. And your phone. What happened to your phone?"

"Samantha! I took an Uber. Didn't you get my note?"

Samantha blinked her eyes. "An Uber? Since when do you use Uber? And what note?"

"It's on the refrigerator. I thought you'd be so proud of me. You think I have no sense of direction in the city, so I took an Uber to keep you from worrying about me."

Samantha, her voice still stern, wasn't ready to let her mother off the hook yet. "And your phone? Why didn't you answer? I worried something had happened to you."

Lillian set the towel on the counter and gave Samantha a hug. "I guess my battery died. I'm sorry I scared you, honey."

Samantha's heart rate slowed to its normal pace. "You're okay, which is the important thing." She turned to Patty. "How are you? Were you able to meet with a lawyer?"

Lillian directed Samantha toward a chair at the kitchen island. "Sit. There's plenty to catch you up on."

Patty walked Samantha through her morning. The mother of Martin's old college friend was an attorney, which was the only way they'd been able to get an appointment on July Fourth. The attorney agreed to take the case and immediately connected with detectives, who intimated that they might want to talk with Patty again as early as next week.

"What does the lawyer say?" Samantha bowed her head, concerned about the detective's continued interest in Patty.

"She pulled no punches. Said it doesn't look good with my fingerprints on the murder weapon." Patty threw her soapy sponge into the bottom of the sink and stomped toward the counter, where she sorted through a stack of bills.

"What was the murder weapon?" Samantha glanced at her mother, trying to read in her face whether she should drop her line of inquiry for now.

Lillian raised her eyebrows, but it was too late. Patty responded. "One of those blasted shovels for the ceremonial groundbreaking. My fingerprints were all over them. The construction workers had splattered them with mud, and as much as I hate the tennis center project, I wanted everything to be perfect for the festival, so I cleaned them."

Martin, who'd been hanging back in the dining room, strode into the kitchen and glared at Samantha. "Mom, you should get some rest. We'll discuss it in the morning."

Samantha, not eager for further interactions with Martin, took that as their cue to leave. "Mom, we should head home. It's getting late."

Lillian hugged her friend and followed Samantha out the front door.

After buckling her seatbelt, Lillian turned to Samantha. "We've got to help her. Patty thinks she can handle everything herself, but she can't deal with this."

"She has a lawyer now. Hopefully she's a good one? If she's not, I can talk to David for her." Samantha looked over at her mother and frowned at the resolute expression on her face.

"The lawyer seems competent, but lawyers can only do so much. We're in the best position to help investigate."

Samantha sighed. "I know you want to help, Mom. But it's one thing to ask a few questions at a festival and an entirely different thing to investigate a murder. You realize my last investigation almost got me killed?"

"I know, honey. And of course, I don't want you to do anything dangerous. But this is my best friend. I'm not leaving her to fight this on her own."

"Mom, this just doesn't seem—"

"Samantha, you can help or not. That's your choice. But I'm doing this. I've got the rest of the week off. I'm a librarian. Research and looking up records are my job. Plus, I've got a friendly face. People are always telling me things, whether or not I ask them."

Samantha's resolute voice belied a certainty she did not feel. "All right, Mom. We'll see what we can do."

When they arrived back at Samantha's apartment, it was after midnight. As she reached for her toothbrush, Lillian pondered out loud how to begin her investigation. "We need to learn more about any other potential suspects. Who else might have wanted Angela dead?"

Samantha remembered her early appointment at Angela Clawson's home the next day and filled her mother in on her planned meeting with Angela's daughter-in-law. "I might learn something while I'm there."

Lillian grinned. "That's fantastic, honey. I know you've been worried about getting more business. Plus, you can be our eyes and ears on what the family is thinking."

Samantha wished her mother good night and headed to her couch, expecting another night of fitful rest. But Ruby's soft purring lulled Samantha to sleep.

* * *

The next morning, Samantha rose early and dressed in black slacks and a gray silk blouse, hoping to strike the right note with the grieving family. She left her mother the newspaper and the password to her laptop for when she woke up, and slipped out the door around seven thirty AM.

Angela's home was only fifteen minutes away, on a tree-lined avenue in the heart of the Highlands. The home, a Greek Revival–style cottage with ionic fluted columns and the wrought iron detailing found throughout New Orleans, was beautiful, but smaller than Samantha had expected. She parked her car on the street out front and walked up a grand staircase to the main entrance, where she overheard shouting coming from inside.

"You never liked her! You were only ever interested in her money and how it could help you and that worthless brother of mine." The voice began in a shriek and ramped up in intensity. "She told me about the latest loan to bail out another of his business disasters. And now that she's dead, you're so sure your problems are over. If I have anything to say about it, they're just beginning."

"I may not have been her biggest fan, but at least I was honest about my feelings. I think she respected that." Samantha recognized the second voice, calmer than the first, but somehow sharper, as Olivia's.

"She was so angry on Friday, she told me she was going to write Matt out of the will!" The first voice grew shrill.

"That's preposterous, Christina. You know how dramatic your mother was when she got angry about something. I believe they disagreed about certain financial matters, mostly about her sticking her nose in where it didn't belong. But don't worry—Angela kept detailed records. You'll find that we've made regular payments on every loan. The files are right there in your mother's office, if you care to go over them." Olivia's tone was clipped. It was clear she was taking no nonsense.

"You never appreciated what she did for you and Matt. She always had your best interests at heart." The voice rose in crescendo as the speaker moved toward the door.

"That's debatable. But I'm not interested in arguing." Olivia's voice also grew louder, and Samantha heard heels click on hard tile.

What am I getting myself into? Samantha nearly turned around to walk back down the steps, when the front door flew open, and a petite brunette stormed out onto the porch.

"Who are you?" The woman eyed Samantha with a scowl.

Samantha stammered. "Oh, excuse me. I'm sorry. I've got an appointment at eight to meet Olivia Clawson?"

The woman rolled her eyes and pointed with her thumb behind her. "You'll have no trouble finding her. She's already made herself quite at home." The woman pushed past Samantha and ran down the steps to a silver Cadillac SUV parked in the driveway.

Samantha steeled herself before stepping into the foyer, attempting to ignore the awkward scene she'd just witnessed. She recognized Olivia right away. The woman's auburn hair was pulled back into a French twist, and she wore a floral mid-length dress better suited to a garden party than funeral planning.

"Samantha, right?" Olivia reached out her hand and shook Samantha's firmly in her own. "I'm sorry you had to witness that. Christina has always been high-strung."

With a smile, she led Samantha into a formal living room, with a dark cherrywood coffee table and two overstuffed blue and green striped couches.

"Thank you again for coming over on such short notice. As you can imagine, we're in a time crunch. We need to nail down plans today, if possible. The funeral is scheduled for Thursday, and we'll host the reception here at the house. I'm trying to take care of everything so my husband and Christina don't have to worry about it . . . not that she appreciates my help."

Samantha took notes on a small tablet she carried inside her purse.

"We're probably talking about a hundred and twenty people over the course of the afternoon. We want a light lunch—a buffet is best, as people will come and go. And of course we want the standard cocktails available. In addition, Matt, my husband, wanted a special drink to honor his mother. Can you accommodate that?"

Accommodate? "Um, sure. Can you give me an idea of what she liked? I'll come up with a few options."

The woman offered a wan smile. "Gin. Angela was a gin drinker."

Samantha made a few notations in her notebook. "Any other particular flavors she liked or that represented her well?"

"Something icy." The woman frowned. "I'm sorry, forgive me, that was inappropriate. Angela was a complicated woman. You would never have known her small-town West Texas roots from the high-society matron she'd become over the last fifty years of her life."

Eager to dig for inspiration, Samantha jumped on the tidbit. "I never would have guessed she was from West Texas."

Olivia smiled. "Small-town girl—the whole bit. She met her husband, Jack, in Odessa in high school. She was a farm girl, and he came from oil money, which he spent to go to medical school. When he proposed, she never looked back." Olivia absentmindedly patted the cushion next to her. "Of course, I heard all of this from Jack before he died. She would have hated that he'd told me that story."

Samantha's imagination sparked. "Hmm . . . I'm thinking something complex, with bitter notes but an underlying sweetness. That's doable. I'll come up with a few ideas and send you a list. It's important that you're happy with what I come up with."

"Whatever you choose will be fine. I'm doing this to humor my husband."

"How about food? You mentioned a buffet. Do you have any thoughts on what you'd like served?" Samantha sensed that Olivia was not overly interested in the details, but she wanted to ask anyway.

"Oh, just a nice buffet. I'm sure Angela would have had a full menu planned out, but I'm more than happy to delegate that to you." Olivia sniffed. "I can practically sense her disapproval from beyond the grave. It's so hard to believe she's gone."

Normally, Samantha might have reached out to comfort the grieving party, but she wasn't sure if that description fit Olivia, exactly. Though her eyes betrayed her tiredness, Olivia appeared as if her mother-in-law's death was one more chore to attend to. Samantha gently probed Olivia on the family's opinion regarding the investigation.

"It is shocking. Angela was so alive on Friday when we last spoke. How is the . . . uh . . . investigation going?"

Olivia rubbed her temple with one hand. "According to police, they have a strong case against that lodge woman. I didn't see it, but apparently there was an altercation between them on Friday night. Angela angered many people over the way she crammed that tennis club down their throats. She never took to heart that adage about catching more flies with honey—not when she could take the steamroller approach."

Samantha uttered a noncommittal "Mmm," wondering if she could press further.

Olivia pinched the bridge of her nose, closing her eyes and showing the depth of her exhaustion. "I shouldn't say such things. She was a complicated woman, but her heart was usually in the right place. My husband and children are devastated. They can't bring themselves to believe that someone wanted her dead."

Samantha was about to formulate a reply, but before she could speak, Olivia stood up. "I'm sorry to rush you, but I have another appointment this morning. Once we finalize everything with the funeral home, I'll send over the details. If you want to email me a proposed menu, that's fine."

Samantha stood up and followed Olivia to the front door, doing one last quick scan around the space before trailing Olivia outside.

"Thank you. I'll be in touch soon." Olivia turned back toward the front door to lock the house.

Samantha drove back to her apartment, hoping to touch base with her mom before going to pack everything up at the festival grounds.

* * *

Back at her apartment, she filled her mother in on the argument she'd overheard between Olivia and her sister-in-law.

"Christina made some pretty wild accusations. She even said Angela planned to write Matthew out of the will."

Lillian gasped. "We've got to find out more. Wouldn't it be great if the daughter-in-law or son did it?"

Samantha's eyes widened. "Um, no, not that great, given that they just hired me for a pretty big job."

"Still, it's two more suspects. Did you learn anything more?"

Samantha told her mother the brief backstory Olivia had told her about Angela.

"Interesting. A rags-to-riches story, but sounds like she wanted to forget the rags." Lillian had been taking notes in a small notebook and clicked a pencil eraser against her teeth. "Wonder if her past might have come back to haunt her."

Samantha walked into her bedroom to change into shorts before returning to face her mom. "Are you sure you'll be fine on your own? It will take me a few hours to clean up at the festival, and then I'll need to meet Beth for a bit to go over plans for next week, so I'll meet you back here afterward. Maybe we can get dinner."

"Oh, honey, I'll be fine. I'll call Patty and do a little research. And I promise, I'll keep my phone on me and fully charged up."

Samantha gave her mom a quick hug and left, bounding down the stairs as she rushed to the festival grounds to pack up and collect her check.

Back at her booth, Samantha stacked bottles and wiped down counters as she improvised some ideas for gin drinks for Angela's funeral reception. *Never imagined I'd be working a funeral, but it's another opportunity to showcase my cocktails.* With half of her mind occupied with plans for later that week, Samantha didn't notice the man standing in front of her cart until she glanced up.

"Oh, Karl! How are you?"

The burly man's face fell. He looked as though he hadn't slept. "I wanted to ask if it was true. I heard a rumor the police were going to arrest Patty."

Samantha grimaced. "Where did you hear that?"

Karl rubbed his hands through his hair. "One of the guys heard from a cop buddy that they were going to charge Patty. So, is it true?"

Samantha didn't want to add to the rumors. "We don't know. Her lawyer is concerned about it."

Karl frowned. "This is terrible. I've been trying to reach Patty but haven't been able to get through. Can you pass a message on for me?"

Samantha nodded, expecting platitudes about keeping her strength up or something equally well-meaning but useless.

"Let Patty know that me and some of her friends have a plan. I can't say more about it now, but we'll make sure the police don't single out Patty in this investigation."

Samantha's forehead scrunched as she took this in. "What do you mean? What kind of plan?"

Karl grimaced. "The more left unsaid, the better. I don't want Patty to think her friends have abandoned her. Now, I've got to head over to help clean up the grill tent."

Samantha watched as Karl walked away, wondering what trick he had up his sleeve.

She worried that whatever it was might end up blowing up in Patty's face.

Chapter Seven

With her booth packed up, Samantha headed to the lodge office to pick up her check. In line, she greeted a woman she'd met during some of the festival planning meetings. "Alice, right? It's Samantha, from the cocktail booth. So how did the festival end up for you?"

The woman sold hand-carved and dipped candles and had a booth in the marketplace. "Oh, hi, Samantha. It turned out pretty well, considering. I had a good bit of business, even despite all the happenings on Friday. It's a shame we may never have a festival of that size again."

Samantha tilted her head. "What do you mean?"

"Apparently, inspectors found a drainage problem with the tennis center construction and wouldn't approve any more permits until planners come back with a revised plan showing everything spaced out more. The rumor is they'll have to expand into at least half of the space we used for the festival."

Samantha's mouth dropped open. "I had no idea! When did you hear this?"

"The news spread all over the craft booths on Friday night. There hasn't been much more said about it since Angela died, but it's only a matter of time. It's such a shame."

They'd reached the front of the line and picked up their checks. Samantha felt cheered at the total written on her check. When she deducted her expenses, she figured she and Beth would net at least five thousand dollars for the weekend. *Not too shabby.*

After pocketing the check, Samantha called to ask Beth to drive their catering van over and help pick up their supplies. Because they still only rented a kitchen part-time at the kitchen incubator downtown, they stored all of their supplies at Beth and Marisa's house.

Beth arrived twenty minutes later, and they began to transfer the boxes of bottles and syrups into the catering van.

While they worked, Samantha filled her friend in on the latest news regarding Patty and the investigation. "Oh, and I lined up a new job for us—Angela Clawson's funeral on Thursday. I met with her daughter-in-law, who wants to hire us to serve a buffet and cocktails for the reception."

Beth paused midway in lifting a box, to stare at Samantha. "Are you serious? You want us to work the funeral of the woman your mom's best friend is accused of murdering?"

"All those rich people? If we impress a handful of them, we'll have an in with some of the most influential people in the Highlands. I just need to wow everyone with the perfect gin drink to represent Angela Clawson's life."

"So you're not considering the funeral an opportunity to snoop? I know your mom is worried about Patty." Beth raised her eyebrows as she locked her gaze with Samantha's.

"If I hear or see something interesting, so be it. But I promise, I don't want the kind of trouble I had last month."

"I trust you, Sam. But the business needs to be our priority. We can't afford to have our name connected with any controversy."

Samantha's face burned. "I would never jeopardize our business, Beth. We've both worked too hard."

Beth sighed. "I know you wouldn't. And you're right—this reception could be a lucrative opportunity."

Tensions soothed between them, Samantha and Beth packed up the last of the supplies and planned to meet the next day to discuss the funeral reception.

* * *

Back home, Ruby pounced on Samantha, sashaying around her legs and mewing insistently. While Ruby was a friendly cat, she rarely lingered this long around the ankles unless she was hungry. Samantha bent down to pick her up. "What is it Ruby? Did you miss your lunch? Mom promised to feed you."

The cat leaped out of her arms and ran toward her empty food bowl. Samantha poured food into the dish and called out, "Mom? Why didn't you feed Ruby? She's acting like she's starved."

Samantha made a quick tour of her apartment and realized her mom was gone again. She extracted her cell phone from her purse and called Lillian.

"Hi, Samantha." Her mother answered after the first ring.

Samantha unclenched the hand she hadn't realized she'd been holding in a fist. "Mom! Where are you? I just got home and found Ruby starving and you nowhere in sight."

"Oh no. I knew I had forgotten something. Ruby will forgive me. I'm at Patty's."

"Is there anything new regarding her case?" Samantha sat at her kitchen table while she talked.

"For now, it's good news. She hasn't been charged yet. Her lawyer checked in with the police department, and they wouldn't say anything other than that they weren't ready with an arrest warrant yet. But Patty heard from a friend with a son in the department that the police are investigating some new suspects."

"Really? That is good news! Does she know who?"

"Not yet. All she knows is that several tips came over the tip line. Her friend is hoping to get more information soon."

The news sounded promising to Samantha. "I wonder if it relates to the person Karl's friend saw messing with Angela's car on Friday night. Make sure Patty's lawyer mentions that to the police. The person who tampered with Angela's car might be her killer."

"Good idea. I'll mention it." Lillian's voice suddenly became muffled as she called out to someone else in the room. "Anyway, Martin, Patty, and I were going to go out for dinner. They were telling me about this great little pasta place in Montrose that makes its own pasta. Want to come join us?"

Samantha's heart sank. She'd been looking forward to taking her mom out for a nice dinner, just the two of them. And the idea of sharing a meal with Martin made her stomach turn. "No, thanks, Mom. I'm pretty beat after today. And I need to plan for the funeral. I'll pick up dinner and hang in tonight."

"Are you sure, honey?"

"Yeah, Mom. Try to have some fun, and I'll see you later."

Samantha tried to stifle her annoyance. Patty was facing a grave situation, so of course Lillian wanted to spend time with her, but was it too much to ask to have her mom spend a little one-on-one time with her daughter?

Oh well. I do need to work on Angela's special cocktail.

She ordered pork pad ke mao from the Thai place down the street and retreated to her kitchen, her happy place, to experiment with different flavor combinations.

Since she and Beth had begun their business last month, she had amassed a decent inventory of her favorite bitters creations. Most she sold to a handful of local bartenders who used them to create custom cocktails, but she sold some through an Etsy page on the internet. Those sales supplemented her income between big gigs, like the Independence Day festival, or the few weddings—and now a funeral—they'd been hired to cater.

Given the tight time line for the funeral, she needed to create a cocktail out of existing ingredients she had on hand. Custom bitters took the better part of two to four weeks to finish because of the infusion time. But the idea of serving a roomful of the Highlands' upper crust even an updated version of an old drink wouldn't help to build her brand. The best cocktails told a story, with bitter notes to cut the sweetness, or an unexpected flavor that served as a plot twist for a traditional standard. Samantha needed to create a signature drink that represented the family's image of Angela, helping to tell her story.

Without time to handcraft new bitters, Samantha decided she would make a shrub, an acidic syrup made of fruit, sugar, and vinegar, which could add complexity to any cocktail. From what she knew of Angela, Samantha decided the more complex, the better.

She pulled out the notes she'd taken during her visit with Olivia Clawson. A gin-based cocktail with underlying notes of bitterness and a hint of sweetness. *Yes, a shrub will be perfect. But what fruit should I use?*

Gin drinks always made her think of cool, which also seemed to fit Angela Clawson. Samantha dug through her fruit crisper to see what she had on hand. Behind the lemons and limes she always had on stock, she found a pint of fresh blackberries she'd bought on sale at the farmer's market. *Hmm . . . blackberry. That might work.*

After pureeing the berries, Samantha mixed them with vinegar and sugar in a pot and set it on the stove. The mixture simmered for an hour before Samantha pureed it further and strained it back into the pot for more simmering.

A pungent vinegar aroma had overwhelmed the apartment, but the thick, slightly sweet and deeply flavorful blackberry syrup that sat cooling on the stove would serve as a nice counterpoint to a sharp gin flavor. The syrup needed to rest in the refrigerator overnight before reaching its full flavor, but so far, Samantha's experiment was a success.

Lillian wrinkled her nose upon walking into the apartment a few hours later. "What is that awful smell? Are you pickling cucumbers in here?"

"It'll dissipate eventually." Samantha explained how she made the shrub before offering her mom a seat at the kitchen table. "Want anything to drink?"

"Absolutely. I could use one of your cocktails. Surprise me." Lillian leaned back in her chair and watched her daughter.

Samantha prepared two Army & Navy cocktails with gin, lemon juice, and homemade orgeat mixed with a dash of her special lemon bitters. The cloudy white drinks had a lemony zing to them, and Samantha's tongue tingled as she took her first taste. "Did you learn more about the police's new suspects?"

Lillian sampled the drink and smacked her lips. "Mmm, this is tasty. No, we still don't know much. Patty's friend, whose son works at the police department, said they had a bunch of tips come in through the tip line last night and that the police will be busy for days following up on them. Patty's lawyer said she should be able to get more information from the police herself in the next day or two. I made sure to mention the person seen messing around Angela's car."

"So how is Patty doing?"

Lillian sighed. "Patty is Patty. She's always been a glass-half-empty kind of woman. Of course, her glass has been more than half empty too many times in her life. She doesn't believe the police will focus for long on anyone but her. How about you? Did you learn anything today?"

Samantha recounted her strange conversation with Karl and the news she'd learned from Alice, the candle seller, about the tennis club needing to expand further into the festival grounds because of flooding concerns.

"Oh no! Patty will be even more on edge than before." Lillian filled Samantha in on the research she'd conducted on the lodge and the tennis club controversy earlier that day. "The only reason most of the lodge supported the tennis club idea is because Adam Muller promised members that once the club was built, they would have plenty of land left for other activities, including future festivals."

Lillian reached for a stack of papers at the end of the kitchen table and flipped through them until she found the one she wanted. It was an article printed from the local Highlands paper.

"This Muller guy is the son of a former longtime lodge president who died five years ago. The president who succeeded Adam's father neglected the upkeep and let the grounds get run down. Maintenance was long overdue. Lodge members elected Adam to restore the organization to financial solvency."

Samantha reached for the article and scanned it herself. "Wow, the building must be in terrible shape. This story says the lodge needs nearly a million dollars in repair work. Members had been considering selling off some land to afford it."

Lillian nodded. "Yes, but they didn't because of the tennis club proposition. Angela approached Adam with the idea of starting the club. She helped him convince everyone it was the only way to save the lodge. Patty said he laid it on thick, saying he wanted to honor his father's memory and keep the lodge going."

"This article mentions a German history center and archives being part of the overall plans." Samantha scanned the rest of the printed pages.

"Oh yeah, that was Muller's other big idea. He said his father wanted nothing more than to preserve the history of Germans in Texas and their contributions to society. He was going to name the archives after his dad."

"I wonder what happens to the archives now. This article says they were going to build it next to the tennis center complex, but now, with the center needing to expand, I wonder if there will still be space for it."

Lillian finished her drink. "That's the least of our concerns now."

Samantha finished her own drink and grabbed her mother's glass, along with her own, to wash them in the sink. "Well, it could be important. The candle woman said the news about the flooding concern was circulating throughout the festival on Friday. Seems to me information like that might make somebody even more unhappy with Angela."

Lillian stood up to help her daughter dry the drinkware. "You have a point there. Oh, I almost forgot, but I did a little digging on Angela at the library today too. She's had quite the career in organizing fundraisers in the last twenty years, but there wasn't much information regarding her life before then. She has one sister who still lives out in West Texas, but I didn't find many details. I'll have another go at it tomorrow."

Samantha stacked the dishes in a cupboard and wandered into the living room. "Speaking of tomorrow, what's on your agenda?"

"Not much." Lillian settled in on the couch. "You and I haven't spent much time together. I don't want to disrupt your work, but maybe we can do something."

The words lifted Samantha's mood. Though she didn't want to begrudge her mother the time she spent with Patty, she was happy to have her mom to herself for the day.

"That would be great, Mom. Tomorrow I have to deliver bitters to a few of my bartender customers. You can tag along, and we can stop for a bite to eat."

"That sounds nice, honey." Lillian yawned. "For now, I'm tired. I'm going to read a bit before heading to bed a little early."

"'Night, Mom." Samantha selected a book of her own and curled up on the couch, with Ruby balanced on her left thigh.

* * *

In the morning, Samantha woke to the smell of freshly brewed coffee and a simmering pot of cinnamon, raisin, and pecan oatmeal.

"It smells amazing in here, Mom." Samantha popped her kettle onto the stove to heat water for her tea and spooned oatmeal into a bowl. "You're taking me back to my childhood with these breakfasts. I haven't eaten oatmeal in years."

"You should make it for yourself. It's easy, and it provides the fiber that will help carry you through to lunch." Lillian sat at the table, drinking her coffee and flipping through the newspaper. "Nothing in here discussing Patty's case."

Samantha poured the hot water in her favorite mug as the scent of cinnamon and cloves from her chai tea mingled with the other spices from the oatmeal. "I guess the city has moved on." She sat at the table with her steeping tea and leafed through another section of newspaper while she ate. "Too many murders and other crimes in this city to keep the focus on one."

"I was hoping for a story about the tips to the police hotline." Lillian took a bite of her oatmeal. "It would be great if a tip pointed police to the killer."

The women ate their breakfasts in companionable silence, skimming through the rest of the newspaper. When Samantha stood to wash the breakfast dishes, her mother went to the bedroom to change.

After her shower, Samantha boxed up five cartons of fresh bitters, with six bottles each. Lillian scrutinized each bottle—macadamia nut bitters, aloha bitters, and pineapple bitters. "These sound like a Hawaiian vacation."

Samantha laughed. "Good. We're going to drop them off at a local tiki bar. They asked me to create some new flavors for fall cocktails."

"I'm so proud of you, Sam." Lillian tucked the bottles back into the boxes. "I know you loved being a reporter, but I really think you've found a new calling. From your drinks at the festival, to these bitters, I am so impressed."

Samantha smiled. "Thanks, Mom."

As they drove to their first stop, Lillian spoke. "I've been thinking more about that argument you overheard between the daughter and the daughter-in-law. We need to find out why the daughter is suspicious."

Samantha scrutinized her mother's face. "And how would we do that, Mom?"

"I've come up with a few ideas . . . What if you contacted Christina, the daughter? Asked to meet her? You could ask for her input on the menu for the reception. That seems reasonable, right?"

Samantha kept quiet, considering. She had to admit, her mom's idea wasn't a bad one. But would Christina suspect anything? Or worse yet, would it anger Olivia? Samantha didn't want to alienate the woman before cashing her check. "I'll consider it."

Samantha saw Lillian's smile out of the corner of her eye. *What is she getting me into?*

At their first stop, Samantha dropped off the box of bitters and chatted with the Hawaiian shirt–clad bartender while her mom oohed and aahed appreciatively at the kitschy decor. The walls were lined with bamboo, and the ceiling was hung with fishing nets and surfboards. Lillian reached out and touched a dashboard hula girl on the bar, setting her off on another round of hip swaying. "This place is darling." Lillian smiled at the bearded bartender behind the counter.

He rolled his eyes and grinned, handing Samantha a check. "Bring your mom back when we're open. I'll make her a 'darling' drink, and she can see how we use your bitters."

"I'd love that!" Lillian hopped off the barstool she'd been sitting on and followed Samantha out the door, offering a wave at her new friend.

As they drove to their next stop, Samantha again considered her mom's suggestion. It had been fun to spend time with her, so Samantha decided she wanted to pay her mom back. "Okay,

Mom, I'll do it. I'll try to talk to Christina and find out more about Olivia. But first, I need her phone number."

Lillian grinned. "Leave that to me."

As they parked outside the tequila and agave bar, Lillian was already writing a phone number down on a piece of paper. She might not be great with directions, but she was a whiz with finding information.

When they returned from dropping off the second box of bitters, Samantha took the plunge and called Christina, hoping she might get her voicemail so she could leave a message.

The phone rang twice before the same loud voice she'd heard outside of Angela's house answered. "Yes?"

"Oh, hi. Is this Christina? I'm so sorry to bother you right now, and I'm very sorry for your loss. I'm Samantha Warren. We briefly met the other day. Your sister-in-law, Olivia, hired me to create custom cocktails for your mother's, um, funeral?"

"Oh yes. I saw you as I was leaving Mama's house. I'm sorry I was so rude. I wasn't at my best then." The woman's voice was soft, but friendly.

Maybe this will be easier than I thought. "Again, I'm sorry to bother you, but I wanted to get some inspiration from someone who knew Mrs. Clawson's best qualities. Olivia didn't seem . . ."

"You don't have to say it. I know just what you mean. Olivia didn't think my mother had any good qualities. But what can I do for you? How can I help?"

Christina seemed nice enough so far, so Samantha decided to come right out with her request. "I hate to be an imposition, but I wondered if I could meet you somewhere or stop by your home and talk to you for a bit about your mother and what she liked and didn't like, and what flavors best represented her."

Christina paused long enough that Samantha worried she'd annoyed the woman, but when she spoke, Christina's voice cracked. "Thank you for that. Olivia jumped in to take charge of everything, and she hasn't even stopped to ask me what I might want. Angela was my mother . . ." Christina let out a sob. "I'm sorry . . ."

Samantha fumbled for her words. "No, *I'm* sorry. If this is a bad time—"

"No, no. I'll be fine. You can stop by my place around two PM."

Samantha gave her mom a thumbs-up. "Thank you so much. I'll see you then."

When she hung up the phone, Lillian squealed. "You handled that perfectly! So, when do we go meet her?"

Samantha gave her mom a look. "*We?* We are not going to meet her. *I'm* going to meet her at two PM. I can't show up with my mother at a business meeting. Besides, Beth needs to come with me to discuss the food."

Lillian face fell for a moment before she nodded. "You make a good point. We'll just have to brainstorm before you go." Her face brightened. "I think you mentioned something about lunch?"

Samantha checked her watch. It was not quite eleven, but close enough to start contemplating lunch, or at least brunch. They dropped the last box of bitters off at another bar on the west side of the Highlands, and Samantha turned toward the Elgin, a glass-walled restaurant filled with chandeliers and Victorian furniture overlooking the Buffalo Bayou, the brown water that ran like an arterial vein from west Houston all the way to the Gulf of Mexico. The restaurant was a cozy spot, with a 'ladies who lunch' vibe and a nice selection of brunch and lunch items she thought her mother would appreciate.

After making themselves comfortable at a small wicker table in a corner, with a view out to the muddy, swirling water, they strategized about Samantha's upcoming meeting.

"Samantha, you need to get Christina talking about Olivia and her brother, Matt. If she really thinks one of them could have murdered her mother, we've got to have more details."

"But I don't want to sound like a gossip." Samantha tucked a stray hair behind her ear.

"Of course not. From that scene you described, I'll bet the acrimony will be obvious at the mere mention of Olivia's or Matt's name." Lillian looked adamant as she took a slice of the hot French bread and spread it with the butter a server had dropped off at their table.

"I hope you're right." Samantha buttered her own slice of bread. "What are you going to do while I'm gone?"

"I'll check back in with Patty, see if she's learned any more from her lawyer about those tips the police are running down."

The two enjoyed a lunch of grilled cheese sandwiches and tomato basil soup while Samantha pondered how best to approach Christina with her questions. If she dug hard enough, she hoped Christina could provide some answers that would help Patty.

Chapter Eight

After lunch, Samantha picked up Beth for the meeting with Christina.

"So, we're just going to go over the menu? Ask her opinion on what she wants?" Beth began jotting in her notebook.

"Olivia is technically the client, but she flat out said she didn't care. And Christina is Angela's daughter. She should have a say in the plans."

"Sure, that makes sense." Beth looked sideways at Samantha. "But tell me the truth: Is there another reason for this trip? Anything to do with Patty?"

Samantha shrugged. "It won't hurt to ask a few questions. But I want you to know, Beth, I would never jeopardize our business with my snooping."

Beth raised one eyebrow. "I know that, Sam. But I also care about you. I don't want you doing anything dangerous."

"This will be plenty safe." Samantha pulled into the visitor parking space at Christina's condo in the Highlands. Though nowhere near as grand or charming as Angela's Greek Revival–style home, Christina's condo exuded money. Christina opened the door, dressed in a casual but elegant romper, and motioned for Samantha to come inside.

The high-end furniture appeared intentionally minimalistic. Samantha took a seat on a bone-white modular sofa that took up three-quarters of the living room, and pulled out her notebook. Beth joined her on the sofa. "Thank you so much for meeting with us. Olivia didn't offer much input on the menu, and I want to make sure that Angela's immediate family is happy with what Beth and I serve at the reception. There's you and your brother, but I understand Angela also had a sister?"

"Thanks for coming." Christina sat in a chair opposite the couch. "Anyway, technically yes, Mama had a sister, but they haven't spoken for years, so we don't need to worry about her feelings."

That's interesting. Samantha wished she could ask more about Angela's sister, but with no easy way to ask for further details, Samantha ignored the comment and pressed on with her questions. "Olivia suggested a buffet, so Beth wants to start out by running through a few of her food suggestions, and I want to talk cocktails with you. I want to come up with something that will reflect Angela's style. Olivia didn't offer much in that regard either."

Christina, sitting across from them in a jewel-toned plush chair, sniffed. "No surprise there. She hated my mother. They were always fighting about something. And after what my Mom told me on Friday, well . . . let's just say I'm not entirely convinced she had Mama's best interests at heart."

Beth lowered her eyes and flipped feverishly through her notepad, while Samantha raised her eyebrows, maintaining eye contact. "Really? What did Angela say?"

Christina lowered her gaze briefly. "I probably shouldn't repeat it." Samantha's hopes were temporarily dashed, but when the grieving woman lifted her gaze from her lap, her face reflected a new resolve. "You know what? I'm going to say it, because what if Olivia or my brother had something to do with Mama's death? Mama and Matt had a big fight on Friday night. Mama was so mad, she told me she was going to write him out of her will! If that's not a motive, I don't know what is, especially after he had just lost major money in a stupid investment. I know for a fact that he and Olivia had to borrow a significant sum from my mother recently."

"But surely you don't think either one of them is capable of murdering her, do you?" Samantha blinked slowly, shocked at Christina's brazen accusation.

"The last time I spoke with Mama, right before her death, she was practically foaming at the mouth, she was so mad at Matt. And with her threat to write him out of the will, what else am I supposed to think? That gives either of them motive." Christina's chin jutted out, as if she was waiting for one of them to contradict her.

Samantha's eyes widened. "You saw your mother right before she died? When did you speak with her?"

Christina's eyes pooled with tears. "It was right before seven thirty. She'd roped me into volunteering as a judge for the pie contest, and that's when my shift began. By eight PM, police found her body." Christina pulled a tissue from a box on the coffee table and wiped at her eyes.

Samantha wished she could find a way to comfort the woman without it seeming awkward. "Did you tell the police?"

Christina sniffled. "Of course I did. The detectives said they would look into it, but it's just my word against theirs."

Samantha opened her mouth to ask another question, when Beth coughed to bring them back on track. "So, where were we? Let's discuss the menu items. We're a farm-to-table catering service, so we prepare everything with fresh ingredients from local gardens. We're in the late-summer growing season, so we have some lovely options. Since we're talking about an upscale lunch buffet, how does blackberry-and-ginger-glazed salmon with potatoes and green beans sound? Maybe a nice kale salad? I've got a great recipe for flatbread with blackberries and goat cheese. We can add a pasta dish for those who don't like fish."

Christina rolled the tissue she held into a tight little ball. "That sounds nice. What about mini quiches or something? Mom always served those at her fundraising lunches. Or . . . I don't know. I've never been great at planning menus. That was Mama's thing. She always served the right meal, wore the right clothes, and invited the right people. I wish I'd listened to her more."

The pain was etched on Christina's face, and it appeared like she was ready to cry. Samantha wished again that she could comfort Christina, but wasn't sure how.

Christina breathed deeply and closed her eyes for a fraction of a second, seeming to center herself. "I'm sorry. You mentioned a cocktail too, right?"

"Yes, if you're okay to talk now?" Samantha used her soothing voice, the one she'd used as a reporter when trying to interview families who had lost loved ones. Christina nodded her assent.

"Well, as I mentioned earlier, we'll have the standard bar, but your brother wanted a signature cocktail to honor your mother. All I got from Olivia is that she was a gin drinker."

Christina offered a half smile. "She got that right, at least."

"With blackberries in season right now, a blackberry cocktail would be lovely. The berries will bring a bit of sweetness, but it will still have plenty of complexity. It sounds simple, but it will look beautiful and taste delicious."

Christina's eyes were unfocused as she stared off into the distance. "I think Mama would like that." After a short pause, Christina's eyes came back into focus as she gazed at Samantha. "I'm sorry. All of a sudden, I'm not feeling great. Do you mind reaching out later if you have any further questions?"

Samantha stood up and Beth followed. "Of course. Thank you for taking the time to meet with us. Please, don't get up. We'll see ourselves out."

* * *

The friends remained silent as they walked to Samantha's car, but as soon as she'd closed the car door, Samantha turned to Beth and spoke. "That was interesting."

Beth nodded. "I sympathize with her. She's clearly grieving. But I'm not sure it was worth the trip. She offered little to no input on the menu."

"She appreciated being consulted, so in that respect, I'm glad we went. I don't want complaints about our menu after the fact. Anyway, do you suppose she really believes Matt is guilty?"

Beth tilted her head slightly, appearing to consider the question. "It's hard to say. I can't get a great read on her. But she says she mentioned her suspicions to the police, so hopefully they can figure it out."

"It won't hurt to mention it to Patty, just in case."

Samantha drove back to Beth's house so they could finalize the menu and confirm they could locate the necessary produce from their local growers. Once they'd made arrangements and booked time slots for Wednesday and Thursday at the kitchen incubator, Samantha gathered her things to go.

"Let's touch base tomorrow to make sure we're on track. Tell Marisa I said hi." Samantha waved as she stepped out the front door.

* * *

Back at home, Ruby greeted Samantha at the door by sashaying around her legs. Samantha bent down to grab the cat, who squirmed in her arms before jumping to the ground and racing into the living room. Samantha spotted a note on the kitchen table. Her mother said she'd be back soon. *Hmm . . .. wonder where she went. Maybe the library again.*

Samantha walked into her bedroom to change into more comfortable clothes and text David. She wished she could talk to him about the case, knowing his analytical mind might make connections that she had missed, but she didn't want him to question her involvement. She decided to keep it simple and truthful.

I hope your trip is going well. Staying busy here but missing you. Ready to see you when you get home! She finished off with a smiley face and two heart emojis before pressing "Send." A minute later, she heard the door open.

"Sam? Can you help me?"

Samantha ran back into the kitchen to see her mother balancing two full bags of groceries in one arm while she tried to close the door with her other. Reaching past her mother, Samantha shut the door and grabbed the bags. "What's all of this?"

"Groceries." Lillian unpacked chicken breasts, carrots, onions, and asparagus.

"I can tell they're groceries, Mom. But what are they for?"

"Dinner. I'm making my homemade chicken pot pie. I promised Patty I would bring over dinner tonight. Oh, and I might have promised one of your special cocktails."

The prospect of her mother's chicken pot pie made Samantha's mouth water, but almost as instantly, she registered the second half of Lillian's comment. "Wait, you're making food to take over to Patty's? And I'm supposed to go there?"

Lillian gave Samantha the "are you feeling okay?" look she usually wore before reaching over to check her daughter's forehead for a fever. "Of course you're supposed to go. She needs all the support she can get right now. She had bad news from her lawyer."

Samantha wanted to hear the bad news, but the prospect of being thrown together with Martin flustered her. "I suppose Martin will be there? I can make something for you to take, but I don't want to go over there."

Lillian laid down the knife and the onion she had been about to chop, and locked eyes with her daughter. "What is wrong with you? I thought I detected some weirdness with you and Martin the other day. What's it all about? You've known each other since you were kids, and you probably haven't seen each other in more than a decade."

"Yeah, and if I don't see him for another decade, that would still be too soon." Samantha huffed.

Lillian tilted her head as she pursed her lips. "Samantha what has gotten into you?"

"Didn't you ever wonder why we'd stopped hanging out in college?" Samantha raised her eyebrows.

"Patty and I just figured it was because you'd broken his heart. We'd honestly been afraid it was going to happen at some point or another, so we were a little relieved when it ended before anything too serious had happened." Lillian shrugged, picking up her knife again to resume chopping.

Samantha felt her limbs turn numb, rooting her to the spot. "Broke his heart? What are you talking about? I know he was mad that I went out with his roommate a few times, but it's not like Martin and I were ever anything more than friends."

Lillian paused in her chopping again and fixed her daughter with a stare. "You were always oblivious to it, but that boy had a crush on you since high school."

"No way." Samantha waved her hand as if to swat the very idea away. She combed through her internal memories, trying to pinpoint anything to make her mother's words make sense. She closed her mind to the memories, anger clouding her thoughts. "But regardless of his feelings, nothing excuses his behavior toward me later."

Lillian stopped chopping again and moved quickly to Samantha's side, reaching out to her arm. "What happened?" Her voice came out in a rush. "He didn't hurt you, did he?"

"Of course he hurt me! He ruined three months of my hard work, making me look like an idiot in front of my editors." Samantha fumed as she told her mother the story about how she'd worked for several months on an article for the student paper about hazing incidents at the university, and how she'd nailed down an interview with one of the fraternity members who'd been involved in one of the incidents. The interview would have provided the confirmation she needed to publish the story, but Martin convinced the guy not to talk to her. "I'd worked so hard on that story. It could have been my ticket to an internship at a major paper, but he ruined it because of his petty jealousy."

Lillian watched her daughter intently during her story, sighing at the end of it. "That does seem mean—at least the way you're telling it—but, honey, that's ancient history. You can't still be mad about it, can you? You're not even a reporter any longer."

And just like that, with the efficiency of a surgeon, Samantha's mother managed to gut her twice—first by discounting her feelings, and second by reminding her that she'd given up her dream job. Though she was happy in her new career, a huge part of her still felt a sense of loss over her reporting career. For so many years, that had been all she had ever wanted, and to have had it snatched away from her because of layoffs felt like the death of an important part of her. It hurt that her mom didn't understand that, but if she was honest, her mom was often oblivious to things like that. "Maybe it doesn't seem important to you, but it was a big deal to me." Samantha deflated. Even saying the words made her feel silly, but she wasn't ready to let it go. "Besides, he's not been exactly friendly to me either. I appreciate that you want to support your friend. I like Patty too, but I don't have to be friends with her son."

Lillian took a step toward Samantha, her face registering concern as she appeared to try to take in her daughter's emotions. "No, of course you don't have to be friends with him. I understand if you don't want to go."

Despite the words, Samantha saw that her mother really didn't understand. *Am I being too stubborn? It was a long time ago. And she's right, I'm not even a reporter any longer, so it shouldn't matter.*

Samantha picked up the bag of carrots and grabbed a peeler, turning away from her mother and toward the sink. The repetitive motion of the peeler calmed her down. *Maybe I am just being silly, especially with everything else that's going on.*

Samantha finished peeling the carrots while her mother went back to the cutting board to chop the onion and chicken. They worked silently together for a while before Samantha asked about Patty. "So, what was Patty's bad news today?"

Lillian began to sauté the onions and carrots in butter, with salt, pepper, and fresh thyme. "Oh, it was those calls into the hotline. It turns out it was a bunch of Patty's friends from the lodge. Karl arranged it, hoping it might take the suspicion off Patty if everyone called in and accused someone else."

Samantha rubbed her eyes. "You're kidding me. He mentioned a plan, but I never imagined it would be as dumb as that."

Lillian added flour and sherry to the pot on the stove before whisking in chicken broth and heavy whipping cream. "It gets worse. The police are blaming Patty for the stunt. Her lawyer says they may bring charges against her soon."

"That's awful. Did the lawyer ask the police about the person Karl's friend saw messing with Angela's car?" Samantha watched as her mom spooned the chopped-up chicken and asparagus into the bubbling sauce on the stove, and breathed in the tantalizing aroma.

Lillian focused on her daughter as she stirred. "Oh, that was another disappointing bit of news. The police found Angela's car unlocked, but there was no damage—only food spilled in the back seat. They figured Angela was attacked after leaving the car to clean up the mess. Patty mentioned to her lawyer that there was normally a camera trained on that parking lot, but the police checked, and the camera was off on Friday night. There's no way to prove anyone was messing with Angela's car, and even if they did, the police said it might have nothing to do with her murder."

Samantha clenched her jaw in frustration. "Why was the camera off? That's ridiculous." She pulled a casserole dish out of a cabinet, for the chicken pot pie. "Oh, I need to fill you in on my weird visit with Angela's daughter today. She hinted that she thought her brother or her sister-in-law might be involved in her mother's murder."

Lillian looked up from the pot. "Really? Did she have any evidence?"

Samantha poured the remaining cream in, along with flour, salt, and baking soda, for the ultra-rich biscuit dough that was the secret to her mother's recipe. "She didn't mention anything specific. Honestly, it was hard to determine whether she actually believed it or she just has an axe to grind. She said she spoke to her mom a half an hour before Angela's body was found, and Angela had complained about a quarrel she'd had with Matt. I'm hoping to learn more at the funeral."

"That seems like our most promising lead yet." Lillian watched as her daughter kneaded the dough lightly on the counter.

Samantha relaxed into the moment, enjoying the aromas of the simmering cream sauce and the time spent cooking with her mother. *Maybe Mom is right. All that stuff with Martin should be water under the bridge by now. I can be civil.* She watched Lillian pour the steaming filling into the casserole dish. "All right, Mom, I'll go. I want to be there for Patty."

Lillian squeezed Samantha's arm. "Thanks, honey. It will mean the world to Patty."

Samantha used a chicken-shaped cookie cutter to cut the biscuit dough, placing the pale chickens on top of the bubbling filling and watching them sink slightly. "I'll be on my best behavior."

Lillian slid the pot pie into the oven as Samantha paged through her recipe book, searching for a complementary cocktail. Deciding that nothing paired well with the chicken pot pie but white wine, she opted to serve a bourbon smash after dinner while they contemplated the next options for Patty.

* * *

Two hours later, sitting around Patty's kitchen table, dishing out the piping hot chicken pot pie, Samantha tried her best to ignore Martin without seeming awkward. But every time she tried to focus her attention in some other direction, she felt his gaze on her. His appearance had matured since college. He'd grown into his lanky body, and his face had filled out nicely. *But I've been burned by a handsome face before. I won't let my guard down now.*

Her thoughts straying, Samantha tuned back into the conversation as Patty explained what her lawyer had said that afternoon.

"The police were angry about having to chase down the rumors. Apparently, Karl had organized a dozen people to call in tips, accusing each other of the crime, hoping the police would see that more people than me disliked the woman. But since most of them were my friends, the police decided I'd orchestrated the plot."

Lillian looked indignant. "That's ridiculous. You want the police focused on finding the real murderer!"

Martin tightened his lips. "Of course, the police are convinced that Mom is the murderer, and this little stunt did nothing to help change their minds. Mom, tell them what your friend Wanda said."

Patty made a shooing motion with her hands. "Oh, Wanda has an overactive imagination."

"Tell them, Mom."

Patty took a few bites from her dinner before launching into her story. "Wanda said Karl organized the whole thing, making sure each accused person had at least one other person to corroborate their alibi. The idea was to sow reasonable doubt, but not at the risk of setting up another innocent person to take the fall for the murder."

Samantha rolled her eyes. "What a stupid plan."

"But that's not the important part, Mom. Tell them what else Wanda said." Martin's voice carried an edge.

Patty took another few bites of dinner and swallowed some water. "This is the most ridiculous part. Wanda pointed out that Karl hadn't included himself on the list of people to be accused, which she thought was strange. Then, she says she remembered seeing him heading in the direction of the construction site not too long before Angela's body was found. She said she specifically remembers thinking it was odd for him to head in that direction, since he was allegedly working at the grill in the opposite direction."

Lillian gasped. "Does she suspect that nice man . . .?"

"She's certainly suggesting it's a possibility." Martin widened his eyes. "I've told Mom she needs to get Wanda to tell the police what she saw."

"But it's ridiculous. Karl wouldn't have committed murder, any more than I would," Patty scoffed, flapping her hand as if to even wipe away the suggestion.

Martin raised his voice. "Mom, I'm just saying you need to have the police considering every alternative. Don't you realize how much trouble you're in right now?"

He turned to Lillian. "Can you convince her? I'm not saying to throw the man under the bus, but how much do we even know about him? For all we know, he could very well be responsible."

"Martin, that is not the way I want to approach this." Patty gave her son a look designed to end any further discussion on the topic.

At the firmness in her voice, Martin's gaze shifted to his plate as he concentrated on eating his food. The room fell silent for a while, with nothing but the sound of forks scraping against the porcelain plates.

"Oh!" Lillian glanced over at Samantha. "Honey, tell them what you learned today from the daughter."

Samantha's cheeks burned, not wanting to be subject to any more attention from Martin. But she sipped some ice water and composed herself, recounting her meeting with Christina, and her accusations against her brother and sister-in-law.

Patty's eyes brightened. "Do you think it could be true? Do the police know?"

Samantha felt guilty at raising the woman's spirits with a story that could prove to be false. "Christina said she mentioned it to the police, and that they are investigating it. I personally have a hard time seeing Olivia or Matt as a killer, but you never know. Anyway, I'm hoping to learn more when I cater the funeral."

Martin raised his eyebrow and fixed Samantha with an annoyed stare. "So you're profiting off this situation now? I shouldn't be surprised. You were always searching for an angle and never really giving much thought to how it might impact anyone else." He picked up his plate and carried it to the sink.

Patty jumped up after him. "Martin! Don't talk to her like that."

Samantha clenched her fist as she felt fury bubble up inside her. "And what exactly does that mean?"

Martin turned to face her, but shook his head and turned away. "Never mind. Forget I said anything." He walked out of the room, heading, Samantha assumed, to his own bedroom.

"I'll go talk to him." Patty followed in the same direction Martin had taken a few seconds earlier.

Samantha focused her gaze on her mother. "See? I told you he was a jerk. Why is he acting like I'm being selfish? Yes, I took a job to work the funeral, but part of the reason I did that was to see what news I could pick up. Patty has to know that, right?"

Lillian smoothed her daughter's shirt. "If she doesn't know it, I'll make sure she does. I don't know what got into him."

Samantha felt heat flush through her body as the anger resurfaced. "I told you it was a bad idea for me to come here. I'm leaving." She grabbed her purse. "Are you coming with me, Mom?"

Lillian picked up her purse as well. "Yes. You go ahead to the car, and I'll meet you there in five minutes. I just want to tell Patty we're going."

Samantha hurried through the living room to the front door. She paused momentarily, playing back Martin's words, wondering what he could have meant. *It's true, I did go out with his roommate when I knew he didn't like the guy.*

Her mother's earlier comments ran through her mind. *Does it change the calculation if I know that he had feelings for me?*

She pursed her lips. *No, what he did to me was inexcusable.* Suddenly she wanted a confrontation. She threw her purse on the foyer table and followed the hallway to his room.

Chapter Nine

Standing outside Martin's bedroom, Samantha spotted Patty at the other end of the hallway, huddled with Lillian. Steeling herself, she knocked on Martin's door and waited.

"Look, I'm sorry. I already said I'll apologize." The voice, muffled behind the closed door, sounded softer than earlier.

Samantha opened the door and peered inside. The sight of a grown man sitting in his childhood bedroom, surrounded by the trappings of his youth, briefly quieted her anger.

"Oh, it's you." Martin glanced at Samantha before lowering his gaze to the ground. "I guess you already heard my apology. Sorry . . . I didn't know you were some great detective now." His petulant sarcasm made Samantha's temper boil once again.

"What is your problem? Why are you even mad at me? I went out with your roommate a few times. Big deal. You're the one who tried to ruin my career."

It was Martin's turn to look confused. "Ruin your career? What are you talking about?"

Samantha stared him down, not allowing him to shift his expression from her gaze. "My interview with Brian Salazar? The one I needed to finish the piece I'd been working on for three months about the hazing problems? The one that made me look like a fool when I couldn't turn it in? I know it was you who told him not to talk to me. He told me right before he canceled my interview."

Martin chuckled. "Brian Salazar? That's why you're mad at me? I saved you from him. Not that I ever expected you to show any gratitude, but he had been bragging about his plan to tell you a bunch of lies to discredit you. I threatened him that he'd better not go through with it, or I'd turn him into the fraternity's disciplinary committee."

Samantha bit her lip, trying to make sense of the new information. "How is that possible? I had to hunt to find Brian and convince him to talk to me. It's not like he was eager. It took weeks to get him to agree to an interview."

Martin shrugged. "I don't know what to tell you. Probably some of what you found was real, but a lot of the fraternity guys were mad about all of the press coverage. I got wind of Brian plotting to 'teach the media a lesson.' Even after the way you'd treated me, I didn't think it was fair of him to tank your professional reputation, so I put a stop to it."

Samantha face reddened. *Can this be true? Could I have been taken in that easily?* She'd always liked to think her reporter's instinct was solid, but she'd been young, and she could see how, in her eagerness to write a big story, she might have missed some warning signs. *I probably would have figured it out before we ran the story, but if Martin's telling the truth . . .*

She sat down on the edge of the bed and rubbed her temples before looking back up at Martin. "If that's true, I guess I owe you a debt of gratitude. So, thank you. But I still don't get what you mean about how I treated you. I know you didn't like Eric and would have preferred for me not to date him, but we only went out for a few months. What was the big deal?"

Martin sat on top of what seemed to be a miniature desk in relation to his now muscular frame, and stared at a spot on the floor. "All that stuff you told Eric about me . . . even if you didn't . . ." He glanced up at her face and swallowed before turning his face back toward the floor. "I mean, I thought we were friends. So to have him tell me you thought I lacked confidence and was too sensitive and that you weren't sure I'd ever have a normal relationship after my dad died . . . it was like a punch to the gut."

Samantha's face warmed and her heart pounded. "Martin, I never would have said that. I've never thought that." She stood up and walked toward him, wanting to close the distance between them. She laid her hand on his shoulder. "I might have told him I wished you believed in yourself more and that I know it was hard on you growing up without your dad, but I swear, I would never have said any of those things." She felt nauseous. *What must he have thought of me for all of these years?*

Martin looked up, seeming to search her eyes for some hint of whether she was telling the truth. "I'd like to believe that."

Samantha held his gaze, willing him to believe her. "It's true."

They stared at one another for a few seconds before the tension was almost unbearable. Martin took a deep breath and exhaled. "You know what? Forget it. It's all in the past. I know you're trying to help Mom now, and I appreciate that. Can we just start over?"

Samantha, whose emotions had been on a roller-coaster ride over the past five minutes, was more than ready to de-escalate the situation. She scanned Martin's face, seeing both the boy she had once known and the man he had become, staring back at her. The weight of everything, from the lost years of their friendship to the regret over words spoken and unspoken, pressed down on her. She was tired. "Yes. Should we go find our moms and reassure them that we no longer want to kill each other?"

Martin offered a half smile as he stood up. "Yeah, good call. Mom doesn't need any more worries right now. I need her to focus on herself."

Samantha stood and followed him into the hallway. "Right. From now on, Patty is our main focus."

They found their moms sitting at the kitchen table, eating chocolate chip cookies from a plate, their knees bouncing with nerves.

Samantha offered a wan smile. "We're fine now. We've called a truce. Anybody still up for a cocktail?"

Lillian jumped up and hugged her daughter. "I'll help—or at least I'll try."

Martin opened a kitchen cabinet and pulled out some glassware. "No, let me help. It's the least I can do."

Lillian looked at Samantha, her expression conveying a willingness to intervene.

Samantha waved her mom off. "Thanks, Martin. Why don't you cut up some lemons for me?"

She strode back to the front door, where she'd left her stuff on the table, and scooped up a bag of lemons and a handful of mint she'd picked from her container garden. Back in the kitchen, she handed the lemons to Martin to slice, and muddled them with the fresh mint and some simple syrup in a cocktail shaker. The muddling process released the citrus and mint oils, creating a clean, tangy aroma, perfect for the recent clearing of the air between the two of them.

Bourbon and bitters completed the smash, which she poured out into the four glasses Martin had lined up on the counter.

Martin sampled the drink. “This is good. Nice and refreshing.”

They collected their drinks and moved into the living room.

“So tell me about this business you’ve started. You create cocktails?” Martin was obviously making an effort to be friendly.

Samantha filled him in on the catering company she ran with Beth, explaining how it focused on fresh, locally sourced ingredients. “We’re still trying to build up a steady clientele, which is one reason I wanted to take the funeral job.”

Martin stared at the floor. “I’m sorry about the selfish crack. I know how hard it is to start a new business.”

Samantha raised her eyebrows. “I thought you were a teacher?”

“Oh, Martin also makes handmade furniture on the side. He made this table right here.” Patty beamed, touching the cherry coffee table.

Samantha took in the carved legs and the intricate design. “It’s beautiful, Martin. I can tell it took time and care.”

Martin coughed as a blush reddened his cheeks. “So, what were we discussing before . . . the funeral, right? Do you have a plan for how you’re going to investigate? I’m guessing you won’t have much time for extra snooping.”

Samantha’s skin prickled again. She couldn’t tell if Martin was trying to imply something or not. “Yes, I’ll be busy. But I’ll do what I can.” Her voice carried a slight edge to it.

Martin’s face blossomed pink. “Oh, I wasn’t suggesting . . . Anyway, what I meant was, what if I came with you? I could be your caterer’s helper or server, or something.” He peered at Samantha as if to detect how his words were landing. “You wouldn't have to pay me or anything. I could be an extra set of eyes or ears."

Samantha relaxed, thankful they weren't going to come to blows again. She considered Martin's offer. "What if someone recognized you?"

Martin shook his head. "I doubt there will be many of the original lodge members attending Angela's funeral. And even if there were, I doubt any of them would recognize me. Most of them haven't seen me since I was a teenager."

Samantha considered his logic. It might be awkward if anybody in Angela's family realized who Martin was, but if he kept a low profile, there was no reason for them to find out. "If you're sure nobody will recognize you, an extra pair of hands is always helpful. But I will make you work."

Martin smiled. "Of course. I'll be at your beck and call."

Samantha nodded. "I'll have to clear it with Beth, but that could work. I'll message you tomorrow."

Patty rose from her chair to take her glass into the kitchen. "Samantha, this drink was lovely. It was just what I needed to help me relax. But now, I have to confess, I'm a little tired."

Samantha rose as well, picking up her mother's glass. "Of course. It's getting late anyway. Mom and I should head out." She followed Patty into the kitchen.

Standing at the sink, Patty took the two glasses from Samantha. "I'm so glad you and Martin worked things out."

Samantha smiled. "Me too. And it's good to have a united front for our primary goal, to get you cleared."

Patty hugged her. "I'll be fine. I don't want you or your mom to worry too much."

Patty handed Samantha the now clean casserole dish and bar supplies. They walked into the living room to rejoin the others.

Lillian stood, following her daughter to the door. "Get a good night's sleep, Patty. We'll talk again in the morning."

They waved to Patty and Martin as they walked down the driveway to Samantha's car.

On the way home, Lillian scrutinized her daughter. "Are things really okay with you and Martin now?"

Samantha stared ahead, considering her answer. "He explained a few things. It turns out he was actually watching out for me back then, though he should have told me at the time. And there were some misunderstandings caused by his old roommate. Anyway, we're putting it behind us for now, at least until we help Patty clear her name."

"That's great. And who knows? Maybe you can become friends again." Lillian raised her eyebrows and shrugged, as if considering the possibilities.

Samantha drove for a few minutes in silence, replaying her conversation with Martin in her head. By the end of her short relationship with Eric, when he'd turned out to be the entitled, egotistical jerk Martin had always said he was, she still wouldn't have believed he would have twisted her words and used them to attack Martin the way he had. *I can only hope my judgment of character has improved since then.*

Samantha pulled into her parking space on her landlord's driveway, shaking her head at this alternative reality of her life, wondering what might have been different if she had known all she'd learned today. *I'll never know.*

Once inside the apartment, Lillian sat at the kitchen table while Samantha put away the clean dishes she'd brought back from Patty's. "Mom, can you handle another cocktail?"

Lillian yawned. "I don't know, honey. I'm pretty worn out after today, and that last drink made me sleepy."

"Just half of one then. I need to test out my recipe for the funeral reception. I need to figure out if it's any good or not, because otherwise I'll have to come up with a plan B."

"So this is research? That's my specialty." Lillian offered a grin. "How can I help?"

Samantha pulled out her hand juicer and handed it to her mom. "Squeeze these limes. I need three-quarters of an ounce of juice."

Lillian sliced and squeezed the limes while Samantha began measuring out the remaining ingredients into her shaker. After shaking the lime juice with the blackberry shrub and gin over ice, she strained the mixture into a rocks glass. A healthy dose of prosecco finished it. The result resembled a foggy sunrise over the bayou, with the deep red rising into the dawn. *It looks good, but how does it taste?* "You taste it first, Mom, and tell me your impressions."

Lillian sniffed the drink before taking a sip. She appeared to savor it for a few seconds in her mouth before swallowing. "This is fantastic, Samantha. I would never have guessed that horrible vinegary syrup could transform into this, but yes, it's quite nice."

Though she appreciated her mother's opinion, Samantha realized she wasn't exactly an unbiased party. She took her own sample of the drink. The blackberry and vinegar flavors came on strong at first, but the lime juice brightened it. The prosecco's effervescence offered a pleasing and refreshing mouthfeel. *Yes, this could work.* "It's not bad."

"Not bad? It's divine. And you came up with it on your own? I already said it earlier today, but I am so impressed with all you've learned to make this business a success."

Samantha smiled, taking a seat again at the kitchen table to share the rest of the cocktail with her mother. "Thanks, Mom. So, what's on your agenda for tomorrow?"

Lillian yawned for a second time. "I may try to take it easy in the morning. Then, Marisa promised to get me into the university library in the afternoon. I want to look around there."

Samantha pursed her lips, surprised that her best friend had made plans with Lillian without mentioning anything to her. "That's nice of her. What are you going to do there?"

"I want to explore the Houston history archives. I'll dig around to see what I can find about the lodge or its history before the lodge meeting tomorrow night."

Samantha tilted her head. "Lodge meeting? What meeting?"

"They're having their first meeting to discuss the preliminary festival results, and they'll update members on the tennis center construction. Patty can't go for obvious reasons, but she cleared it with her friend, the membership chairwoman, to let me go instead. I'm going to keep my eyes and ears open for anything noteworthy."

Though doubtful much could happen in the middle of a crowded room, Samantha still didn't like the idea of her mom going to the meeting on her own. "I'm going with you. We'll just tell Patty's friend that I'm your ride. I've got to do some shopping tomorrow morning to prepare for the funeral, but I'll be free in time to take you to the meeting."

Lillian wished her daughter good night and prepared for bed. With her mother safely ensconced in her bedroom, Samantha made up her bed on the couch and crawled under the covers. She made a mental to-do list of items she needed to pick up tomorrow at the farmers market to supplement what Beth would gather from the local farms they worked with. Then her mind turned to the events of this evening and her truce with Martin. How had she missed the supposedly obvious signs of his crush when they were younger? She wasn't sure how she would have reacted if she'd known, but now? He'd been solicitous toward her at the end of the evening, and his entire demeanor had changed once they'd talked. There was no denying he was attractive. From there, it wasn't a far leap to consider other possibilities. But then her memory drifted to David, who should come home from New York City in a few days. She pictured his tousled hair and his warm green eyes, and she pushed any other thoughts from her mind.

Chapter Ten

Samantha woke early the next morning, determined to make it to the farmers market in time to get the freshest produce. Beth was busy making the rounds of several local farms, so Samantha had promised to pick up the fresh blackberries, green beans, and potatoes, along with the goat cheese for the flatbread. She also wanted time to explore. You never knew when a special at the farmer's market might inspire a menu addition.

Her mother still fast asleep, Samantha made a mug of chai tea to go, then left her mom a note promising to check in on her later. She arrived at the market just as the big delivery trucks pulled out, on their way to deliver fresh produce throughout the city. The market on a Tuesday morning was a very different affair from the hustle and bustle of a Saturday, with its lively conjunto soundtrack and the scent of roasting elotes wafting through the air. Saturdays were for families, but Tuesdays were for the professional foodies. It had taken a while, but Samantha was starting to feel at home among the rest of the restaurant managers and chefs wandering the aisles.

Samantha smelled the sweet blackberries, and handling one, felt a slight softness at her gentle squeeze. They were perfectly ripe and would serve as a unifying element to connect all of their dishes. She picked up the other ingredients Beth had ordered and made one last pass through the market stalls to see if anything else caught her eye. As she rounded the corner, she spotted the familiar face of the woman she'd stood in line with at the festival as they waited for their checks.

"Alice! What a surprise to see you again so soon. What are you doing here?"

The stocky woman arranged candles on a counter facing the aisle. "Samantha, right? I rent a stall here two or three times a week. I do a decent amount of business selling my candles. Of course, it's busier on Saturday, but since I was working the festival last weekend, I swapped my Saturday for today."

Samantha stopped to sniff a candle. "These really are lovely." She breathed in the scent of rosemary and mint. "So, are you going to the lodge meeting tonight?"

Alice nodded. "I wouldn't miss it. There should be fireworks once Muller gives his construction update. I heard he's got a new proposal for the tennis center and a new design for the history center and archive. But no matter what he's come up with, lodge folks will be angry about losing more club property to the tennis center."

Samantha raised her eyebrows. "Sounds like it could get heated. But what I have never understood is why everyone is still so upset about the tennis center. From an article I read, the lodge either had to join in with the tennis center or sell off part of the property to fund necessary repairs."

Alice pulled out another stack of candles from a box on the floor and began setting them up on the counter. "Well, that's true. But at one point, the city offered to buy a few acres of the land to build a new softball field. Some lodge members liked that idea better. If we had sold a small parcel of land and earned enough money for repairs, we might have avoided any clashes."

Samantha blinked. "So why didn't the lodge accept that deal?"

Alice opened one of each variety of candles, releasing the heavenly aromas of pine, honey, and sea salt into the air. "Several people refused to sell any of the land. Plus, Adam Muller laid it on thick about the heritage museum and how it would have meant the world to his grandfather and father."

Samantha picked up a lavender candle and sniffed deeply. "It sounds like I don't want to miss the meeting. I guess I'll see you there." Before she said goodbye, Samantha remembered last night's conversation about Karl. While she had a hard time believing the genial man capable of murder, she wondered what someone who had known him longer might say. "On another note, do you know Karl Brandt?"

Alice looked up from her candles. "Karl? Oh, sure. He's been a member of the lodge for as long as I can remember. Why do you ask?"

Samantha didn't want to give away too much, but she wanted the woman's honest assessment. "No real reason. I met him briefly, and he seemed so nice. But I've heard rumors."

Alice frowned. "I've heard the rumors. Silly gossips suggesting he killed Angela. I don't believe it for a minute. Karl's a big teddy bear. You didn't hear this from me, but I suspect the only reason he organized that little plot to throw suspicion on others is because he's got a crush on Patty."

This was news to Samantha. "Really? Does she know?"

"I doubt it. Poor Patty hasn't given romance much thought in the twenty-five years since her husband died. I'm not sure she'd recognize the signs anymore."

Samantha nodded. Patty had been alone for so long, Samantha had trouble picturing her dating anyone. She filed the thought away for later and made her excuses to Alice. "I've got to finish up my shopping. I guess I'll see you tonight."

Alice waved and went back to arranging her shelves.

As Samantha paid and loaded up her car, she replayed Alice's comments in her mind. This was the first she'd heard about the city offering to buy part of the land for a softball field. Adam Muller's insistence on moving forward with the tennis center plan intrigued her. He clearly was desperate for the heritage center and archives to be built, but perhaps there was another motive at play. Also, Karl's crush on Patty was interesting. But rather than eliminating him as a suspect in Angela's murder, it might give him more of an incentive, given how much grief Angela had caused Patty.

* * *

At the kitchen where she and Beth rented space, Samantha unloaded her car, carrying the boxes of blackberries, green beans, and potatoes inside. She put the vegetables in the refrigerator right away but chose several mounds of the ripe blackberries to prepare a bigger batch of the shrub for the reception. Although her mother had raved about the cocktail the night before, Samantha wanted to tweak the original recipe. She roughly chopped the blackberries and smashed them into the bottom of a pot on the stove. Along with the sugar and vinegar, she added a new ingredient—fresh thyme from Beth's garden. She thought it should add an herbal note to the drink and offset its sweetness. She left the syrup to simmer and reduce. It was too early to begin prep work on other items. She and Beth would tackle those tomorrow, but her shrub needed to cool in the refrigerator for over twenty-four hours before being used.

With her prep work done for now, Samantha headed home to grab some lunch and catch up with her mother before she left for the university library to meet Marisa. Now that she had some extra time, Samantha planned to tag along. She'd loved digging through archives ever since her first job at a small central Texas newspaper. Interesting stories popped up when you looked in the right place.

As she climbed the stairs to her garage apartment, she spotted her mother's silhouette in the kitchen window. "Mom, hey! I finished early and wanted to tag along to the . . ."

Entering through the kitchen door, Samantha's last few words stuck in her throat as she noticed a shadow on the opposite wall in the living room.

"Mom, watch out!" Samantha launched herself at her mother, pushing her out of the kitchen and away from the living room, into the hallway that led into her bedroom.

Lillian crashed into the bedroom's doorway. "Samantha! What is wrong with you?"

As Samantha ran back into the kitchen to grab her large butcher's knife, the shadow took shape, and she saw Karl's face peer around the corner of the kitchen. Her brow wrinkled as her mind flashed back to her earlier suspicions about Karl's potential motive for murder.

"You! What are you doing here?" She stood her ground with the knife out in front of her, trying to impress on him that she was ready to run at him should it become necessary.

A red hue climbed up the man's face, obvious despite his beard. "I'm sorry for scaring you, but I needed to talk to your mother."

Samantha's jaw dropped, and still holding the knife out in front of her, she glanced at her mother. "My mother? Why?" She raised her eyes in a question to Lillian.

"Put the knife down, honey. I invited him." Lillian reached out to take the knife from her daughter.

Samantha's hands dropped to her side as she took a step back. Her heart rate slowed to a more regular beat as she realized she might have overreacted. "I'm sorry. I'm a little on edge these days."

Karl dropped his chin to his chest as he gazed downward. "Patty won't talk to me. I heard my plan backfired and caused even more suspicion to fall on her. I never meant for that to happen." He swallowed hard and looked up at Lillian. "She has to believe me. I was trying to help her."

Samantha sat at her kitchen table, her breathing back under control. Though she couldn't totally rule Karl out as the murderer, she no longer feared for her life in his presence. "How did you imagine that scheme would help her, Karl? She needs the truth to come out, not more confusion."

The man stared at the ground. "Well, part of me thought she actually did it. Killed Angela, I mean." His gaze rose. "It's stupid, but my idea was to present the police with a list of folks with as much motive as Patty to kill Angela. I wanted to create reasonable doubt. You gave me the idea when you mentioned the tip line."

Samantha couldn't believe Karl was blaming her for his crazy idea. She certainly hadn't meant for him to do anything like this when she brought up the tip line. But something else puzzled her. "If you assumed she was the killer, why help get her off?"

The man blushed again. "If she'd done it, it had to have been an accident, and only because that awful woman must have pushed her to it. Patty's an old friend, and I know she wouldn't intentionally hurt a fly. I was just trying to help her out. But I screwed up, and now she won't even talk to me."

Lillian patted the man's hand. "She doesn't hate you, Karl. But she is annoyed with you. Your entire scheme has caused her more trouble."

Karl lowered his head to his chest, nodding in agreement. "I know and I'm so sorry for it."

Samantha wasn't quite so ready to accept that he was completely innocent. "Tell me this, Karl. Why didn't you put your own name in the suspect list? You included so many others, but you didn't include yourself."

Karl looked up at Samantha, his eyes locked on her face. "I didn't want to implicate myself. It sounds terrible, but the rule was, we wouldn't include anyone on the list unless they had an alibi. And the simple fact is, I don't have an alibi, or at least not one I could prove."

Samantha wanted to give Karl the benefit of the doubt, but he kept opening himself up for more suspicion. "Why don't you have an alibi? Where were you when the murder happened?"

Karl leaned down to pick up Ruby, who had been weaving around his legs. He stroked her fur as he cradled her in his arms. "I was looking for Patty. I'd originally planned on going to see my son, but realized I had time before I needed to relieve him at the grill, so I went to find her and ask if she needed any help."

Samantha watched as her cat purred and rubbed her head insistently against Karl's meaty hands. "And where did you go? What did you see?"

Ruby finally leaped from Karl's hands, and he shrugged. "I went to the office to see if she needed any help cashing out the tickets, but she wasn't there. There was nobody there."

"What time was that, Karl?" There were so many moving parts, Samantha wanted to nail down the time line.

"My shift started at eight PM, so it was probably a half hour before that." The man stared at his shoes. "I wish I had seen her, or at least seen something useful."

Samantha recalled the volunteer who had mentioned Angela fighting with an unidentified man at the festival around 7:10. That was not too far from the time when Karl had no alibi. Could he have been the mystery man? "Karl, did you speak with Angela on the night she died?"

Karl blanched. "No, I didn't say a word to her. I never did, if I could help it. Talking to her made my blood pressure boil."

Samantha tried to gauge his reaction but found it difficult to measure his truthfulness. Though he denied any role in the killing, Samantha didn't think she could cross Karl off her list.

Lillian glanced down at her watch. "Oh, look at the time. I'm sorry to rush you, Karl, but I've got an appointment. I'll tell Patty you asked after her."

Karl shuffled toward the door. "I'm sorry to keep you. Thanks for hearing me out. And please, tell me what I can do for Patty."

He followed Lillian to the front door and walked outside and down the steps.

When Lillian closed the door, she turned back toward her daughter. "Really, Samantha! Why did you pull a knife on that poor man?"

Samantha crossed her arms over her chest. "I can't believe you invited him into my apartment when you were here by yourself. You heard him—he doesn't have an alibi. He could be the murderer."

Lillian waved her hand, as if dismissing Samantha's concern. "You're being silly. That man wouldn't hurt a fly."

Samantha shrugged. "I'll grant you that he seemed sincere. But if he's truly interested in Patty, doesn't that give him more of a motive to have killed Angela?"

Lillian stooped to lift her purse. "I sure hope not. He and Patty would make a great couple. I'd hate to think he was a murderer. Anyway, I need to get going. I'm going to be late getting to the library, particularly since I have no idea where I'm going."

Samantha walked back into the kitchen and opened up the refrigerator, scooping up a container of hummus and a bag of baby carrots. "Let me eat something, and I'll take you."

Lillian beamed. "Oh, honey, you don't need to do that."

Samantha dipped the carrots into the hummus and ate. "But I want to. I'm always up for a trip to the library. My mom's a librarian, you know!"

Lillian laughed, grabbed a carrot of her own, and dragged it through the dip. "If you don't mind, I won't argue with you. I hate driving in the city."

After a few more snacks, Samantha and Lillian gathered their things and drove to the university's library. Marisa waited out front.

"Lillian, hi!" Marisa leaned in for a hug. "And Sam! I didn't know you were coming too."

Samantha hugged her friend. "I finished up early at the kitchen, so I tagged along with Mom."

Marisa waved the women into the building. "Well, come on in. Lillian, I'll check you into the history archive."

Samantha followed them into the library and watched for a few minutes while her mom geeked out over the room filled with musty books. Marisa showed them how to check out the microfilm and where to locate the indexes before apologizing that she needed to head to her next class at the law school.

Samantha pulled up a chair next to her mother, trying to show interest in the database Lillian had pulled up on the computer. Her interest waned after a few minutes. She tapped her mom on the shoulder and whispered. "I'm going to browse the stacks. Come find me when you're done."

Lillian waved her off and turned her attention back to the screen.

Samantha explored stacks filled with books and bound journals. Though she wasn't the research expert her mom was, she wanted to find what she could about the lodge. A librarian directed her toward a section on the history of social organizations in Houston, and among the books, she found a small booklet detailing the history of the German lodge, created for its seventy-fifth anniversary forty-five years ago.

Samantha flipped through the booklet and learned that the lodge had moved to its current site five years after its inception. A founding member had donated the land, which originally had consisted of twenty acres. A few parcels had been sold off years earlier. Scanning the pages, Samantha spotted familiar names among the founding members, including the name Muller, the same last name as the current lodge president.

According to the booklet, lodge members had first brought up the idea of a history center and archive in the 1930s, but during World War II, because of anti-German sentiment, lodge members had opted to lie low and not promote their heritage. Later, in the 1980s, Wilhelm Muller attempted to start the heritage center, but the lodge never could get enough money together, and they set the project aside.

Samantha poked around further but couldn't find any more about the lodge among the stacks she'd been browsing, and without relevant dates, she wasn't sure how to search newspapers or any other publications.

She turned her attention to her other group of suspects—Angela Clawson's family. There had been plenty of innuendo from Christina about Olivia and her husband, Matt, borrowing a vast sum of money from Angela because of a poor investment. Samantha realized she needed to focus her attention on Matt Clawson.

She sat at one of the research computers in the library and plugged his name in, hoping to find a website or at least a LinkedIn profile to give her information on his career.

The first thing she found was a website—The R&C Group, with Matt Clawson's boyish face front and center; he was listed as director. The website didn't offer many details describing the company's purpose, but a few minutes of searching helped Samantha piece together that its primary activity was land speculation for the oil industry.

Paula Lindsay, an old reporter buddy of hers from the paper, had written several stories a few years ago about companies traveling across rural Texas, trying to buy up land and mineral rights identified by geologists as ripe for oil or natural gas drilling. Sometimes, they hit it right and made tons of money, but sometimes they guessed wrong and lost millions. It was a high-stakes gamble, and few people had the nerve for it. Samantha had a hard time picturing the man in the photograph in front of her winning a hand of poker, much less a million-dollar gamble on the location for the next hot drilling spot.

From Samantha's limited experience, researching land and mineral rights in Texas was a complicated affair and well beyond her expertise. She made a mental note to message Paula to see if she could give her any tips on how to investigate Matt's company and find out how well his gambles had paid off.

Samantha wandered back to the research room to find her mother.

Lillian still sat in front of the computer, taking notes on a yellow legal pad next to her on the desk. She looked up as Samantha drew closer. "Oh, hi, honey. I'm nearly done here. Can you give me five more minutes?"

Samantha nodded and sat beside her mother, pulling out her phone to check her messages while she waited. She'd had her phone on vibrate at the library and hadn't noticed a new text message. Her pulse quickened when she saw it was from David.

I hope everything is going well. I'm flying back tomorrow afternoon and would love to see you. Let me know!

Samantha grinned at the formality of the message. Others were content to communicate with abbreviations or emojis, but David refused to send a message without complete sentences or proper punctuation. As a writer, it was one of the little things about him that she found alluring.

How should I respond? She'd been looking forward to seeing him, but she wasn't sure she wanted to introduce him to her mother yet. It would only give Lillian ideas. Not to mention, if he got one whiff of her trying to investigate another murder, he wouldn't be thrilled. *I'd better put him off.*

Hey. It's good to hear from you. I can't wait to see you again, but tomorrow's going to be crazy. My mom is still in town, and Beth and I need to prep tomorrow night for a big event we're catering on Thursday. Maybe Thursday night or Friday? Safe travels!

She pressed "Send," hoping she'd been breezy enough. This whole dating thing was hard. She hated second-guessing herself and trying to convey just enough of one thing and not too much of another. She knew David didn't buy into the traditional "rules" on dating, but she feared making a misstep so early in whatever it was they had going.

Lillian closed down the computer. "Ready to go, honey?"

"Yeah. Did you find anything good?" Samantha sorted through her purse.

"I found out a bit more about Angela's family in West Texas, but nothing very interesting." Lillian filled Samantha in on Angela's youth in Kermit, Texas, a small town near Midland. Her parents had both died more than twenty-five years ago, leaving only Angela's younger sister, Mary Hawkins, who still lived on the ranch where she and Angela had grown up.

Samantha held the library door open for her mother, and they walked to the car. "I asked Christina about the sister, and I got the impression there's no love lost there. She said they haven't been in touch in years."

Lillian pursed her lips. "If there's bad blood there, maybe she's worth adding to the suspect list. But that's not exactly the kind of thing you can find out at the library."

"There are plenty of other ways to find out information." Samantha pondered their next move. With a little time to kill before the lodge meeting, she suggested they stop off for tacos at a new fusion taco spot, near downtown, famous for its blending of Latin food with different cuisines.

The smell tantalized them as they walked into the former hat shop on Main Street, one of a dozen of the city's oldest commercial buildings, which had been repurposed into a lively restaurant and bar scene. The walls of the shop were painted in the colors of the Mexican flag, but the spices and aromas that filled the air contained a blend of Eastern and Western elements. The exposed kitchen revealed a hive of bustling activity, with chefs attending to simmering pots on the stove, or slicing meat that had been slowly roasted on an indoor grill. A line of patrons stretched to the door, allowing Samantha and Lillian the opportunity to scan the extensive menu, which included traditional Mexican favorites such as carne guisada and beef fajita, but also included tacos with Asian, Turkish, Indian, and Middle Eastern influences.

When they reached the counter, Samantha opted for a Thai chicken curry taco with a pungent green curry filling, while her mother chose a Korean barbecue taco with a blend of charcoal grilled beef in a tangy sesame and brown sugar sauce. They sat at a scarred wooden table, with a window facing out to the small pocket park across the street, and dug into their tacos.

"What do you think will happen tonight? I'm hearing there could be fireworks." Samantha sopped up the flavorful sauce with an extra tortilla.

"I don't know. It should be interesting. I promised Patty I'd give her a full report." Lillian bit into her first taco, and her eyes widened. "Yum! I've always thought tacos were the perfect food, but this place has figured out how to improve on perfection!"

Samantha filled her mother in on the old booklet she'd found and about earlier failed efforts by a Wilhelm Muller to start a history center and archives. "The current president has to be related somehow. It'd be too big of a coincidence, otherwise.

Clearly, the history center has been important to his family for a while."

Lillian twirled her fork, as if preparing to launch into lecture mode. "It's an interesting history. German settlers played a huge role in Texas, and then, for a while after World War I, they had to hide their heritage because of a wave of anti-German sentiment."

Sometimes Samantha was annoyed by her mom's off-the-cuff history lessons, but in this case, she wanted to hear more. She nodded, not wanting to interrupt her mother.

Lillian took another bite of her taco before continuing. "It wasn't really until the fifties, long after World War II ended, that the Germans could reclaim their place in history. I can understand the club's desire to preserve the heritage."

Samantha munched on the chips and a trio of tangy salsas they'd ordered on the side. "It is interesting. If the lodge can ever get that history center built, I bet it would be fascinating."

With her tongue burning after consuming a particularly spicy pepper, Samantha guzzled her water. Finished eating, the two women cleaned off their table and headed outside. It was still muggy enough to make Samantha's curls stick to the back of her neck, but the heat had broken earlier in the day. She wondered how much things would heat up tonight at the lodge meeting.

Chapter Eleven

Samantha and Lillian caught a bit of downtown traffic on the way to the lodge but made it a few minutes before the meeting began. On the outside, the low-slung concrete building had been painted with fake wooden beams and stone, to resemble a Bavarian chalet, but the interior, with its dark wood paneling, speckled terrazzo floors, and a drop ceiling of asbestos tiles, was much more institutional. As she opened the door, a wave of ice-cold air-conditioning blasted her in the face as she and her mother stepped into the cave-like interior.

Walking through the hallway toward the great room, where tonight's meeting was being held, Samantha glanced at the portraits of old white men, which lined the walls. Lillian pointed out a man with a particularly droopy moustache, and Samantha noted the name—Wilhelm Muller.

The great room itself was another blast from the past, though this time it hearkened back to Samantha's elementary school cafetorium, with the same institutional flooring and walls, plus a small stage at one end, framed with red velvet curtains. The walls were decorated with bunting, with half of the room covered in red, white, and blue, and the other half proudly displaying the black, gold, and red color of the German flag. A large disco ball hung from the ceiling, hinting at the all-purpose nature of the room, which must serve double duty as a dance hall.

As Samantha and Lillian signed in with Patty's friend, Samantha noticed that more than a hundred plastic chairs lined up in front of the stage were already full. A large crowd had formed, and loud, angry voices filled the air.

"You people are trying to cheat us out of more of our land!" A strapping blond man, whom Samantha recognized from the beer tent at the festival, stood with a sneer on his face, pointing angrily at a crowd of what Samantha thought of as the tennis club set.

"It's written in the contract that we are entitled to more land if drainage becomes a problem. It was there from the beginning." A suit-clad man with distinguished gray flecks in his wavy brown hair spoke loudly and firmly, but his voice was drowned out by those shouting around him.

Samantha gazed at her mom and raised her eyebrows. "Looks like the fireworks have already started!"

The two women opted for seats together at the back of the hall, trying to avoid the chaos, and waited for the official meeting to begin. Within ten minutes, Adam Muller, the man Samantha recognized as having introduced Angela during her welcome speech at the festival, walked onto a small stage, accompanied by a familiar-looking blonde woman with big hair and a designer suit. The crowd hushed and pressed toward the front of the stage, but appeared ready to boil over now that a new focal point for their anger had arrived.

"Please, please, take a seat. I know everyone is angry, and justifiably so. We've been hit with a huge curve ball. But Ms. Beech and I have come up with a plan that should satisfy everyone."

Some in the crowd still jeered, but others quieted down, wanting to hear what the pair had to say.

Muller took a seat at table near the stage, joined by Calista, who seemed more in command today than she had at the pie tent.

Muller banged a gavel and spoke. "First, we need to acknowledge the tragedy that happened at our festival and to one of our members last weekend. Let's take a moment of silence to remember Angela Clawson and her contributions to our little community."

Many on the tennis club side of the hall bowed their heads, while the dull roar softened to a quiet murmur on the other side. After a minute, Muller banged the gavel again. "Ordinarily we would start with a report on the festival and go through our budget, but I've asked the rest of the board to dispense with that for now so we can bring forward the most pressing concern, the drainage issue and the construction permits."

A man in the front row of chairs stood up and yelled. "So it's true? I didn't believe you would give away more of our land to those people. Your father would be ashamed!"

Muller stood stoic, ignoring the comments thrown at him. "I'm aware that rumors have been circulating, but I want to give you the full truth right now. City inspectors denied the permit for the tennis club based on drainage concerns. And yes, more land is now required for the tennis club to be built."

The crowd roared. Shouts of "How long have you known about this?" and "This was their plan all along!" rang through the large meeting hall.

Muller attempted to shush the crowd, but when that failed, he spoke over them. "I learned about these problems last Friday. And trust me when I say I was not happy. This could have been anticipated." He seemed to glare in the general direction of the tennis club crowd. "Nevertheless, it doesn't do any good to relitigate it. We need a solution. And I think what Ms. Beech has come up with is our best bet."

The lights dimmed as a projector in the back lit up, casting a PowerPoint presentation onto a screen mounted on the side of the stage. The screen showed a bird's-eye view of what Samantha recognized as the original proposed tennis court project, with the ten new courts, the lodge's one existing court, and the stadium court in the center, along with an impressive two-story clubhouse structure.

Muller aimed a laser pointer in the general direction of the screen, circling features of the design. "I'm sure you recognize the original plan for the tennis club project. Ms. Clawson had informed us that city engineers approved the design, but the city inspectors now say the tennis courts are too close together. They are requiring us to space them out further and build a retaining pool to alleviate any flooding concerns."

His voice was clipped, and he appeared to be making an effort to keep his expression neutral as he progressed to the next slide. The new design showed the tennis courts spaced out on a larger swath of land, eating into more of the festival grounds, and an even larger clubhouse structure next to the courts.

Audience members were squinting to make out the design, and one man near the front audibly gasped. "Where's our lodge building? It's not there."

Other audience members joined in. "Yeah, where is it? What kind of new plan is this?"

Muller raised his palms as if to stop the crowd from getting more riled up. "Yes, as you can see, the current lodge building is gone, and in its place, you see the expanded clubhouse, which includes a similar amount of space to our current facilities, combined with the clubhouse space. It also contains a dedicated space for our archive and heritage center."

A middle-aged man standing two rows in front of Samantha yelled out, "What kind of plan is that? You want us to give up our lodge too? This is crazy."

Calista Beech stood up, her voice rising to speak over the crowd. "You are not giving up your lodge. This is a compromise. As you'll see if you follow along, you will gain as much as you're losing."

She forwarded through a series of PowerPoint slides showing outdoor and indoor schematics of the new clubhouse building. One man several rows in front of Samantha continued heckling, but others had quieted down and were watching the presentation. Samantha tried to gauge people's reactions. While many still seemed to be very skeptical, others appeared more open to listening.

Lillian leaned over and whispered into Samantha's ear. "It actually looks nice, doesn't it?"

Samantha nodded. The design of the proposed clubhouse on the screen was a beautiful Spanish Revival–style building that would replace the low-slung boxy lodge headquarters, which had been built in the 1950s after the founder's home and previous lodge quarters had been demolished. According to the schematic, the new clubhouse would contain traditional clubhouse amenities such as locker rooms, a restaurant, a ballroom, and lounge areas. However, it would also include meeting space for the lodge and a dedicated space for the archive and heritage center.

Calista flicked through a few slides showing an architectural rendering of the proposed new heritage center, with archive and exhibit space for the historical artifacts the lodge had in its collection. Further slides showed additional exhibit space throughout the clubhouse property, comingling the tennis club and lodge space, making them more entwined rather than separate entities.

Adam highlighted this aspect of the plans for the audience. "If you'll notice, this new design will help to marry lodge and tennis club activities in a much more cohesive way than in our original plan. In this space, we can both grow together in a way that simply wasn't possible before."

The comments drew jeers from some in the crowd. "We're the ones with the history and tradition. How can we be comfortable surrounded by all of this?" A lodge member threw his mesh ball cap emblazoned with lodge insignia onto his chair. "It's not right."

A man from the tennis club section of the hall responded angrily. "Well, what about us? We're paying very high fees for the use of these facilities, but the German Club will get to use them free of charge? What happens when we're trying to host a club event or a tournament, and they're playing bingo or whatever it is they do over there?"

The exchange drew louder jeers from both sides of the aisle, and Muller banged his gavel, trying to restore order to the meeting space. "We will make every effort to ensure that calendar events do not overlap, but if they do, we will work out a compromise scenario. We will do what we can to satisfy everybody."

While some grumbling continued, most had died down, and there appeared to be a greater willingness to at least listen to the presentation. Calista advanced a few more slides, showing the proposed retention pond, with a fountain in the middle; and the tennis courts, spaced out throughout more of the property.

When the slide show finished, the lights came up in the lodge room, and the crowd scrutinized each other, as if trying to judge individual reactions. Muller banged his gavel. "All right. I know this was a lot to take in, but if we want this project to remain on track, we need to move forward. The board needs to vote to approve the redesign by the end of the week to seek the go-ahead from the city to continue construction. Time is money, and each day this project is delayed, we lose more of it."

Muller wiped his face with a handkerchief and stared at the crowd. "This presentation and the renderings will be saved on our website for everyone to review. We will accept comments through close of business on Thursday, and the board will vote on Friday."

Muller walked off the stage, refusing to answer any further questions. Calista followed him and they left the room. The crowd that remained slowly dispersed, but some groups clustered together to discuss the news.

Samantha and Lillian searched the audience for a familiar face, wanting to gauge the audience reaction to the presentation. Samantha spotted Alice in a corner by the refreshment table. "Alice!" She hailed the woman with a wave.

Alice waved back and strode toward her. "Hi, Samantha. I told you it would be interesting tonight."

Samantha nodded and introduced her mother. "So, what was your impression? How'd people react where you were standing?"

Alice slurped some lemonade and bit into an Oreo. Samantha grimaced slightly. She had never understood why people combined those items on a refreshment table.

Alice wiped the smear of Oreo crumbs from her lips. "I thought it was a very professional presentation. Which then made me wonder how long they were aware of these permit problems. It seems suspicious to me that they completed such detailed renderings in only a few days."

Samantha agreed. "I see what you mean. It's almost as if someone had that entire presentation tucked into their back pocket, waiting for a chance to use it. But even if that were true, what difference would it make?"

Alice raised an eyebrow. "It would mean they've been conspiring behind the lodge members' backs for quite some time. And that makes me wonder why. Who gains from this deal?"

Samantha pondered the question but couldn't answer it. "So, what do you think will happen?"

Alice groaned. "What always happens. They'll approve it and do what they want, and we'll be stuck living with it. Anyway, I've got to run. See you around, Samantha."

Samantha waved and shifted to face her mother. "What now?"

Lillian gestured toward the tennis club side of the aisle. "Let's listen to the comments over there."

Most of the tennis club group had left, but Samantha followed her mother toward a cluster of well-dressed ladies who lingered in a corner. Samantha and Lillian stood just outside the circle, close enough to eavesdrop, and pretended to search for someone in the crowd.

A woman with a stiff blonde wedge cut spoke conspiratorially to the other ladies in the group. "This doesn't surprise me. Angela never could stay on budget to save her life. She never settled for less than perfection."

A tall brunette woman piped up: "Angela herself practically promised me we'd have more space than what the original plans showed. She must have been aware of the flooding issue."

Another blonde with frosted highlights nodded. "The new proposed grounds look much better. It's a shame that we have to share our clubhouse with those lodge members though . . . and that awful exhibit space."

The original woman shrugged. "Oh, I don't know. It might be pretty unique to have a heritage center and archives on the grounds."

The blonde with highlights harrumphed, and the group split up. Samantha and Lillian exchanged glances and shrugged. While the overheard tidbits didn't seem all that useful to their investigation, Samantha found it interesting to note the various opinions.

The pair glanced around, trying to spot anyone else worth talking to or overhearing, but most of the crowd had filtered out, leaving few options for further eavesdropping.

Samantha led her mother to the parking lot. She looked around at the property, trying to imagine tennis courts sprouting here and there among the foliage. "I think it might look quite nice, actually."

Lillian was more noncommittal. "Maybe, but underhanded sneakiness is making me question the spirit of cooperation. Those tennis folks better be happy that I don't get a vote. I would vote against this proposal just for spite."

Chapter Twelve

As they drove back to Samantha's apartment, Lillian called Patty to fill her in on the details of the meeting. Samantha could overhear Patty shouting about the hybrid tennis club and lodge design on the other end of the line, even with the radio playing.

When they arrived, Samantha left her mother in the kitchen to finish her conversation, while she called Beth to discuss plans for tomorrow.

Her friend picked up after the first ring. "Hey, Sam. I was about to call you. We had a last-minute request to cater a light luncheon for twenty-five tomorrow afternoon for an art gallery and its board of directors. Apparently, their usual caterer couldn't handle it, and one of the board members gave them our name!"

Despite the excitement in Beth's voice, Samantha's stomach clenched. "A light luncheon tomorrow? How can we cook for a luncheon and prep for the funeral on Thursday too?"

Beth paused. "It will be tight, but we can't turn down this opportunity. It could open up a lot of doors for us. Plus, the pay is pretty good for sandwiches and soup plus dessert for twenty-five."

Samantha sighed. "Okay. You're right. We're not in a position to turn opportunities down. Do they need any cocktails?"

"Nope. Just lunch. I can handle the soup and sandwiches on my own. My chicken salad is usually a hit, and I'll pair it with my green minestrone, and a watermelon and tomato salad, with some brownies for dessert. Please tell me we can juggle both."

Squeezing her eyes shut, trying to force herself to be calm, Samantha took a deep breath before responding. "I think we can make it work. We'll get the luncheon stuff done in the morning. Leave me your recipes and instructions for the funeral reception food, and I'll get as much done as I can while you are serving the luncheon. We'll make it work. Cheers to being busy. It's a good problem to have."

Though their catering venture was holding its own for now, they were skating on thin financial ice. Checks came through barely in time to make the payments for ingredients for the next job. Eventually, Samantha knew, they would turn a real profit, but for now, it was slow going as they waited for word of mouth to draw in new business. Given their circumstances, Samantha supported Beth's decision to jump on the art gallery job, but the prospect of preparing most of the food for the funeral petrified her. Everything needed to go right at this funeral, not only for their business's sake, but for Patty's as well.

Samantha considered Martin's offer to help work the funeral. Could she somehow convince him to assist her in the kitchen tomorrow? Their truce was short-lived, and she hated to derail it by asking for a favor.

She bit her lip as she contemplated a way to approach him. If she had an extra body to help her, she could pull off both events.

After hanging up with Beth, Samantha walked to the kitchen to check on her mother and, by extension, Patty. "How's Patty doing?"

Lillian offered a half smile. "Patty is Patty. She's worried about every little detail of the new construction plans but can't be bothered to worry about her own case. I suppose a little distraction is good for her."

Samantha filled two glasses with water and offered one to her mom. "My plans for tomorrow just got busier. Beth found another new client, and I need to help as best as I can while trying to prepare everything for the funeral on Thursday. I was wondering . . . do you think Martin might be willing to help me out a bit tomorrow?"

Lillian looked up from the table, raising an eyebrow. "Martin? Are you sure? I've no doubt he'd be glad to help. I just want to make sure you're not compelled to ask on my account."

Samantha shook her head. "No. I seriously need some assistance!"

Lillian shrugged. "I'll give him a call."

Normally, Samantha would have protested her mother's interference, but for now, it was easier to have her serve as go-between.

Fifteen minutes later, Samantha had her free labor lined up, ready to meet her at the kitchen incubator at eight AM.

"Thanks, Mom. That will be a big help. What will you and Patty do tomorrow?"

"I'm not sure. She's supposed to meet with the lawyer tomorrow morning to get an update on the case. The lawyer told her to prepare for the fact that the police might arrest her. I'm so scared for her, Samantha."

The idea that Patty might be arrested tomorrow sent a chill through Samantha. Although she'd known it was a possibility, the vision of the police slapping cuffs on her mom's oldest friend was hard to picture. "How did she sound?"

"Honestly, she sounded resigned to her fate, which scares me. Patty is a fighter, and I don't want her to give up that fight." Lillian seemed tired, and Samantha realized that she was also exhausted.

"Mom, try not to worry too much. Hopefully, we'll make more progress and find information to help Patty's case." She yawned. Although it was only ten thirty, she was already anticipating her five AM wake-up call. "I'm sorry, but I need to call it a night. I've got an early morning tomorrow, and I'll be worthless unless I get enough sleep."

Lillian patted her daughter on the back. "Don't work too hard. Good night." She retired to Samantha's room with a book.

Samantha headed to the bathroom to change and brush her teeth. As she made up the couch for bed, she remembered her plan to connect with her friend Paula from the *Gazette* to learn more about Matt Clawson's investments and whether they might give him a motive for murder.

Samantha grabbed her phone and dashed off an email.

Hey Paula—Long time, no talk. I was hoping you might be able to help me with your oil and gas expertise. I'm researching a company called the R&C Group. They've been buying up properties and mineral rights, searching for new sites to drill. Rumor is they made a bad gamble, but I'm trying to figure out how bad their losses were. Do you have any tips on where I should start? Help me out, and you've got a bottle of my tiki bitters with your name on it! Thanks a million. Sam

She pressed "Send" and made her bed on the sofa. After pulling up the covers, she called for Ruby to join her. The cat jumped up and curled tightly next to her. She drifted off to sleep with contented purring in her ear.

* * *

In the morning, Samantha's cell phone alarm went off before sunrise. She awoke, took a shower, and made a cup of hot tea, trying to keep as quiet as possible, to avoid waking her mother. The caffeine gave her the jolt she needed to face the day.

When she arrived at the kitchen incubator, she found Beth busy kneading dough for the fresh French bread she planned to make for the sandwiches. The scent of roasting chicken tantalized Samantha.

"How's it going? You must have gotten an early start." Samantha noticed Beth's glassy-eyed expression, wondering how much sleep her partner had gotten the night before.

"I've been here a couple of hours. I got a little nervous last night after we talked, and decided I should get going early. So, are you sure you're all set for today?"

Samantha smiled. "I've recruited backup. Patty's son, Martin, is going to help me out. If he familiarizes himself with the food, it should help him blend in better tomorrow at the funeral."

Beth nodded, noncommittal. "You'll have to keep a close eye on him. Our reputation is on the line with these jobs, so the work has to be up to our standards."

"I know how important this all is. We'll make it work." Samantha perused Beth's proposed menu and picked up a knife. "I'll make the watermelon and tomato salad for you."

She chopped up bright pink watermelon and heirloom tomatoes, fresh from a local farm, into large chunks and placed them in two serving bowls for Beth's art gallery event. She would season the mixture with fresh basil, red onions, and a handful of feta cheese and top it all with a light oil and vinegar dressing. Samantha's mouth watered. The salad was one of her favorites, with vine-ripened tomatoes and juicy watermelon combining the best flavors of summer.

As she worked, Samantha filled Beth in on the events of the meeting last night, and her friend Alice's suspicion regarding the timing of the new design being released.

"So your friend thinks the Tennis Club Committee was aware of the drainage issues before Friday? But why wouldn't they have been honest from the beginning? This just complicates the project." Beth covered the bread dough to let it rise.

"The assumption is that if the lodge members had been aware, they wouldn't have approved the project." Samantha finished the salad, wrapping the bowls tightly with Saran wrap and storing them in the refrigerator.

"But is that a motive to commit murder?" Beth pulled the roasted chicken out of the oven and left it to cool for a few minutes before shredding it.

Samantha inhaled the scent of the freshly roasted chicken, and her stomach rumbled. "You never can tell what will drive someone to murder. Anyway, do you need help with the brownies?"

Beth's eyes went to the clock on the wall, which read eight AM. "I guess it wouldn't hurt. If you can make the brownies, I can chop the ingredients for the soup."

Samantha pulled out another bowl and measured dry ingredients. "So how is Marisa doing? I saw her for a few minutes with my mom yesterday, but I haven't had much of a chance to talk to her since this mess began."

"Me either, to be honest. We've been running ourselves ragged with these jobs, and she's so busy with her classes that by the time we see each other, we're so tired that we just want to go to bed." Beth sighed. "But, she's fine. She understands the pressure we're under, and she's being supportive. How about you? Heard any word from David?"

It was Samantha's turn to sigh. "He's getting back into town today. I want to see him, but I put him off for now, saying we'd be busy because of the funeral. In reality, I'm afraid to tell him about Patty and this new murder investigation."

Beth popped her head up from the table where she'd been peeling zucchinis. "Why would you be afraid to tell him?"

Samantha fingered the end of her ponytail before realizing she'd have to wash her hands again. "I don't want him to think I'm nosy or someone who takes dumb risks. But I also don't want him to make me second-guess my decisions. I've lived with too much of that in my life."

Beth dropped the zucchini peels in the compost bin. "I don't know David that well, but it sounds to me like you're projecting your own worries on him. He's a reasonable guy, and he's really into you, by the way. You should give him the benefit of the doubt."

"You're probably right. I just worry I'll screw up." Samantha scrubbed her hands at the sink before turning back to the brownies.

Beth rummaged through the refrigerator for more zucchini and continued peeling. "Meanwhile, what's the deal with this Martin guy? The last I heard—"

The kitchen door opened, and Martin walked through the door. "My ears are burning. Did I hear my name?" Martin offered a lopsided grin as his gaze tracked back and forth between Samantha and Beth.

Samantha's cheeks warmed at the thought of Martin overhearing Beth's words. "Oh, I was just telling Beth how grateful I am that you agreed to help today. I can't thank you enough. We're swamped."

Martin reached out a hand to Beth, who merely waved with the hand holding the vegetable peeler. "It's nice to meet you, Martin, but my hands are a bit slimy from the zucchini. Anyway, like Samantha said, we appreciate you coming to our rescue today."

Martin walked over to the sink and washed his hands. "No problem. My mom and I could stand a bit of time apart. We've been driving each other crazy the last few days." He tied on an apron hanging up on a peg on the wall. "Anyway, put me to work."

Samantha put the brownies in the oven and pulled out Beth's recipe list for the funeral. She started with the pasta salad, which she knew would benefit from several hours in the refrigerator, to allow the flavors to soak in a bit. She dug out the recipe from Beth's book and handed it to Martin. "You can cook, right?"

Martin rolled his eyes as he read the index card and perused the ingredients. "I've been living on my own for the past decade. Of course I can cook."

He filled a stock pot from the rack with water and set it to boil on the stove. Samantha watched for a bit, but figured he couldn't screw up boiling pasta, so she turned back to tomorrow's menu.

With most of the meal plan revolving around blackberries, Samantha had ordered two flats from a local grower. The fleshy purple fruit nearly overflowed the two plastic trays. Samantha grabbed several handfuls and threw them in a food processor, releasing a scent that reminded her of sultry afternoons in the Texas sunshine.

The scent seemed to call something similar to mind for Martin, who inhaled and closed his eyes. "Remember when we were kids, and we used to go picking dewberries in the summer? We'd eat them right off the bushes. They tasted like candy."

The memory reminded Samantha of a time when she and Martin had been great friends, long before the incident in college had come between them. "Those were fun times." She smiled at him.

The three worked silently together, focused on their separate tasks. Beth punched down her dough and began forming small loaves of bread for the sandwiches. Martin boiled the pasta and sliced vegetables for the pasta salad. Samantha parceled out the blackberries to be used for various recipes.

The morning passed quickly, and by ten thirty AM their pace became more frantic as they worked to assemble the gallery lunch and pack everything in the catering van for Beth. "Good luck," Samantha called to her friend. "Get us some new customers!"

When they turned to walk back toward the kitchen, Martin looked at Samantha. "What now, boss?"

"Now, we have lunch." Back in the kitchen, Samantha made two plates piled with Beth's chicken salad sandwiches and bowls of the watermelon-and-tomato salad. She glanced over at Martin, who had settled onto one of the bar stools in the corner of their workspace. It was amazing how quickly they'd been able to fall back into an easy camaraderie. She felt another pang of regret over how easily she'd let a few misunderstandings derail their friendship so many years ago. She wanted to reach out another olive branch. "I don't know what we'd have done without you today. Beth and I have been so stressed out lately, trying to make a go of this business, that we have to jump on every opportunity that comes along."

Martin dug into his food, eating as if he wouldn't get another meal. "I have no doubt you'll make a success of it. You usually do. Anyway, this food is delicious. I'm impressed."

"The food is really more Beth's thing. She's a skilled chef and an excellent teacher. She's taught me so much in the last few weeks."

"Don't sell yourself short. I've been watching you in here. You're pretty good with that knife." Martin's grin lit up his face, and Samantha caught herself admiring his angular chin.

For the second time that day, her cheeks burned. She shifted gears in the conversation. "So, how is your mom really doing? She seems remarkably well put together, given the circumstances, but that's pretty typical behavior for her."

Martin nodded. "She is the epitome of that deodorant commercial—never let them see you sweat. Ever since my dad died, and she had to take care of me by herself, she's refused to show any sign of weakness. I'm not sure if she fully realizes how much trouble she is in right now. Hopefully we can find out something tomorrow to help her case, because I'm getting pretty worried."

Samantha cleared their empty plates and washed them at the sink. "I'm worried too. There's no shortage of suspicious activity, but I'm struggling to figure out how to connect any of it to Angela's murder. Maybe tomorrow we'll learn something that will eliminate your mom as a suspect."

She tied her apron on again. "You've already put in several hours. Do you have it in you to do a few more? It's okay if not." Samantha desperately hoped Martin wouldn't abandon her. There was plenty left to do, but she wanted to give him an out in case he was tired.

Martin found another apron and fitted it around his muscular frame. "No problem. I promised to help. I can stick it out until we're done."

They continued to work companionably, growing more and more comfortable as they chatted about what had happened in the intervening years since they'd seen each other. He laughed at amusing anecdotes from her newspaper career, and she listened intently to his stories about life as a high school history teacher.

During a lull in the conversation, Samantha stopped her chopping. Though they had already cleared the air the night before, Samantha wanted to say more to make sure Martin understood the depths of her regret, especially after all he'd done for her today.

"Martin, I've been thinking a lot about what you said yesterday, and I want to apologize again. Eric was such a jerk. You were right about him from the beginning, and I should have listened to you." Though she wanted to look away, she forced herself to hold Martin's gaze, wanting to be sure he heard what she was saying. "I just want to be sure that you know I never would have intentionally hurt you. Back then, I was overly confident and way too sure of myself. Trust me, life has knocked me down a few pegs more than once in the last few years."

Martin nodded. "Don't worry. I've learned plenty of lessons myself. It's like I tell my students: every mistake is an opportunity to learn something. Anyway, I'm glad we can move forward."

They dove back into their respective recipes, and after a few more hours, they'd baked the flat bread, prepared the toppings, snapped the green beans and marinated the salmon. Samantha felt more confident that everything would be completed in time for the funeral tomorrow. She wanted one more quality-control taste of her special cocktail and offered to make one for Martin.

"Sure, I never mind a little day drinking. Will you join me?"

Samantha considered. With the early start time that morning, she'd put in more than an eight-hour workday already, and she would do more later this evening. "Why not?"

She mixed the blackberry shrub she'd prepared the previous day, with gin and lime juice in a cocktail shaker, and poured the icy concoction into two coupe glasses, which she topped off with prosecco. She handed one of the violet-colored drinks to Martin and took one for herself.

As they clinked glasses, the kitchen door opened, and a tall man with wavy black hair and green eyes stepped into the room. Samantha yelped. "David!"

David laid a package he'd been holding on the counter and tilted his head slightly, offering a wary smile. "I'm sorry. I know you said you couldn't see me until tomorrow, but I have a little gift for you. Am I interrupting?"

Samantha recovered from her momentary shock and realized how the scene he'd walked into probably looked to him. She sat her glass down on the counter and rushed to embrace him in a hug. "It's so great to see you! David, this is my friend, Martin. Our moms are best friends. We've known each other since we were kids." Her words tumbled out in a rush of reassurance.

They seemed to hit their mark, as David's smile broadened and he walked over to Martin, holding his hand out to shake. "Nice to meet you, Martin. I'm David."

Martin's stance tensed, but he gripped David's outstretched hand and shook it. "Likewise."

Samantha, suddenly buzzing with nervous energy, wanted to keep the conversation going. She walked over to the counter where she'd left her bar supplies. "David, can I offer you a drink? Martin and I were sampling my newly created cocktail for an event I'm catering tomorrow."

David eyed the purplish liquid. "It's a striking color. I can't really stay, but I'll try yours. I hate to miss a Samantha Warren original."

Samantha passed her glass and watched as David took a small sip and nodded his head. "Mmm . . . this is delicious. What is it?"

"Gin, blackberries, and prosecco."

Martin swirled his glass. "I taste another flavor in there? Something slightly sour?"

"The sour comes from vinegar. Do you think it tastes okay? Will it satisfy the blue bloods at the Clawson residence?" Samantha looked back and forth between Martin and David, hoping for reassurance.

"Anyone would love this drink." David took another small sip and passed it back to Samantha.

"They'll be begging for more." Martin finished his drink.

Samantha grinned. "Thanks, guys. I hope the family likes it."

David picked up the small package he'd left on the counter and handed it to Samantha. "Before I go, open this. I found it while strolling through a farmer's market in Brooklyn. When I saw it, I immediately thought of you."

Samantha unwrapped the small package, revealing a small bottle of garam masala bitters. "Ooh, this is intriguing!" She screwed off the top and sniffed, breathing in the scents of cinnamon, cumin, and coriander. "My brain is going into overdrive thinking of different drink combinations. Thank you!"

Her pulse quickened at the thoughtful gesture, pleased both that David had missed her while he'd been out of town and that he knew her well enough to pick out the perfect small gift.

David smiled. "I knew you'd come up with a creative way to use it."

As she was screwing the top back on the bottle, Samantha's cell phone rang. Seeing Beth's name on the caller ID, she answered. "Hey, Beth. How'd the luncheon go?"

"The luncheon was fine. Our catering van, not so much. I'm on the side of the road near Montrose and Gray. The van is smoking." It took a lot to rattle Beth, but her voice shook as she told her story.

"Oh no! I'll come pick you up. See you in a few." Samantha wondered what else could go wrong. She pictured the money they'd just earned from the luncheon disappearing before they could even deposit it. But there was nothing to be done—a working van was crucial to their business.

She clicked to end the call and glanced back and forth between David and Martin. "I'm sorry, guys—I've got to pick up Beth. Our catering van apparently stalled out and started smoking. She's stranded, waiting for the tow truck on the side of the road."

David's eyebrows knit together in sympathy. "That's awful. I can drive over with you and wait for the tow truck if you need to run Beth and any of your catering supplies back here."

Martin grabbed for his keys. "I can come with you. I've got tools in my truck, and I know a bit about engines. Maybe there's something I can do to help."

Samantha picked up her purse, frowning, her mind already calculating whether they had enough money in the bank to pay for repairs. "Thanks to both of you, but I doubt there's a quick fix for this. The van made a few screeching sounds last week. I sort of ignored it, hoping it would hold up until we finished a few jobs and had the time and money to get it fixed, but I've secretly been afraid something like this might happen. We'll sort it out when I get there."

She waved the men out the door and locked up the kitchen. "David, it's great to see you. Thank you for the bitters. Martin, I'll call you later." She didn't look back as she headed toward the garage and her car.

Chapter Thirteen

Samantha's stomach clenched as she drove to pick up Beth. Their business ran on such a tight margin; a busted catering van was the last thing they needed. As she drove, she contemplated worst-case scenarios. *What if our van can't be fixed? How will we get everything to the funeral tomorrow?*

Eventually, she spotted the turquoise and green van on the side of the road. It hadn't been that long since they had bought it and painted it with their name and the slogan "Cocktails and Catering: From Our Garden to Your Table." The slogan was so lovely, painted in charming cursive. She hoped the van could be resurrected.

Samantha parked behind the van and called out to Beth, who was sitting on a bench at a nearby bus shelter. "Beth! What happened?"

Beth stood up, frowning. "I don't really know. It made some awful noises and then suddenly it sort of shuddered and stopped. I eased it over to the side of the road and flipped on the hazard lights. I hope it's nothing too serious."

They took a seat on the curb to await the tow truck. Samantha stared at the van as if trying to will it back to health.

"So, how much did you finish for tomorrow?" Beth bit her lip, her worry etched on her face.

"I made good progress. Martin helped a lot. I think we're in pretty good shape . . . provided we have transportation to the funeral." Samantha tried to reassure her friend.

They fell silent as they waited for the tow truck, which finally appeared. After several minutes of maneuvering, the driver secured the van on the back of a flatbed truck, and Beth and Samantha headed back to the kitchen incubator to talk strategy and await the bad news from the garage.

Back in the kitchen, they checked the to-do list for tomorrow. They still needed to grill the salmon, steam the potatoes and green beans, and finish adding toppings to the flat breads Samantha had baked earlier that day. The salads and pasta dish were done; the blackberry shrub and lime juice were ready for the specialty cocktail; and a chocolate sheet cake topped with toasted pecans, known as a Texas funeral cake, was chilling in the refrigerator. For a second dessert option, Samantha had made a modification to her grandmother's homemade prune cake, subbing out the prunes for figs.

As Samantha began chopping up dried figs for the cake, Beth surveyed the table linens, china, and silverware that had arrived that afternoon from the rental company. She counted and packed the supplies, making certain everything was ready for the party tomorrow.

Within an hour, the garage called to tell them they had diagnosed the problem. Their engine had lost compression because of two worn compression rings on the piston. It was fixable but expensive at one thousand five hundred dollars. Samantha mouthed the figure to Beth, who grimaced but then nodded.

"All right, we'll do it. Please tell me you can have the truck ready for tomorrow." Samantha groaned. The van would take two days to fix, but the garage offered them a loaner van.

After ending the call, Samantha groaned again. "The loaner is basically a U-Haul van. We won't have any of our equipment inside."

Beth wrung her hands. "We'll make do. There's a kitchen at the Clawson's house. We'll just wrap the food as well as we can and warm up everything in the kitchen. It will be alright."

Worry lines etched across Samantha's face as she pulled up their business bank account on her phone. They should have enough money to pay for the repairs, but she wanted to be certain. After perusing the numbers, she called Beth over. "Hey, Beth, you know what's weird? The check from the lodge hasn't cleared yet."

Beth walked over to where Samantha peered at her phone. "That is strange. It should have cleared by yesterday, I would have thought. We'll give them until tomorrow and call them."

Samantha nodded and returned to her cake, placing the sheet trays in the oven and anticipating the warming scent of cinnamon and cloves to permeate the air, signifying, much like it had in her grandmother's day, that with a little bit of cinnamon and sugar, everything would be just fine. "I'll wait for this cake to finish baking, but other than that, we should be in good shape for tomorrow."

Beth sighed and leaned against the metal worktable. "Thanks for handling preparations today. The gallery luncheon went pretty well. I passed out several cards. We might get new business out of it. I'm pretty beat, though. Marisa can drive me over to pick up the loaner van this afternoon."

Samantha waved goodbye to her friend as she mixed up the cinnamon and powdered sugar glaze, getting it ready to pour over the cake as it came out of the oven. With that done, she headed home to see her mother and check in with Martin to finalize the details for tomorrow.

* * *

On her way home, Samantha called David. She knew he would worry about her and the van, but she also wanted to make certain he hadn't misconstrued anything between her and Martin.

"Samantha! How's Beth?"

"Hi David. She's okay. The van, not so much. The compressor failed or something. They can fix it, but it'll be expensive and will take a few days, unfortunately. Anyway, I just wanted to call and say I'm sorry for rushing out on you."

"No, I totally understand. You told me you were going to be busy. I just didn't want to wait another two whole days before I saw you."

His words warmed her like a shot of smooth bourbon. It had been sweet of him to stop by the kitchen. "I didn't get a chance to ask—how was your trip?"

"I sold two paintings!" David's voice betrayed his pride. "And the gallery owner wanted to keep two more paintings. She thinks she can find another buyer for them."

"David, that's fantastic. I'm so proud of you."

"Thanks. I'm pretty excited. So, how about you? What's the big event tomorrow? And who was that guy? You said he was an old friend of yours?"

David's question sounded casual, but Samantha picked up a slight note of caution in his voice. She wasn't sure how to answer either of those questions without arousing more of his curiosity, so she kept things simple. She really didn't want to get into the whole murder aspect with him yet.

"It's actually a funeral. The woman was rather high society, so Beth and I hope to attract new business if we can impress the right people. And Martin—yeah, he's an old friend. I told you we grew up together, sort of. He's going to help us out at the funeral tomorrow."

Conversation paused as David absorbed the information.

"High society? Who is it? Maybe I know the person."

Samantha frowned to herself. He might know Angela. He certainly mingled with Houston's upper crust in his life as a lawyer, and she didn't want to have to explain to him her involvement in another murder investigation. Though he'd never lectured her during the last situation, she didn't feel up to defending her choices to embroil herself again. "Angela Clawson. Apparently did a lot of fundraising for Houston hospitals."

"Hmm . . . the name doesn't sound familiar. But I'm sure you'll wow the rest of them with your food and drinks. Anyway, I'd love to see you again. Are you free tomorrow night?"

Samantha breathed a sigh of relief, glad David didn't know Angela and had missed the news of her murder. "Sort of. My mom is still in town, and I'm not sure what she has planned. But let's try to arrange something. Can I call you after the funeral?"

"Of course. I look forward to it." David hung up.

Samantha had reached home and parked in front of her landlord's house. She held the phone in her hand and stared straight ahead at nothing, letting her thoughts linger on David for a little while. He was so sweet, and she felt guilty for misleading him about her activities, but she was afraid he wouldn't understand why she needed to help Patty. Or even if he could understand, he'd still try to convince her to leave it to the authorities, unlike Martin, who was clearly invested in the investigation.

As she walked up the driveway to her garage apartment, she replayed her morning with Martin. It was strange to admit that she'd enjoyed herself, and she couldn't help but wonder again how life might have been different if they had cleared the air years ago. Her mother's comments about Martin's old crush came to mind. *Would a relationship have ever worked between us?* After their easy morning together, a little part of her couldn't deny that it was possible.

At the top of her stairs, she fit her key in the lock and opened the door. Inside, she found her mother pacing in the living room, practically wearing a hole in the area rug. "Samantha, honey, it's awful. Patty's been arrested."

Samantha dropped her purse and drew her mom in for a hug. "Oh no! We knew this was likely, but I didn't think it would be so soon. When did it happen?"

Lillian pulled away and resumed her pacing. "This afternoon. Martin and her lawyer drove her to the police station. They'd arranged with the prosecutor that if she turned herself in, she could immediately go before a judge who would set her bail. This way, she can at least avoid spending any time in jail. I told them to come straight here when they were done, but I haven't heard from them yet."

Though they had been expecting the news, Samantha still felt a knot in the pit of her stomach. She had a hard time picturing Patty facing a judge. "I'm sure we'll hear something soon."

Filled with nervous energy, she glanced around for some way to occupy herself. She strode into the kitchen and pulled out a stack of take-out menus from a drawer, carrying them back into the living room. She pulled her mom down next to her on the couch. "Here, let's look through these and pick something for dinner. We'll have the food delivered, so it's nice and hot when they get here."

They flipped through the menus, unable to concentrate on the food descriptions with their minds racing with concern for Patty. Almost at random, Lillian pulled two menus from the stack. "Either of these look good." She handed the two menus to Samantha and threw the remaining stack on the coffee table, standing up to resume her pacing.

Samantha studied the two menus as her thoughts kept turning to Patty and Martin, wondering how they were dealing with this latest setback. Unable to concentrate, she picked the menu on top. "Let's go for Vietnamese." She skimmed the menu and selected a few specialties.

It was too hot outside for pho, so they ordered lemongrass chicken, shaking beef, and shrimp spring rolls to share. While they waited for the food to arrive, Patty called Lillian to let her know that she and Martin were heading over.

The food arrived a few minutes before Patty and Martin, so Samantha pulled out plates and set the table to prepare for their visitors.

When mother and son shuffled through the door, both appeared drained. Lillian jumped up to hug Patty, who shook off the hug. "Martin insisted we put up the house as collateral. I told him I could have handled a few days behind bars, but unfortunately, my lawyer seems to think it would be more than a few days."

Samantha caught Martin's eye, trying to reignite their childhood ESP and get an accurate gauge of how well Patty was really doing, as opposed to the show she was putting on for Lillian. He shook his head, which Samantha assumed meant Patty's situation was even more dire than Patty had suggested.

"What does your lawyer say about the evidence?" Samantha spoke matter-of-factly, knowing Patty wouldn't appreciate an overt show of sympathy.

Patty sat at one of the kitchen chairs and put her head in her hands. "It doesn't look good. Apparently my fingerprints were the only ones on the murder weapon, so the police seem to think I'm the only one who could have killed Angela. I don't think they are even considering anyone else."

Samantha dished out food onto plates, her appetite suddenly gone. "So what's next?"

Martin piped up. "The lawyer is filing a discovery motion to find out if the police have any fresh evidence, but she said it will be a long process."

Lillian filled glasses with ice water and placed them on the table. With a glimmer of hope in her eyes, she glanced at her daughter. "Hopefully you can uncover something at the funeral to get the detectives off Patty's back."

With nothing left to say, the four ate the food in front of them. Samantha was glad for the spiciness, which appeared to bring color back into Patty's and Martin's faces. Samantha's mouth puckered with the delicious taste of lime and pepper on the grilled meat.

Martin dipped a spring roll into the creamy peanut sauce. He coughed, appearing eager to change the subject. "How was the rest of your day? Did you get your van fixed up?"

Samantha groaned. Patty's troubles had superseded her worries about her own bad news, but Martin's question brought her concerns back to the forefront. "Unfortunately, no. Beth is picking up a loaner van today. It's going to cost an arm and a leg to fix the van, but we can't run our business without it. Thanks again for your help today, by the way."

Martin's face was still clouded with worry, but he nodded. "It was a nice distraction for a few hours. Though it seems stressful, preparing food for so many people."

Samantha bit her lip, anxiety about tomorrow creeping back into her mind. "The reception will be even more nerve-wracking. Serving the food to a crowd is hard enough, but keeping it hot is the other half of the battle when you're feeding a lot of people."

"But you will both take some time to keep your ears open tomorrow, right?" Lillian directed a pleading look at Samantha.

The dual worries about her business and Patty's situation caused Sam's throat to tighten, but she shook it off and bobbed her head in assent. "Speaking of which, we should probably discuss strategy. Mom, why don't you and Patty go into the living room, and Martin and I can make drinks. We'll bring them out, and we can talk about how to approach tomorrow."

The older women moved into the living room and settled on the couch while Samantha led Martin to her bar area. After the long, hot day, she opted for beachy but simple, selecting the Island Old Fashioned, made with aged rum, velvet falernum, simple syrup, and Angostura bitters.

As she placed one large ice cube in each rocks glass, she handed the shaker to Martin. He shook the ingredients and strained them over the ice while Samantha garnished them with a twist of orange peel. She placed the glasses on a tray and carried them out to the living room, passing the icy drinks out to everyone.

"Delicious." Lillian's demeanor had changed from morose to slightly hopeful. "So, what's the game plan for tomorrow?"

They determined that Lillian and Samantha would attend the actual funeral while Martin helped Beth get ready at the Clawson residence. Samantha planned to leave the funeral early, to arrive in time for the final setup. They would listen and talk to as many funeral goers as possible, hoping to pick up on anything interesting or unusual.

"Is there anyone we need to focus on in particular?" Lillian appeared ready to take notes.

Samantha pondered. "Obviously, I want to learn more about Olivia and Matt. See how they act around everyone else. Also, after the meeting the other day, I'm interested in Mr. Muller. I guess those are the top suspects on my list."

Martin finished his drink. "I'll pay attention to the other relatives as well. They are the ones most likely to benefit from Angela's death."

Patty took a last swallow and placed her glass back on the tray. "But I want everyone to be extra careful. I don't want anyone putting themselves at risk for my benefit." She yawned and offered Martin a look, signaling her readiness to head home.

"We'll leave in a minute, Mom. I'm going to help Sam clean up." Martin picked up the tray and carried it into the kitchen.

Samantha followed him and took her place at the sink, pouring some dish soap onto a sponge to clean the dishes. "I'm glad you came in. I wanted to run something by you without our moms hearing."

Martin picked up a hand towel to dry the dishes. "I'm all ears. What's the big secret?"

Samantha peeked back at the living room and saw her mother and Patty talking, and decided it was safe to continue.

"When I was at Angela's house, meeting Olivia for the first time, I overheard her fighting with her sister-in-law about a loan Angela gave Olivia and Matt."

Martin nodded. "Yeah, you told us that earlier."

"Well, Olivia told Christina that Angela kept extensive files detailing every loan and that the documents were in the library in the next room. I was thinking if we had time before the guests arrived, we could snoop around." Samantha handed Martin a glass, watching his expression.

Martin nodded. "Sure. Anything that might help Mom. So what would we be looking for?"

"Any folder with Olivia's or Matt's name, or the name R&C Group on it. Depending on how big the loan was, it could point to motive for one of them."

Martin finished drying the glass and set it on the counter. "So just hope there's a folder and take photos of any contents? Seems easy enough. I can do it while you're at the funeral. Anything else?"

"Christina mentioned something about Angela threatening to write Matt out of the will. I would love to take a look at that will, if it's around." Samantha paused her scrubbing to glance at Martin, who raised his eyebrows.

"That might be a tall order, but I'll give it a try. Clearly, I need to make sure Beth doesn't catch me snooping. I get the impression she wouldn't like that idea."

Samantha laughed. "You're not kidding. She definitely wouldn't. We can't afford to mess up our business right now, and she's worried my sleuthing is going to cause problems."

"Don't worry. I'll be stealthy as a cat. No one will notice." Martin lifted the next clean glass out of the dishrack and began drying it with the towel.

Samantha smiled at him, and they were quiet for a few minutes as they finished up the dishes.

After a few moments, Martin paused and gazed at Samantha. "So, who was that guy at the kitchen? He your boyfriend or something?"

Samantha felt heat rise up her cheeks. "David? He's a friend."

Martin eyed her carefully. "That's all? He seemed like more."

Samantha sighed. "We started seeing each other a few weeks ago. But I just got out of a long relationship, and I'm not totally sure what I want yet."

"He didn't seem to have any doubts about what he wanted." Martin tried to conceal it, but Samantha picked up a hint of annoyance. She recalled their easy connection as they worked together that morning, and for the first time, wondered about Martin's current relationship status. It seemed unlikely that he could be developing an attraction to her so quickly after so many years of bitterness between them, but she couldn't deny a hint of curiosity about what might have been that had crept into her mind today. Still, David was her focus. He'd been the one who'd been there to help her and support her over the last month. And the butterflies she felt in his company were real.

"We're taking things slow." Samantha set the last dish on the rack to dry and stepped into the living room. Her face still burned, but Lillian and Patty didn't seem to notice.

The four said their goodbyes and made plans to reconvene in the morning.

* * *

Samantha woke at six AM and set her teakettle to boil. Normally, she enjoyed a nice cup of chai in the mornings, but this morning required an extra dose of caffeine, so she brewed a plain black tea to jolt herself awake. After a quick shower, she made it to the kitchen incubator in record time and prepared the flat bread with blackberries and goat cheese and the blackberry-glazed salmon for the grill.

As she was checking on the blackberry shrub for the cocktails, Beth walked in, carrying a steaming cup of coffee. "Well, the loaner van is not bad. It's nice and clean and has plenty of room for our stuff. I brought extra coolers from home to carry food over to the Clawson's house."

Samantha sniffed the shrub and was pleased with the fruity and vinegary aroma. "Thank goodness. I wasn't sure how we were going to get the food to the Crawford's house in time for the funeral, without a van."

They worked silently together for an hour, packing up the food to finish cooking it at the Crawford's house before the guests arrived after the funeral. Samantha provided strict instructions on how to prepare the cocktails and told Beth that Martin would meet her at the house by nine AM to help with the setup and serving.

"I'm off to change." Samantha sighed as she took off her apron and located the bag she'd packed with a black sheath dress and black flats.

"Are you sure you want to attend this funeral?" Beth picked up her own change of clothes, which included her standard caterer's uniform of all-black slacks, black blouse, and black shoes—an all-purpose outfit that helped her blend into the background at events.

"I think it would be good to show my face. Not to mention, I need to keep an eye on my mother." Samantha walked into the bathroom to change.

A few minutes later, she inspected herself in the bathroom mirror. Clad in a black dress with three-quarter-length sleeves and a boat-neck collar, Samantha pulled her hair back in an elegant bun. The outfit was versatile, allowing her to easily transition from the funeral to serving at the reception.

When she left the bathroom, Beth headed out with the van, and Samantha hopped in her blue Sentra and drove toward the Highlands' Episcopal Church, where the funeral service was being held.

The parking lot was nearly full, and church workers were setting up an overflow area next door, but Samantha was able to snag one last slot. As she walked into the red-brick building, underneath a marble arched doorway, the first person she spotted was Calista.

After glancing around to try and spot her mother, Samantha approached the woman.

"Hi, Calista." Samantha smiled at the woman dressed in an elegant black wrap dress with her blonde hair blown out as big as a rodeo queen's.

"Oh, hi. Samantha, right? It's nice to see you again, though obviously under such unfortunate circumstances." Calista smiled at Samantha and gazed around at the rest of the crowd.

"Yes, I'm so sorry for your loss. It's a nice turnout today." Samantha took in her surroundings. Sunlight streaming in through the stained-glass windows glinted off the white stone arches that supported the interior walls of the church. Elaborate candelabras wrapped around columns, bringing more light into the cavernous space. An array of flowers decorated the alter. Under different circumstances, Samantha imagined the space would be lovely for a wedding, but the white lilies were a reminder of the circumstances of the day.

Calista surveyed the nave and nodded her head in agreement, making no move to walk away. Samantha wanted to be respectful, but she also wanted to take advantage of the opportunity to question the woman more about what she knew.

"I saw your presentation the other day at the lodge meeting. You did a great job keeping your cool in the face of all of that yelling. What a mess to have to deal with the city inspection issues on top of these unfortunate circumstances." Samantha gestured at the pews in front of them. "Though, I guess the leadership had to have known about the flooding concerns?"

Calista stopped looking around the room and focused more directly on Samantha. "Yes, flooding was always a concern. It was fortunate that we'd had the architect draw up those alternative plans, along with the original ones, so the project wouldn't be delayed further if the city forced us to build the retention pond."

Interesting. I'm surprised none of the other members seemed to know about it. While Calista was talking, Samantha decided to press further. "How about the lodge president? Had he seen the alternative plans? I heard he was furious on Friday when the city refused the permit application."

Calista coughed. "I wouldn't know. Angela was charged with liaising with Muller and the rest of the lodge leadership. I'm not sure what she told him, or when he learned. Anyway, it was nice to see you, but if you don't mind, I'm delivering a eulogy, and I really need to clear my head a bit before I have to speak."

Samantha felt her face burn, ashamed to have appeared insensitive. "Oh, forgive me. I'm sorry again for your loss." She stepped away and searched the room again for her mother, finally spotting her in a row near the middle of the church.

Scooting into the pew next to Lillian, Samantha gave her mom a side hug. "How long have you been here?"

Lillian smiled. "Oh, I arrived a few minutes ago. I saw you talking to that tennis club lady and thought I'd grab us a seat."

Samantha picked up the program her mother had placed next to her on the pew. "Seen anything or anyone interesting yet?"

Lillian gestured toward the front row. "Not too many in the family pews yet. Though maybe they will file in as the service begins. I noticed Mr. Muller come in after me. He's a few rows in front of us."

Samantha found the man's head in the crowd and noted that he appeared to be sitting alone for now. She looked around the rest of the nave, trying to find anyone she recognized. A few well-dressed ladies from the VIP tent seemed familiar, but apart from Muller, she didn't spot anyone else she recognized from the lodge.

As an organ began a solemn hymn, the church filled, and pallbearers wheeled the closed casket to the front of the church, covered with a spray of lilies, roses, and chrysanthemums. Samantha's breath caught in her throat for an instant. Though she didn't know Angela well and had found her overbearing in life, the sight of the casket and the flowers reminded her that a life had been lost and that friends and family grieved that loss.

Ushers led the family up the aisle to the front pews. Samantha recognized Olivia, walking up the aisle, appearing to help support a sobbing man who must have been her husband, Matt. Two preteen boys followed behind them, dressed in black suits. At a close distance, Christina walked up the aisle alone. As the family filed into their pew, Samantha caught the death stare Christina directed at her sister-in-law.

The pastor, clad in white robes, began the service with readings from the *Book of Common Prayer*, after which the sounds of "Jesus Christ Is Risen Today" spilled out from the choir loft at the back of the church.

After the gospel reading, the pastor said a few words describing Angela's devotion to her family and the church. A woman from the Medical Center Auxiliary Board praised Angela's fundraising efforts on behalf of various projects, including a new cancer wing at one of the major hospitals. The recitation made Angela sound very efficient and effective. After the woman finished, Calista Beech strode to the altar and stood behind the lectern, her face somber.

The tone in the room immediately shifted from official to emotional as Calista took the mourners on a more personal journey, telling the story of Angela's youth in West Texas, of her romance with the famed heart surgeon who had become her husband, of her dedication to her children and the causes most dear to her heart.

A young brunette woman sitting two pews ahead of Samantha audibly scoffed, muttering under her breath. Samantha took note of the woman, curious about her objections to Angela's story. She appeared on the younger end of her twenties, and something about her expression struck Samantha as familiar. *I want to hear her story.*

Samantha elbowed her mother and pointed to the woman, whispering. "See if you can talk to that woman after the funeral. She seems like she might know something about Angela's early years."

Lillian nodded, training her eyes on the young woman, as if trying to memorize her profile.

With no further reaction from the woman, Samantha turned her attention back to Calista, whose words brought Angela to life. For the first time, Samantha wished she had gotten to know the woman better.

Calista finished with a story about Angela's latest project, the tennis club, and why it meant so much to her.

"In my last memory of her, she is standing on the stage at the festival, resplendent in her navy dress and her trademark white pearls, pretty as a postcard, but not willing to take no for an answer when it was something she wanted. The tennis club scholarship program was so important to her because Angela believed in supporting our youth. She always gave her all to the causes that were most dear to her heart, and we will honor her memory by finishing what she started."

Calista closed with a poem, which left many audience members in tears, including Christina, who was openly sobbing. Samantha figured if there had been a donation box, Calista could have single-handedly raised enough for ten scholarships with that one speech.

The choir sang "We Walk by Faith and Not by Sight," and Samantha realized the funeral was ending. She whispered to her mother that she needed to leave and raced out to her car to get back to the Clawson's house and help Beth prepare for the guests to arrive.

Chapter Fourteen

When Samantha hurried into the Clawson home, Beth and Martin were assembling the buffet station before the first guests showed up. Samantha jumped in, helping to arrange chafing dishes of blackberry-glazed salmon and flatbread with blackberries and goat cheese on an immense table already filled with steaming buttered potatoes and green beans, and a kale and blackberry salad loaded with fresh vegetables from the garden.

Samantha loaded up the bar cart with wine, beer, and enough liquor to prepare most basic cocktails. She laid out the ingredients for Angela's specialty cocktail, hoping that Olivia's husband and Christina felt it represented their mother well.

With everything finally ready, they had the time to catch their breath, and Martin asked Samantha about the funeral.

"I had an interesting conversation with Calista Beech. She admitted that those construction plans had been prepared well before this week in case there were flooding concerns. I tried to ask her how much Muller knew, but she dodged the question. I think she knows something but was hesitant to gossip. Maybe I can try to press her more this afternoon." Samantha arranged a few bottles of champagne in ice to chill.

"I'll ask around about him too. Anyone else interesting show up?" Martin dabbed a napkin at his forehead to wipe away sweat.

Samantha nodded. "There was a young woman sitting in front of me who seemed annoyed by the eulogy. I had to leave before I could talk to her, but I told Mom to try to seek her out after the service ended."

Martin's eyes were pensive as he considered Samantha's words. "Anything else?"

Samantha rocked back on her heels. "No one else stood out to me. The family was there, obviously. The daughter, Christina, shot daggers at Olivia, but there's clearly no love lost between them. I think it's worth watching them today. How about you? Did you make any progress on that little project we discussed yesterday?"

Martin grinned. "My snooping time was limited. I couldn't find a will, but I did find a few folders with Matt's name on them. I didn't understand everything I saw, but I took photos of all of it. We can peruse them later to see if there's anything useful."

Samantha smiled. "Great work, Martin. Hopefully, we'll find something helpful in those documents."

She moved back over to the bar area to prepare for the guests' arrival.

Beth came into the dining room from the kitchen, carrying a tray of cold pasta salad. She fiddled with the dishes on the buffet table, moving them slightly this way and that. "Are we all ready? When do you think they'll get here? Do we have enough food?" Her words came out rapid fire.

Samantha tried to soothe her. "We're ready. We'll be fine. Once everyone arrives, Martin will circulate with the appetizers. Everyone will love the food. We'll get loads of new customers."

Beth moved one last dish and nodded. The door opened and the first cluster of guests swarmed in. Beth rushed into the kitchen to help Martin plate the hot appetizers, while Samantha took her place behind the bar.

Olivia, her husband, and her two boys were the first to walk into the living room. Olivia ushered her husband into a chair, appearing to fear he'd collapse. She sent the boys upstairs and glided into the dining room, appraising the dishes.

"Everything looks and smells wonderful. I can't thank you enough for handling this on such short notice." Olivia walked over to the bar and lowered her voice. "Can I get one of those specialty cocktails? My husband needs perking up."

Samantha nodded and shook the gin with the blackberry shrub and lime juice until icy crystals formed on the outside of the shaker. She poured the concoction into a stemless Manhattan glass and topped it with champagne, then garnished it with two blackberries and handed it over to Olivia. "It's a bit sour, a bit sweet, and very complex. I hope your husband enjoys it."

Olivia took a little taste of the cocktail and smiled. "Delicious. I'm sure he will love it. Thanks again."

Samantha was glad Olivia was pleased with the drink. With that worry subsided, she contemplated how to investigate. She was most interested in Christina's hints regarding Olivia and Matt, as well as Calista's non-hints about Adam Muller. But stuck behind the bar, there wasn't much to do but keep her eyes and ears open.

Christina slumped inside, looking like a wrung-out dishrag. Her exhaustion did nothing to limit the serious side-eye she gave Olivia when she spotted her. She turned into the dining room and headed for the bar.

"How are you holding up?" Samantha tilted her head, offering a sympathetic smile.

Christina seemed to be on the verge of tears. "It's rough. Can I try one of those cocktails you mentioned the other day? Alcohol is the only way I'm going to get through this day."

Samantha offered what she hoped was a comforting smile. "Of course. Again, I'm so sorry for your loss. I know this is a tough day for your family."

Christina peered at Olivia in the next room and grimaced. "Well, for some in our family, anyway. I can't believe she has the nerve to act like the chief mourner after everything she's done."

"Do you still suspect her?" Samantha kept her eyes mostly on the drink she was preparing but snuck a brief glance at Christina.

"Oh, this is good. I see why mother enjoyed your drinks so much." Christina finished the drink in two large swallows. "Make me another one, please."

While she waited, Christina fidgeted with a pearl necklace around her neck. "I don't want to believe my brother had anything to do with it, but I told you about the loan and my mom's comments about the will. Plus, he and Olivia have been desperate to get their hands on this house for years, and now, since she didn't have time to change her will, they'll get it."

Christina was spilling her suspicions, and Samantha wanted to keep the young woman talking. "Have you asked them about what you heard?"

"Olivia claims it was nothing. She says Mama was always threatening stuff like that when she didn't get her way." Christina sampled her cocktail.

"And did she? Threaten to change her will often?"

Christina shrugged. "Sometimes. But only when she was really mad. And she was really mad that night."

Samantha was as confused as ever. If Angela had a history of threatening to change her will, how much weight should she put on Christina's accusation? She decided to see how far she could press Christina. "If they get the house, what will you inherit?"

Christina seemed taken aback. "Her jewelry and, of course, money. But I'm not the one needing cash—at least not as badly as them. The police are convinced the lodge lady is guilty, but I want them to look harder at those two." She tipped her head toward Olivia and Matt in the living room. "Anyway, thanks for this." She lifted the drink and sauntered off to join a group of ladies in the living room.

More guests streamed through the door, and the line at the bar kept Samantha busy. She surveyed the room, trying to locate Martin. She spotted him in the corner of the living room with a tray of baked brie with blackberries and mini cheese-and-bacon quiche appetizers, an item they'd added to the menu in a nod to Christina's request. Martin appeared to be offering them to various clusters of people crowded together, hanging a bit outside of the circles.

Olivia clinked a knife against a glass and quieted the crowd. "The family wants to take this time to thank you for coming out today to help us celebrate Angela's life. We are grateful for the outpouring of love and support. Please help yourself to food and drinks in the dining room when you are ready."

Samantha searched for Christina again but didn't see her. She prepared for an onslaught, as dozens of mourners milled over to the dining room to take plates.

Beth prepared to serve, dishing out salmon on plates while guests helped themselves to other offerings in bowls on the table.

Samantha caught Beth's eye and offered a smile, trying to buck her up for the final push of their already long day. She turned her attention back to the line at her cart. Most guests asked for the specialty cocktail, but a few asked for basic drinks such as margaritas and martinis.

When the line died down, Samantha gazed out over the crowd, hoping to spot the young woman from the funeral service who had sat in front of her. So far, she was nowhere to be found. Eventually, after a haze of unfamiliar faces, Samantha spotted Calista at the end of the line. As she prepared Calista's drink, Samantha complimented her on her eulogy. "You were wonderful this morning. There wasn't a dry eye in the house after you finished that poem."

A red blush rose up Calista's cheeks. "I wanted people to get a sense of the real Angela."

Samantha placed the blackberry garnish in the glass. "You must have been close to her."

Calista sipped the drink and held it in her mouth for a moment before swallowing. "We've known each other for years and worked on several projects together."

Samantha nodded sympathetically. "You were probably the most clued in to what was happening with the tennis club project. This may sound strange, but since you and Angela were so close, I'm certain you want her killer caught. I keep hearing rumors that the police are trying to find a new suspect. What do you know about Adam Muller?"

Calista swallowed the rest of the drink in one gulp, and she coughed. "Can you make another one, please?" She paused as she watched Samantha shake the cocktail. "I'd hate to say something and be wrong . . ."

Samantha desperately wanted to press her, but she used the old reporter trick of keeping quiet, hoping Calista felt compelled to fill in the silence. She kept her eyes on the drink she was making, pouring the champagne into the blackberry and gin mixture, watching the bubbles fizz, and hoping that answers, like the champagne bubbles, would rise to the top.

Calista lowered her voice. "Okay. I saw Angela and Adam arguing shortly after they appeared on stage together. I can't swear to it, because I couldn't hear everything, but one of them mentioned the detention pond."

With no one else in the drink line right then, Samantha moved slowly with the garnish, hoping to extend her conversation. There was no artful way to ask her next question, but she kept her tone nonconfrontational, with her words coming out less like a question and more like a statement. "That reminds me, I saw you and Angela in what looked like a tense exchange at the VIP tent."

Calista's eyes widened, but she quickly recovered. "Well, yes. We were discussing the city inspection news and how to handle things with the lodge leadership. The rumors were spreading rapidly, and we needed to get out in front of the situation."

"That makes sense." Samantha handed the woman her second drink. Calista thanked her and headed toward the living room to mingle with other guests.

Two elderly women walked up to Samantha and ordered drinks. As she prepared them, she considered Calista's comments. Apart from the brief expression of surprise, Calista hadn't seemed ruffled by Samantha's questions. It made sense that the two women had been conferring about the inspection results, but could there have been another source of tension between them? And what about Calista's mention of Adam's argument with Angela? It seemed likely that Adam was the mystery man the volunteer spotted arguing with Angela prior to her death, so he remained firmly on her suspect list. Equally interesting was the continued insistence from Christina that something was up with Olivia and Matt. Her list was growing, rather than shrinking.

How can I find out more about all of them? She looked around for Martin. At the next break between guests, she signaled for him to come near. "Have you learned anything yet?"

Martin used a handkerchief to wipe his brow. "I've been so busy. It's hard to listen in, but I've picked up a few tidbits here and there. How about you?"

"Same. But listen, I've had two interesting talks with people. We need to learn as much as we can about Olivia and Matt Clawson, Adam Muller, and Calista Beech." Samantha waved Martin away as another group of elderly women stepped toward the bar.

Martin headed to the living room, taking his time picking up discarded plates and silverware from the coffee table and end tables.

Samantha watched him, surprising herself as she admired his muscular stature. He'd grown up nothing like how she'd imagined when they were kids. She shook her head, trying to return to reality, as she turned to a new guest in front of her.

An elderly woman in an elegant black shift dress smiled at her. "I had to try one of those specialty drinks. I've heard they're delicious."

Samantha smiled back and prepared the drink. "I'm sorry for your loss. How did you know Angela?"

The woman fiddled with a gold necklace around her neck. "Oh, I've known her for years. We served on several fundraising committees together. I was one of the first women she recruited to join the tennis club. She wasn't the easiest person to get along with, but she always got things done."

Samantha slowed her preparations, hoping the woman would elaborate. "I only met her briefly, but she certainly seemed like a force to be reckoned with."

The woman chuckled. "Oh, she was that, for sure. But she had her soft spots too. Like that son of hers." The woman glanced around as if to make certain she wasn't overheard, and lowered her voice. "She always coddled that boy. Picked up after his worst messes, bailing him out with loans time after time. But part of that was control. She took the view that giving him money meant she had a say in how he lived his life."

Interested, Samantha took her time placing the garnishes on the drink, hoping to prod the lady into saying more. "What do you mean?"

"Oh, silly things, such as what kind of clubs he belonged to, what kind of car he drove. The latest fight was over where his son should go to school. Angela wanted him to go to Matt's alma mater, but Matt's wife put up a huge fight. Giving Matt money gave Angela leverage, which she used to pressure him to do many things."

Samantha remembered the disagreement she'd witnessed the night of Angela's death, regarding Matt's fiftieth birthday party. The lady's story had a ring of truth to it. She handed the woman her cocktail.

After one taste, she smiled. "One thing Angela knew was quality. And this drink is quality. You've done her justice." The woman raised the glass in a toast to Samantha and joined a group of women clustered in the living room.

Samantha watched the woman go, pondering her insinuations. She needed to explore Angela's meddling and hoped the documents Martin had photographed from the library would give her a better idea of how many times Angela had rescued her son from financial ruin.

With food-table traffic dying down, Samantha decided she might be able to ask Beth to spell her at the bar for a few minutes. She hoped to snoop around a bit. She prepared a few more of the specialty cocktails, placed them on a tray, and called Beth over. "Hey, I'm going to circulate with these cocktails. I need to stretch my legs for a minute."

Beth nodded and took her place behind the bar. Though she wasn't as good a bartender as she was a chef, she could handle most basics.

Samantha maneuvered around groups of people, aiming for the living room with her tray and keeping her eyes peeled for people she might want to talk to or listen in on. She saw Adam Muller in the corner, standing by himself. She walked over to offer him a drink, curious about what he might say to her. As she neared him, he looked up from his cell phone, which he had been reading, and grimaced.

"Care for a cocktail? They were created specially to honor Angela Clawson." Samantha held the tray out toward the lodge president.

He reached for one. "Thanks. You seem familiar. Have we met?"

Samantha smiled. "Well, I served cocktails at the Independence Day Festival the other day. Speaking of which, my check for the festival hasn't cleared the bank yet. Do you know why?"

The man's cheeks flushed red. "Oh yes. I'm so sorry about that. We had a few issues with money being moved around to different accounts because of the tennis club project. But it will be corrected once the board approves the new plans tomorrow. We may need to reissue new checks."

Samantha didn't like the sound of that. She and Beth needed that money to keep their business running. They already had so little of a cushion. "Wait, I'm confused? What does the vendor money have to do with the construction project?"

Muller took a step backward, away from Samantha, and cast his eyes at the floor. "I'm terribly sorry. It should only delay payment by a couple of days. We appreciate your understanding. None of this should have happened, but we will pay everyone soon."

Samantha ground her teeth, trying to bite back her anger. "Do the delayed payments relate to the permit situation? After seeing the presentation at the lodge the other night, it seems like lodge leadership has a lot to answer for."

Muller had sampled the drink Samantha had given him, and he immediately coughed. "We are still sorting everything out, but I assure you, all of the vendors will be paid. Now please excuse me." He hastened away from her.

Darn it! Other than rattling Muller somewhat about the lost payment, Samantha hadn't accomplished much of anything during her exchange with the lodge president. And she was still seething about the late payment. She and Beth had been counting on that money to pay their mounting bills, and now they'd be operating on the thinnest of margins.

Frustrated, she walked back to take her position behind the bar. She was ready to wrap up this event, and hoped that the Clawsons paid faster than the lodge.

Chapter Fifteen

Beth immediately noticed Samantha's glum expression. "What's wrong?"

Samantha clenched her jaw. "I had a little chat with the lodge president. Apparently, they are delaying our payment for a few more days because they don't have the money to cover what we earned yet. Before we can get paid, the board has to vote to approve the latest construction proposal for the tennis courts."

Beth's eyes grew wide. "What does that mean? How is the construction project connected to our money?"

"It shouldn't be. I want answers, but this is probably not the right place to seek them." Samantha rubbed the back of her neck, trying to release tension.

Beth ran a hand over her face. "We need that money, especially after the van repair. I wish you'd never agreed to work at that stupid festival. It's been nothing but trouble since you took the job."

Beth stomped off, and Samantha crossed her arms over her chest, wishing she hadn't told Beth the news.

It's not my fault they aren't paying on time. Samantha huffed, but then breathed deeply and exhaled slowly. She had to remember to view things from Beth's perspective. Beth had given up a lucrative position as a landscape architect to start their business, whereas Samantha had given up relatively little. She'd already been laid off and was used to life on the edge; Beth, on the other hand, struggled when she didn't know when her next paycheck was coming. Everything was fine as long as they were busy and bills were being paid on time, but one late payment was a setback at this early stage of their business.

With few guests to serve, Samantha began to straighten up the bar area. As she cleaned, she kept her eye on the living room, trying to read the room. The party appeared to be winding down. Groups of guests were leaving, stopping to pay their respects, separately, to Olivia and Matt and then Christina.

Matt appeared ready to fall over. If he was playing at grief, Samantha decided he was doing a pretty good job. Christina had visited the bar several more times during the afternoon, yet she was walking around with almost a manic energy.

When another flock of guests left, Christina returned to the bar and asked for another special cocktail. As she mixed up the drink, Samantha hoped Christina wasn't driving.

"It's been a nice turnout." Samantha handed Christina the glass. "I think your mother would have been proud."

Christina took a sip and sighed. "I suppose so. Mama was always one to worry about appearances. I'm sure the turnout would have thrilled her. For myself, I can't take Olivia's faking any longer."

Christina took another swallow before she turned abruptly and stalked into the living room, barreling toward her sister-in-law.

Samantha watched as Christina confronted Olivia and appeared to stumble, splashing the remains of her cocktail onto Olivia's black dress and the white Persian rug beneath her feet.

Christina regained her footing and sneered at her sister-in-law. "Oh, Olivia, don't look so horrified. It's not even your place yet. And if I have anything to do with it, it never will be."

Olivia scowled at her sister-in-law and grabbed the glass from Christina's hand. "You've had enough, Christina."

Christina snatched a half-drunk beer from her brother's hand.

"No, Olivia, I don't think I have." Christina took a long slug from the bottle, her expression challenging anyone to take it from her. "If drinking at my mother's funeral is such a sin, consider all you have to atone for."

A hush fell over the room as the remaining guests tried to eavesdrop on the conversation without telegraphing their interest.

Olivia raised her eyebrows at her husband, as if to will him into action. Matt stood up and walked over to his sister and embraced her. "Oh, Chrissie, I miss Mama too, but this isn't helping."

Christina pushed Matt away and screamed, "Get your hands off me! You're as bad as she is."

Christina ran from the room and tripped on a rug, landing hard on her knee on the tile floor in the foyer. She screamed, her face twisting in agony.

With the remaining few guests frozen, unsure how to react, Samantha raced over to help Christina stand up. The woman moaned as she struggled to stay upright. Samantha wrapped her arm around her, supporting her as she led her toward the area where she assumed the bedrooms were located. "Is there a room where you can rest?"

Christina pointed toward the first door on the right down the long hallway, and Samantha pushed it open to reveal a bedroom decorated lavishly in blue and white floral print. She helped Christina to the bed and settled her in among a mound of pillows, attempting to make her comfortable. "I'll come back with ice."

Christina winced as she elevated her foot.

Samantha raced to the kitchen to fill a bag with ice, which she wrapped in a towel and carried back to Christina, along with a glass of ice water. She settled the cool bag on the woman's knee, which was already swelling, and handed her the cold glass. "I thought you might like some water."

Christina gulped at the water as if trying to quench a fire in her throat. Tears pooled in her eyes and spilled out over her dark lashes. Her words slurred, but Samantha understood.

"You're being nicer to me than my mother ever was, so I don't even know why I should care who killed her. The last time I saw her, she yelled at me for wearing the wrong necklace for my outfit. She literally forced me to switch necklaces with her so I didn't embarrass her in front of her friends. That was the kind of mother she was." Christina slammed the glass down on the adjacent bedside table. "Even so, she didn't deserve to be murdered."

Samantha fiddled with the ice pack, trying to position it to alleviate the swelling. "Of course not. Nobody deserves that."

Christina clutched a nearby pillow and squeezed it. "Everyone thinks I'm just drunk, but I know what I heard. Olivia and Matt are somehow involved in my mama's death. They practically admitted it."

Samantha raised her eyebrows. "Admitted it? How?"

"I overheard Olivia talking to Matt. She said, 'Just keep quiet until next Friday. It will all be over and everything will be fine.' Guess what happens next week? We're meeting my mother's lawyer to discuss her will."

That's interesting. It sounded like the couple was hiding something, at a minimum, though Samantha wished there was some solid evidence of guilt. "Even if they are eager to hear about the will, what makes you think either of them had anything to do with your mother's murder?"

"Remember, Mama threatened to cut Matt out of the will the night she died. It looks pretty suspicious to have them counting down the days until we hear about the will. Plus, there's the simple fact that Olivia disappeared on Friday night. I didn't see her at any point after I talked with mom at seven thirty. She was supposed to be watching the pie contest, but she wasn't there. And it took Olivia more than half an hour to show up after I called Matt to tell him about Mama's death. Where did she go? Who's to say she didn't leave to clean up after killing my mother?"

Before Samantha could respond, the door opened, and Olivia walked in. "I can take it from here, Samantha. I'm so sorry you have had to witness all of this. Most of the guests left, so once you finish cleaning up, I'll leave a check for you in the kitchen."

Samantha stood to leave and nodded. "Thanks." She turned back to Christina. "I hope you feel better soon."

Samantha walked out the door and was about to lean in to see if she could overhear anything from the other side, when she spotted Matt walking down the hallway toward her. "Have you seen my wife or sister?"

"They're both in there." Samantha nodded in the direction of the closed room and continued down the hall. As she walked to the kitchen, she tried to picture Matt or his wife killing Angela, but she had a hard time envisioning it. It wasn't so much their genteel appearance. There was a long history of genteel, properly mannered people committing great atrocities. But the crime was so brutal, and Matt had seemed so broken up at the funeral and reception.

Of course, that could be guilt, particularly if he or his wife committed the murder to help clean up after one of his apparently many financial mistakes.

Samantha reached the kitchen and found Beth packaging up food into containers for the family. She grabbed a sponge and scrubbed the empty chafing dishes. "Where's Martin?"

Beth placed the containers in the large refrigerator. "He told me to tell you he had to leave. Something to do with his mom. But he said he'd call you later."

Samantha raised her eyebrows. "His mom? I hope she's okay."

"I'm not sure." Beth frowned. "Anyway, Samantha, I'm sorry about earlier. I know it's not your fault that the lodge hasn't paid us our money. I'm just on edge about the van repair bill, and worrying about when our next booking will come in. Do you think it will ever get any easier?"

Samantha leaned in to give Beth a half hug. "It's going to get way easier. We knew it would be like this for a time. It just takes a while to build up a regular clientele, but we're doing a good job, Beth. We are going to make this work."

Beth returned the hug. "I know we are. I can't imagine trying to do this without you. Anyway, Martin did a good job today. He was a great worker."

Samantha nodded. "He was a big help yesterday preparing the food too. I misjudged him over the years. He's not so bad."

Beth gave her friend a sideways glance. "Are you sure there's nothing happening between you two? I caught him studying you a few times today, and his gaze lingered."

Heat warmed Samantha's cheeks. *Why does everyone keep asking if there's something going on with me and Martin?* "There's nothing. I'm just trying to help his mom, for my mom's sake. I'm going to see David after we finish up here."

Beth turned her attention back to the dishes. "And how are things going with David? Are you still taking things slowly?"

Samantha nodded as she finished scrubbing more serving dishes. "We are. He's understanding, even though I think he's a little frustrated. I just don't want to rush into anything after my last relationship blew up in my face. I don't want David to be a rebound guy."

Beth dried the clean dishes. "David's a good guy, and he knows you're worth waiting for."

Samantha began sorting the dishes they'd rented from the ones that belonged to them. "I hope so. Meanwhile, what are you and Marisa up to tonight? Got any big plans?"

Finished with the drying, Beth jumped in to help the sorting. "We're finally going to try out that new Ethiopian place. This is Marisa's one night without study group, so we've been looking forward to it."

Samantha was glad her friends were making the time to go out. "That sounds amazing. Have a great time."

With the packing done, Samantha found the check Olivia had promised, lying on the dining room table. She was relieved to note it included a sizeable tip. Beth agreed to return the rental items if Samantha dropped the check off at the bank. They wanted to deposit the money as soon as possible, since it sounded as though they would be waiting a while for the festival check to clear.

Samantha drove to the bank, and after breathing a sigh of relief to see the new balance in their business account, she called her mom to check for any word on Patty.

"Oh, honey, it's been an awful day. Her lawyer wanted to discuss a plea agreement. Apparently, the prosecution offered a one-time-only deal for her to plead to a charge of second-degree murder. She has to decide by the end of the day." Lillian's voice sounded defeated.

"Surely she's not taking it, is she?" Samantha couldn't imagine Patty taking a plea deal when she hadn't committed a crime, but her mother sounded really upset, so she wasn't completely positive.

"Martin talked her down from the ledge. Her lawyer wanted to be sure that she understood her options and why she might want to consider the deal. I get it—she needs to understand those things. But Patty is starting to lose hope."

Samantha wished she'd made more progress on identifying the murderer so she could help Patty get back to her normal life. Then she remembered the woman from the funeral. "Mom, were you able to talk to that young woman I pointed out at the funeral?"

Lillian's voice perked up with excitement. "Oh, how could I have forgotten that? Well, I didn't get a chance to talk to her, but I did follow her."

Samantha struggled to remain patient as her mother took her time telling the story. "And? What happened?"

"Well, after the service ended, I followed her up to the receiving line to talk to the family. She made a beeline for Angela's son and gave him a hug before she raced out of the church. I kept my eye on her and followed her to the parking lot, but by the time I got there, she was already in her car—a beat-up Chevy pickup truck."

Samantha urged her mother to continue. "So you followed her? Where did she go?"

"Oh, Samantha, I had a heck of a time. You know I'm no good in traffic, but the truck was distinctive, so I kept up with her pretty well. I followed her a while, something like fifteen or twenty minutes, until she pulled into a parking garage. Well, I got all turned around, and by the time I figured out which way to go, I'd lost sight of her, and I knew there was no way to find her."

"What kind of parking garage? Do you know what building she went into?" Samantha's heart raced with excitement as she tried to pull the story from her mother.

"Well, no, not exactly, but I know what kind of building it was. Some kind of a hospital. The parking garage was in the Medical Center and seemed to feed into two or three different hospitals. There were people honking behind me, and the space was so narrow it was hard to turn around, and I just had to get out of there."

Samantha's stomach sank as the realization that what might have been a promising lead had slipped through their fingers. "And there's nothing else you can remember about the woman?"

Lillian's voice softened. "I guess I messed up. I tried to keep up with her, but those parking garages stress me out . . . Wait a minute . . ." Then the phone call ended.

Samantha clenched her fist, frustrated by the disconnected call and wondering whether she should call her mom back. Just as she was about to hit "Redial," Samantha's phone rang. "Mom! Why did you hang up?"

"I'm sorry, honey. I was trying to go through my pictures. I remembered that I had taken a photo of the woman and her license plate. We can feed it into one of those internet searches. We'll have to pay a little money for it, but it should pop up with the name of the owner of the truck anyway. Maybe that will help."

Samantha let go of the breath she'd been holding. Finally, some good news. "Brilliant, Mom! Text me the photos and I'll try the search on my computer later."

"I'll do it as soon as we hang up." Lillian's voice had grown stronger, pleased she'd been able to contribute after all.

"Thanks, Mom. Is there anything more I can do to help Patty right now?"

Lillian sighed. "No, honey. Martin and I will pick up dinner and sit with her for a bit. You're welcome to join us, but you must be beat after all that work today."

Samantha was exhausted, but she also looked forward to seeing David. "I am pretty beat, Mom. And I'm meeting my friend David for dinner. Give Patty my love and tell her not to lose hope. Maybe your hot tip will turn into something good. I'll see you later when you get home."

True to her word, Lillian texted the two photos once they'd hung up. The picture of the woman was blurry, but the license plate photo was clear as a bell. She'd look up the owner later tonight, but now, she had other business. She dialed David.

"Hey, stranger." His baritone voice sounded playful, but warm.

Samantha smiled. "Hey back at you. I heard there was a handsome attorney in town who might be free for dinner tonight with a lowly caterer. Did I call the right number?"

"This attorney had plans with a self-starting entrepreneur and creative cocktail genius. But you sound cute. I might be persuaded." David chuckled. "I'm dying to see you. Tell me when and where, and it's a date."

Samantha felt a tingling warmth spread through her body, down to her toes. "How about Paulie's? I need to run home to get cleaned up and change, but I can meet you there in an hour."

"I'll be counting the minutes."

They hung up and Samantha allowed her thoughts to linger briefly on David as she delighted in the fact that she would see him soon.

* * *

Back at her apartment, Samantha greeted Ruby, who circled Sam's feet as soon as she walked in the door, reminding her to top up her food bowl. Samantha fed the cat and showered, hoping to wash away the day. Refreshed, she hunted through her closet for a cute sundress to wear to dinner, and pulled out an emerald-green, spaghetti-strap midi dress, which would contrast nicely with her blonde hair. After applying the barest amount of makeup and throwing on a pair of silver strappy sandals, she was ready to walk out the door and turn her attention to something other than Angela Clawson.

She was a few minutes early at Paulie's, one of her favorite Italian restaurants in the Montrose neighborhood of Houston. Though the floors and furnishings were sleek and modern, the exposed brick walls and large plate-glass windows overlooking the street created a homey atmosphere. The scent of homemade pasta cooking in the kitchen, and the sound of clinking glasses filled with Italian wine, contributed to the pleasant ambiance. Samantha felt immediately at ease. The restaurant was an order-at-the-counter kind of place, so she sat at a table near the front and perused the specials as she waited for David. He arrived within five minutes, dressed in dark blue slacks and a crisp white dress shirt.

At her first glimpse of his green eyes, Samantha broke into a wide smile and stood up to hug him. "It's so nice to see you. Did you just come from court?"

He returned her hug and appeared to admire her dress. "No, a late client meeting. You look fantastic, by the way."

Samantha's cheeks flushed pink with pleasure. "Thanks. You do too."

They ordered dinner, opting to split a salad and a bottle of wine. Gripping the bottle and a couple of glasses, they headed to a cozy table by the window, where a tea candle glowed, it's small light flickering and reflecting off the glass.

"How was the funeral?" David poured her a glass of the red Tuscan blend they'd picked out, before filling his own glass.

She sipped the wine and savored the flavor. "It was a long day, but the food tasted great, and everyone enjoyed the special cocktail I created in the woman's honor. It sounds awful to say, but hopefully we'll attract new business because of it."

Samantha decided she should steer the conversation away from the funeral. She didn't want to let anything slip about the murder or the fact that she was trying to investigate again. She felt a slight pang at keeping David in the dark, but it was better to avoid the subject. "Anyway, I'm much more interested in hearing about your trip. You sold two paintings? That's amazing. I want details."

She listened as he shared amusing anecdotes about people he met at the gallery show, including one about an elderly woman who had bought his largest painting for her summer cottage because it reminded her of her late husband's favorite jazz album.

When he tried to turn the conversation back to her, she offered short answers and asked him about the case he was working on and the sights he had seen in New York.

"Okay, you don't need to listen to me wax poetic about Rockefeller Plaza. Why do I get the feeling there's something you're not telling me?" David stared intently into Samantha's eyes, as if trying to read something in them. "Did something happen while I was gone?"

She pinched the bridge of her nose and pressed her lips together. *I should have known I couldn't keep this from him. He's way too perceptive.*

Before she could think of another answer, the truth slipped out. "There was another murder."

David's jaw dropped open as he stared in shock. "What? What happened? You're not involved, are you?"

Samantha calculated how much to tell him without worrying him too much. "You know that friend of mine you met yesterday? Martin? As I mentioned, his mom is my mom's best friend, and she's been accused of the murder. But she didn't do it." The words spilled out of her, and Samantha had to pause to take a breath.

David reached for her hand. "Please tell me you're staying out of it, after the last time."

Samantha squeezed his hand, enjoying the sensation of his warm palm holding her own. "I'm not in any danger. I've just been keeping my eyes and ears open to see what I can find out."

David let go of her hand. "Sam, you can't—"

"David, it's my mom's best friend, a woman I've known my whole life. She didn't commit this crime, and today the prosecutor offered her a plea bargain." Samantha lifted her chin and held David's gaze.

He stared at her for a moment before glancing down at the table. "Sam, you're a smart and capable woman, but you're not a detective, and this isn't some game."

Samantha picked up her fork and twirled a strand of angel-hair pasta around its tines. "I promise, I'm not in any danger. As far as anyone is concerned, I'm just the caterer."

He lifted his eyebrows. "But you're asking questions, and that kind of thing gets noticed. You have to be careful. And let me help you. I don't want you doing any of this alone."

David asked for details about Patty's lawyer and the case against her. He reassured her that Patty's lawyer was a good one and would mount a vigorous defense. "Just to be clear, are you sure Patty isn't involved?"

Samantha's eyes widened. "I told you—she's my mom's best friend. I've known her my whole life. She didn't like Angela, but she would never have killed her, or anyone else for that matter."

David lifted his palms up in a signal of surrender. "Okay, I believe you. Obviously, I don't want your mom's friend to face charges for a crime she didn't commit. But I also don't want you in any danger. Promise to keep me posted."

Samantha smiled and nodded before changing the subject. "Oh, I have a legal question for you. And so you don't think I'm asking for free legal advice, a cappuccino and cookie are on me." She filled him in on the lodge payment delay and asked if she and Beth had any recourse.

"If it came down to it, your only recourse is a lawsuit, but I'll bet it won't come to that." David rubbed his chin. "I could call this lodge president tomorrow and scare him by threatening to sue. I'd bet you'd get your money before the end of the day."

"Thanks for the offer, but I'll wait a day or two. I'll give them the benefit of the doubt for now." Samantha walked back up to the counter and ordered two steaming mugs of frothy cappuccino and two iced cookies from the mouthwatering array of desserts on display. She balanced the small plate of cookies on top of one of the mugs and carried everything back to the table.

David jumped up, quickly relieving her of the plate and one of the mugs and setting them gently on the table. "I really missed you, Sam. I know I was only gone for a few days, but I thought about you constantly."

Samantha smiled, toying with the thin necklace around her neck. "I missed you too."

They sipped their cappuccinos, gazing at each other over their cups. When Samantha dunked her cookie into the coffee, her phone rang. She glanced at the number and smiled apologetically at David, mouthing, "I need to take this."

Samantha answered the phone. "Martin—what happened with your mom? She didn't agree to a plea bargain, did she?"

After assurances that his mother had not accepted an agreement, and that she was fine for now, Martin reminded Samantha of the pictures he'd taken during the funeral. "You need to see this, Sam."

Chapter Sixteen

Samantha gazed at David, who was reading headlines on his phone while he waited for her. "Okay, meet me at my place. I'll be there in a few."

David glanced up from his phone, an inquiring look on his face. "What's going on?"

Samantha winced. "David, I hate to leave, but something's come up, and I need to deal with it. I really enjoyed dinner. It was great to see you. I'll call you later."

She stood up to kiss him, but he grasped her hand. "Samantha, where are you going? Is this about the murder investigation? I'm coming with you."

She pulled her hand away. "No—that's not necessary. I'm just going to my apartment. I'll talk to you later." She gave him a peck on the cheek and walked out the door before she could change her mind. She'd text him later, thanking him for dinner and suggesting they get together again soon.

On the way back to her apartment, her mind shifted into curiosity about what Martin's photos showed. When she reached the driveway that led to her garage apartment, Martin was already there, sitting on the bottom step of the outdoor stairs that led up to her door. She spied him before he noticed her and admired his profile. Not for the first time since they'd become reacquainted this week, she noted how handsome he had become.

She shook the thoughts out of her head and called out to him. "Martin! Hey. Come on, I'll let you in." She brushed past him, turned the key in her lock, and opened the door.

He followed behind her, and when she turned around to offer him a seat at her kitchen table, she noticed him eyeing her. He blushed. "Sorry for staring. You look great. I hope I didn't drag you away from anything."

Samantha brushed aside the image of David sitting alone at their table at Paulie's. "No, it's alright. I was at dinner with a friend." She didn't know why she hadn't said David's name, but decided it was better to keep the focus on Patty. "How's your mom?"

Martin shrugged. "The same as ever. Honestly, I think she's in denial."

"That's hard." Samantha touched his arm. "So what's the news? What did you find today?"

Martin pulled out his phone and opened the photos he had taken earlier. "I couldn't find the will, but you were right about the folder with Matt Clawson's name on it. I expected to hunt for it, but it was right there on the desk. If you look here, you'll see that he visited the bank of Mom several times over the last few years."

Samantha zoomed in on the photo and perused the itemized list, noting a loan of fifty thousand dollars from four years ago, one for seventy-five thousand dollars two years ago, and the last item—a loan of a hundred thousand dollars from three months ago. "Was there a payment record? I distinctly remember Olivia saying they had been paying those loans off and that there was a record of their repayment."

Martin flipped through a few other photographs. "I didn't have a ton of time in there, but it seemed like there were individual files for each loan, with a signed document and payoff schedule and everything. Seems like Ms. Clawson ran a tight ship. So I found files for the earlier loans, marked as paid."

He flipped to a new photo. "This is the file for the last big loan. It shows a few payments and then this . . ." Martin zoomed in on the photo, revealing a handwritten notation: *Winkler County???*

"What do you make of that?" Martin looked up from his phone.

Samantha pulled out her phone and googled the name. "Hmm . . . it's out in West Texas. Angela's hometown, Kermit, is the county seat. But how does that relate to this loan? And how might the loan relate to Angela's murder?"

Samantha took up Martin's phone, swiping through the photos once more, hoping to find a clue she'd missed earlier. "Something about this doesn't feel right. This loan is from three months ago. From what Christina said, Matt said something to Angela on Friday to make her angry enough to threaten to cut him out of the will, so it seems unlikely that this loan had anything to do with that. What could he have said to make her turn on him that quickly?"

"What if he told her he couldn't pay the loan back? That might make her angry." Martin pursed his lips in thought.

"Maybe, but I have a hard time picturing it. Based on what Christina told me, Angela used money as a way to control people. It seems like Matt being in debt to her would make her happy because she'd have more control over him. He had to have done or said something specific to make her angry."

Martin took his phone back and opened up the notepad app. "What else did you learn at the funeral?" He clutched the phone as if it were a matter of life or death. "I'm afraid we're running out of time to find fresh evidence to help my mom."

Martin's comment about fresh evidence reminded Samantha of her mother's discovery. She picked up her own phone again and pulled up the texted photos from her mom before retrieving her computer.

Martin glanced at the photo. "Who's that?"

"She sat in front of us at the funeral. I don't know who she is, but she's the woman I told you about who groaned during the talk about Angela's early life. Maybe someone from her past? Mom followed her after the funeral but lost her in a hospital parking lot. She did capture this photo of her license plate. Let's look it up and see if we can identify the mystery woman."

Samantha performed the license plate search, pulling out her credit card to pay the sixteen dollars and ninety-five cents required for the computer to spit out what Samantha hoped was the woman's name. For a few minutes, they watched the spinning wheel of death while the internet did its thinking. When a name popped up on the screen, Samantha gasped. "Mary Hawkins? That's Angela's sister. But that woman couldn't have been Mary—she was much too young."

"Angela's sister?" Martin's words woke Samantha from a temporary trance.

"According to Christina, they hadn't spoken in more than twenty-five years. Maybe this woman is Mary's daughter?" Samantha's mind processed the information, and she recalled another detail from her mother. "Mom said she hugged Matt after the funeral and immediately left. But that woman looks younger than twenty-five. She and Matt can't have been close if their mothers haven't spoken since before she was born."

"Clearly, they've had some contact. Probably found each other on social media or something."

Hmm . . . Angela's son openly defying her wishes and speaking with a member of the family she'd cut off contact with . . . That might get Angela's dander up. Samantha followed her train of thought out loud. "There's got to be a connection between this woman showing up and this notation about Winkler County in the loan file. But until we find out what it is, it's hard to know whether or not it's relevant."

Martin started typing on his phone. "Let's take notes about what we've learned so far. Maybe something will pop out at us."

Samantha stood up. "I prefer to write by hand. I think better that way. Do you want a drink while we brainstorm?"

Martin rubbed the back of his neck. "Sure. Anything is fine."

Samantha mixed two Kentucky mules and carried them into the living room. "We'll be more comfortable here. Let me grab my notepad."

When she returned to the living room, Martin sat on the couch with his cocktail. She paused, contemplating the risk in sitting so close, before shrugging and sitting down.

"This is nice. It's got a kick to it." Martin smiled as he placed his drink on a coaster on the coffee table.

"It's the ginger beer. I make it with jalapenos." She sampled hers, enjoying the spicy fizz as she swallowed, before placing it on a matching coaster next to Martin's drink. "I think we should begin with a list of suspects."

Martin grinned at her. "You haven't changed. Even when we were kids, you were always ready with a plan."

Samantha felt heat rise up her neck. "I'm sorry. I don't mean to be bossy."

He nudged her arm with his shoulder. "I was joking, Sam. Remember when we were kids? You'd create these detailed plans for the simplest games. But it was great. You always had the best ideas."

Assuaged, Samantha took the cap off her pen, ready to get down to business. "So, I guess the first people we should list as suspects are Olivia and Matt Clawson, agreed? They could each have their own motivations for murder, but for now, we'll list them together."

Martin nodded as she wrote their names at the top of the list.

Olivia and Matt Clawson

1. *Son and daughter-in-law of victim*
2. *Had outstanding loans of just under $100,000 from victim*
3. *Olivia claims the money is being paid back*
4. *Christina claims Matt and Angela fought before Angela's body was found, and Angela threatened to cut Matt out of her will.*
5. *Christina says the couple will inherit the house after the will reading.*
6. *Christina says she overheard Olivia tell Matt he needed to keep quiet until next week when "everything would all be OK."*
7. *Matt seen hugging mysterious woman from West Texas at funeral.*
8. *Angela made a notation about Winkler County on Matt's loan document.*
9. *Christina says Olivia was supposed to be at pie contest, but was nowhere to be found before or after the murder.*

"Can you think of anything else to add?" Samantha passed the list to Martin, who reviewed it.

"Maybe the mystery woman has her own motivations. Even if she's not an official suspect yet, we can mark her down as a suspicious character." Martin passed the list back to Samantha, who created an entry for the mystery woman.

Mystery woman driving Mary Hawkins' truck

1. *Unknown woman attends Angela's funeral and seems disgruntled about references to Angela's past.*
2. *Woman hugged Matt Clawson before leaving and driving to a hospital.*

"Unfortunately, that's about all we know about her. But there's plenty that we'd like to know. I'll write that down too." Samantha continued to jot her thoughts down on the paper.

Who is she? How is she connected to Mary? Why did she attend the funeral? Why did she go to the hospital? Was she in town the night Angela died?

Martin looked at the list and nodded. "All good questions. So who's next?"

Samantha filled Martin in on her talk with Adam Muller at the funeral and wrote his name down.

Adam Muller

1. *President of the German Lodge*
2. *Seen by Calista Beech fighting with Angela shortly before Angela's death.*

3. *Many people said he was angry about city permit problem.*
4. *Angry that extra money was needed to move forward with the new design.*
5. *Angry the lodge would lose additional land because of the detention ponds.*

"You know of anything else suspicious about Mr. Lodge President?" Samantha twirled the pen in her hand.

"Beth mentioned that your check from the festival bounced. Is that suspicious? The fact that the lodge is suddenly super short on money?" Martin tilted his head, reminding Samantha of her cat Ruby, when she heard a strange noise.

"All it really proves is that the funds were improperly comingled, which is strange. For now, we don't know what's important, so I'll go ahead and write it down." Samantha added the late payment to her list.

She twirled her pen again. "Who else can we add? How about Karl? I know he's got the hots for your mom and all, but he created that entire plan to trick police by having everyone accuse everyone else. Maybe he wanted to shift suspicion away from himself."

Martin laughed. "I know I was ready to pin the whole thing on him at first, but the guy has been calling practically every day, and I'm pretty sure he's harmless. But if we are being equal opportunity with our suspect list, write him down."

Samantha scribbled Karl's name on the notepad and looked back up at Martin. "Anyone else? What about the person Karl's friend spotted in the parking lot near Angela's car right before police found her body? I heard about it from Calista too. If it's true, that's suspicious. So, we add 'Suspect X' to the list?"

Martin nodded.

"Anyone else? I'm going to add Calista Beech to the list. She seemed close with Angela, but I did see them in a tense discussion the night Angela died. She says she was at the pie contest when Angela was killed, but I want to verify that."

Samantha put the end of the pen in her mouth as she contemplated her notebook. "There are a half a dozen other lodge members who hated Angela, but with nothing more specific, other random names would only muddle the list."

Martin tugged at the ends of his hair. "What about Christina? She might be trying to shift suspicion to her brother. Could she have killed her mom?"

Samantha tapped the pen on the notepad. "I don't think so. She was judging the pie contest at the time of the murder, with plenty of witnesses. She couldn't have done it."

Martin sighed. "I can't think of anyone else. What now?"

Samantha flipped to a fresh page in her notebook. "Now, we figure out what other information we can gather regarding our current suspects. I want to start off with Olivia and Matt. We need to dig into Matt's business failings and what caused them. I messaged a friend at the paper to ask her for any intel on Matt's business. I'll check back in with her."

Martin finished his cocktail. "I can talk to Karl—feel him out."

Samantha tapped her pen against the notebook. "Now, about Adam. He mentioned a board meeting coming up over the weekend to approve the redesign of the plans. Is there a board member who can fill us in on what he says?"

Martin shrugged. "I don't know many lodge members now. I haven't been around in a decade. But I'm sure Mom knows someone. I'll check in with her."

"I think the next thing we need to focus on is alibis. Who has one and what are they? That's the quickest way to sort through the list." Samantha made a note on her notepad. "Is there anyone to eliminate off the bat? Anyone with a strong alibi? Karl already told us he has no alibi—he claims he was looking for your mom."

"It seems like someone from the lodge would have seen Adam. I'll ask Mom to ask around." Martin flipped through the notepad. "I don't really know anyone else on this list."

Samantha leaned her head closer to Martin's, looking at the other suspect names. "Christina says Olivia disappeared around the time of the murder, but we should double check. I haven't heard where Matt was at the time of the murder either. As for the mysterious West Texas woman and 'Suspect X,' we need to identify them before we can investigate their alibi."

Martin sighed, leaning back against the couch. "I hope we can make some headway soon. Police aren't focusing on anyone but Mom."

The mention of Martin's mother reminded Samantha that she hadn't talked to her own mother in a few hours. "Speaking of your mom, what were she and my mom doing? It's getting kind of late, and I haven't heard from her."

"As far as I know, they were just hanging out after dinner, but you're right, it has been a while." Martin grabbed his phone to check for messages. "No word from my mom."

Samantha picked up her phone to call Lillian, who answered after the fourth ring.

Lillian sounded out of breath. "Hey honey. Can't talk long. Patty felt like baking, hoping to take her mind off of her troubles, so we're elbow deep in strudel dough."

Samantha groaned. It was 9 P.M., but she realized they could be at it for another few hours. When Samantha and Martin were children, their mothers were known to spend hours in marathon baking sessions, making three different strudel flavors. The result was usually delicious, with an assortment of cherry, apple, and raisin strudels, but it usually meant that she and Martin were on their own to entertain themselves.

"I may spend the night here, if you don't mind, Samantha. We'll be at it for a while." Lillian sounded hurried.

"Sure, Mom. I'll see you in the morning." Samantha ended the call and flipped over to her calendar app. The only item listed for tomorrow was an intimate anniversary dinner Beth had booked for Friday evening. They were catering a romantic meal for two couples at a private home, so Beth planned to handle the actual event on her own. Samantha needed to go into the kitchen in the late morning to help with dinner preparations, including creating a special cocktail for the couples, but early morning and most of the afternoon would be free. She looked over at Martin and pitied him, having to go back to his mother's house to be the third wheel to their moms' midnight baking session. She decided to throw him a bone.

"Bad news." Samantha grimaced at Martin and immediately regretted it when she noticed him tense up. "I'm sorry. Poor choice of words. It's nothing terrible. Just our moms are planning a strudel-making slumber party. I don't envy you going home to that right now."

Martin rolled his eyes. "They'll be up all night, carrying on. But I shouldn't begrudge Mom the fun. She needs time to decompress after her ordeal with the lawyer. I'll find something to do."

Samantha paused, considering the ramifications of what she was about to offer, and made a split-second decision. "You can stay here for a while. We could make another drink and watch a movie or something?"

Martin's face brightened. "Kind of like the old days?"

Samantha laughed. "Yeah, except, I hope you've outgrown the gruesome horror movies by now. Those used to give me nightmares."

Martin flipped through the options on Netflix while Samantha walked into the kitchen to make popcorn and a few more drinks.

Is this a wise idea? What would David think? She pushed the thoughts from her mind as she shook the Bourbon and lime juice together. *We're old friends. Nothing is going to happen.*

When she walked back into the room with their popcorn and drinks, Martin had pulled up *Groundhog Day*, a movie they'd watched a thousand times as kids and had practically memorized. She laughed, and grabbed a throw blanket to cover her legs before calling Ruby up to the couch to snuggle between them.

As Bill Murray relived the same day repeatedly on the big screen, Samantha and Martin laughed through their favorite parts, almost as if no time had passed and they were two children on summer break. She snuck a peek at his profile, noticing the light blonde stubble on his angular jaw, struck that the face she had once known so well, appeared both the same and so very different. She turned away and focused her attention back on the television.

Comfortable and tired after a long day, Samantha curled up under her blanket and fell asleep. When she woke several hours later, she sat up with a start. Martin was curled up on the other side of the couch, Ruby perched on his chest, and the Netflix landing page played in a loop on the screen. She shook her head to wake herself up more fully and scrambled off the couch, turning off the television.

As she stared at Martin, her thoughts turned to David, whom she'd left at dinner the previous evening. *What did I get myself into here?*

She shook off the thought and glanced at her phone to learn the time. It was 3 A.M. She tucked the blanket over Martin's legs and moved to her bedroom, deciding she'd deal with Martin in the morning.

Three and a half hours later, Samantha woke to a knock at her front door and a yell of surprise from her living room. She ran out of the bedroom and crashed into Martin on the floor, tangled up in the blanket she'd thrown over him last night. The knocking persisted.

Chapter Seventeen

"Who is it?" Samantha called out as she tried to extricate herself from the pile of limbs and blanket on the floor.

"It's your mother. I come bearing strudel."

Samantha and Martin exchanged glances. *How can we explain this?* Samantha tried to convey the message with her eyes as she stepped to open the door.

"Oh, Sam, did I wake you up? I'm sorry . . ." Lillian fell silent as she spotted Martin, who was attempting to comb his unruly hair with his fingers. "Did I interrupt something?"

Samantha reached out for the packages of strudel in her mother's arms and ushered her into the living room. "No, Mom. We fell asleep watching a movie last night, that's it. It was a long day for all of us."

Martin tucked his t-shirt into his shorts, continuing his effort to appear less like he'd just woken up. "I hope Mom didn't worry last night. I should have phoned."

Lillian looked Martin up and down. "No. She realizes you're an adult and can make your own decisions."

Samantha walked towards the kitchen. "I'm going to make tea. Anyone want some? We can have it with the fresh strudel."

Martin, still looking sheepish, shook his head. "Nah, I should probably head back to Mom's."

Samantha set the kettle to boil before walking Martin to the door. "Thanks for hanging out last night. Talk to you later."

Deciding to ignore her mother's raised eyebrows for now, Samantha returned to the kitchen to set her chai tea to steep and cut into the fresh apple strudel on her counter. "Do you want yours heated?"

"I'll just have coffee. I had more than my fair share last night." Lillian bustled around the kitchen.

Samantha could feel her mother's eyes on her as she sat down at her kitchen table with the strudel and a steaming mug of tea. "Okay, Mom. Out with it. What are you thinking?"

"I'm just wondering if that was wise, letting Martin spend the night here." Lillian shifted her gaze to the coffeepot, which was emitting steam and the aroma of pecan flavored coffee.

"Geez, Mom. First you were upset that we weren't friends anymore, and now, you're mad that we're trying to be friendly again. I don't get it."

Lillian poured a cup of coffee and sat across from her daughter at the table. "Samantha, I know you're an adult. But I don't want either of you hurt . . . And by the way, weren't you out with that lawyer guy last night?"

David! Samantha realized she'd forgotten to text him last night. She searched for her phone, trying to assess whether it was too early to text him now. It was 6:30. She decided she'd give him at least another half an hour so she didn't seem too crazy, or too guilty to be calling him so early in the morning.

She turned her attention back to her mother. "For your information, I had a lovely dinner with David. Afterwards, I came back here to meet Martin and talk over what we'd learned at the funeral. We spent most of the night discussing the case against Patty." Samantha filled her mom in on the details they'd picked up from the funeral, and the next steps they planned to take in their investigation.

"Oh, and we looked up the license plate you found. That truck is owned by Mary Hawkins, Angela's sister!" Samantha hoped the new information would be enough to get her mother's mind off of Martin.

It appeared to have worked. Lillian's eyebrows lifted. "Now, that is interesting. It's got to be connected to the case; don't you think?"

"I don't know, but it's definitely worth investigating further. How is Patty doing?"

Lillian filled Samantha in on her evening with her friend. "She's not doing so great, to be honest. That meeting with her lawyer yesterday really got to her. She's losing hope."

"All the more reason we need to get into high gear with our investigation." Samantha finished her strudel, savoring the warm apples spiced with cinnamon. "I need to meet Beth this morning to help with a small dinner she's catering tonight, but I want to check into a few items before I leave. Do you have morning plans?"

Lillian took a sip of her coffee. "Not really. I think Patty and I saw plenty of each other yesterday. She could probably use some alone time this morning. I was hoping to tag along with you for a bit."

Pulling out her notepad from the night before, Samantha showed her mom the next items on her to-do list. "I'm going to follow up with my friend from the business desk at the Gazette. Can you read through this list of suspects and tell me what you think?"

Samantha texted Paula, hoping to catch her before she got busy at the newspaper. Her friend messaged her back fairly quickly.

Hey! Was planning on messaging you. You have a minute for a quick call?

Samantha hoped Paula had good news for her. *Sure. That would be great!*

The phone rang.

"Hey, Sam! So I did a bit of digging through Texas Railroad Commission records. Your boy, Matt Clawson, has been busy. He bought several drilling leases in pretty typical areas, but he purchased one big one out in West Texas in Winkler County. The reason it's unusual is that new leases in that area are pretty rare because that region was tapped out long ago during earlier oil booms."

Winkler County again! Samantha buzzed with energy, certain there had to be a connection between the lease and Mary Hawkins. She pressed her friend for more information. "So, speaking as someone totally unfamiliar with how this works, why exactly would someone do that?"

Her friend laughed. "Same reason people place dumb bets at Vegas. Maybe he received a tip that the area was ripe for new exploration. But I haven't seen activity near there in years. Anyway, I can send you the spreadsheet of the leases your guy purchased. Hopefully you'll find what you're looking for there."

Samantha hoped the spreadsheet would contain some concrete information that could explain the connection between Matt and Mary Hawkins. "Thanks so much for your help, Paula. I've got your name on a couple of bottles of my best bitters. I'll send them your way!"

The friends hung up, and Samantha raced into the kitchen to fill her mom in on her call with Paula.

"That's too big a coincidence to not be important, Samantha. We've got to find that young woman, or, at the least Mary Hawkins."

As they discussed next steps, Samantha's phone dinged with an incoming email. It was from Paula, and it contained the spreadsheet listing the land leases Matt had signed in the past year. Scanning through the list, she noted a cluster of five leases which Paula had highlighted, all with the same person.

"Well, this proves it—Matt was doing business with Mary Hawkins. But according to my friend, it was a strange move, because she said there hasn't been any fresh oil or gas found in that area in dozens of years. Why would he risk the wrath of his mother for a longshot at best? It makes no sense."

"That makes it even more suspicious. I think we're on to something with this." Lillian sounded excited. "But how can we find out more?"

Samantha's reporter instincts kicked in. "Mom, can you find out Mary Hawkins' phone number?"

Lillian grabbed Samantha's computer and searched. After paying another fee at a people finder site, Lillian found Mary's home and cell phone numbers, which she wrote out on a notepad and passed to Samantha.

Samantha looked at her phone and saw it was 7:30 A.M. She could call the woman now and maintain the element of surprise, but it was risky. While her journalistic training told her not to ask a question she didn't know the answer to, time was of the essence, and they needed answers fast.

Samantha dialed the home phone first, but as she suspected, there was no answer. *She's probably still in Houston, particularly if she was at a hospital yesterday.*

She dialed the cell phone next, hoping for the best. The call went directly to voicemail, and Samantha made the calculated decision to hang up for fear of scaring off the woman with a message. She would try again later.

Lillian stepped out of the bedroom, freshly made up and ready for the day. "Did you reach Mary, Sam?"

"Not yet. I got her voicemail but didn't leave a message. I don't want to scare her off, so I'll try again later." Samantha picked up her notepad again. "While I think this Mary Hawkins thing may be our best lead, there are still a few other loose ends we need to investigate. Did anything stand out to you on this list?"

Lillian glanced at the notepad filled with Samantha's scribbles from the previous evening. "I support having as many suspects as possible, but I think you should remove Karl from this list. I can't picture him as the murdering type."

"But he doesn't have an alibi." Samantha was reluctant to remove anyone from the list based on nothing more than a feeling. "If you can find anyone who saw him between 7:30 and 8 P.M., we can scratch him off the list, but not until then."

Samantha explained that she wanted to investigate alibis for Olivia, Matt, and the other suspects.

"Christina claimed that Matt argued with Angela before she died. But Adam Muller also admits he and Angela had a disagreement late that night. I wonder if we can get more details on those timelines."

They fell silent for a moment, pondering, before Samantha looked at her watch and realized it was time to meet Beth.

Before they headed to the kitchen incubator downtown, Samantha and Beth would plan the menu at Beth and Marisa's place. They could also pick fresh ingredients from Beth's herb and kitchen gardens. Beth wouldn't mind if Lillian tagged along.

Samantha wrapped up a strudel in foil and grabbed a few bottles from her collection of homemade bitters and cocktail syrups, including a jalapeno tincture. "Come on, Mom. Let's go help spice up someone's anniversary."

Chapter Eighteen

Marisa answered the door and welcomed Samantha and Lillian into the quaint Victorian cottage she shared with Beth in the city's Montrose neighborhood. "Hey, long time no see!" Marisa hugged each of them and led the way into the kitchen, where Beth was sitting with her menu-planning notebook, mapping out a course list for the evening's event.

"So, what's on the menu tonight?" Samantha took a seat next to her business partner, while Lillian sat opposite them across the kitchen island, and Marisa perched on a stool.

Beth flipped backward in her book and started reading out her plan. "The main dish will be beef tenderloin with a cognac cream sauce and au gratin potatoes. I'm growing lovely heirloom carrots in the garden right now, so I'll roast them for a side; then we'll end with peach cobbler for dessert, served with homemade vanilla ice cream. That leaves a salad and cocktails."

Samantha picked up a peach sitting on the counter and smelled it for inspiration. "Hmm . . . your cobbler gives me an idea for a special spicy peach and bourbon cocktail I can mix up for dessert. Before dinner, you can serve sidecars, to hint at the cognac in the tenderloin."

Beth noted the additions in her book. "Sounds like a plan. It shouldn't be too much work."

She led the way to the garden, followed by Samantha, Lillian, and Marisa. Lillian's eyes widened at the bounty of vegetables and herbs Beth had coaxed from the ground. "This is amazing, Beth. Can you give me a tour?"

Beth showed Lillian around while Samantha picked a few herbs for the drinks. With the herbs in hand, Samantha headed inside to place them in water until she needed them.

Marisa followed her. "What's the latest in the case? Beth told me you're still investigating that woman's death."

Samantha looked down. She didn't want a lecture from Marisa, who had plenty of reason to discourage her from getting involved in another investigation after saving Samantha's life a month earlier. Marisa had walked into Samantha's apartment just in time to interrupt a killer who had already stabbed Samantha's arm. "I'm just asking a few questions here and there."

Marisa rolled her eyes. "Please. You can't fool me, girl. I know you. And I won't lecture you—I want to help. If you're going to involve yourself, I don't want you doing it alone."

Samantha looked up in surprise from the notepad, where she had doodled ideas for the peach cocktail she'd been planning for the dinner party. Marisa's eyes shone with an openness that encouraged Samantha to confide in her. She realized she'd missed her best friend. They hadn't hung out one-on-one in a while because of the craziness of starting up a new business, as well as Marisa's heavy schedule at the law school. Samantha didn't want to lose the closeness they'd always shared.

Samantha filled her in on the latest on the case, including what she'd learned that morning about Matt Clawson's purchase of oil rights from his aunt Mary.

Marisa was pensive. "What's your plan?"

"I need to dig more. Mom saw the mystery woman going into one of the hospitals in the medical center. If I could figure out where she is, maybe I could try to talk to her in person."

"Does your mom know which hospital?" Marisa straightened a pile of papers on the counter.

"No, it was one of those garages that feed into multiple hospitals. She got a little turned around and lost sight of her."

"Well, I've got some time this afternoon between classes. Do you want me to call around to some of the hospitals to ask if Mary is a patient?"

Samantha pondered but couldn't see any downside. HIPAA rules allowed hospitals to reveal patient's names and room numbers, though most usually wouldn't report on a patient's condition over the phone. "That would be a big help. Calling a few hospitals certainly wouldn't be dangerous. Thanks! In the meantime, maybe I can reach out to Christina and find out what she thinks of her brother's business deal."

"That's not a bad idea." Marisa packed the papers she'd been sorting into her backpack.

Beth and Lillian returned from their gardening expedition, with Beth carrying a produce basket teeming with heirloom carrots in every shade of orange and purple. "What have you guys been plotting in here while I've been outside?" Beth's gaze went back and forth between Samantha and Marisa, who offered a half smile.

"Oh, don't worry. Sam's just brainstorming." Marisa picked her messenger bag up from the counter. "Sam, I'll text you if I find anything."

Marisa kissed Beth. "Good luck today. I'm headed to class now." Marisa waved to Samantha and Lillian as she headed out the door.

Samantha and Beth packed a few items to carry to their rented kitchen. "Beth, do you mind giving Mom a ride? I'll meet you there in a bit. I've got a quick errand to run."

Beth glanced at Samantha, trying to figure out what she was up to, before she agreed. "Sure. She can help me get started on the cobbler."

They left the house together, with Lillian following Beth to her truck. Samantha climbed into her Sentra. She hoped Marisa would have some luck finding Mary Hawkins, but in the meantime, she'd decided she would try to talk to Christina.

Before she did, however, Samantha knew she needed to apologize to David. She looked over at her wrapped strudel, hoping it would serve as a sufficient peace offering for practically ghosting him after dinner the previous night.

David's law office was in the opposite direction of the kitchen incubator downtown. Samantha steered her car down Westheimer, toward River Oaks, the wealthiest enclave in the city, filled with mansions built by oil money. The law office was in a nondescript tower. Samantha strolled into the lobby and gave David's name to the guard, who waved her toward an elevator and told her to press the button for the ninth floor.

Clutching her package close to her chest, Samantha worried about David's reaction to her appearance in his office and wondered if she should have called first. But she hadn't wanted him to tell her not to come. When the elevator door dinged open, she walked toward his suite. Taking a deep breath, she rang the buzzer, alerting the receptionist to her arrival. The door buzzed as it unlocked, and she strode into the well-appointed lobby with overstuffed couches and dark cherry furniture intended to suggest prestige and power. Only the painting above the reception desk, one of David's own, offered any hint of softness to the decor.

"May I help you?" A blonde woman in a gray pencil skirt and ivory silk blouse looked up from her desk and studied Samantha.

"Oh, I was wondering if David is in? I don't have an appointment. I just wanted to give him something." Samantha held out the bundle in her hand.

The woman stood up and reached for the bundle. "I'm happy to deliver it for you."

Samantha took a step backward. "That's okay. I was hoping to do it myself. I just wanted a quick word with him."

The woman frowned. "I'll call and ask if he'll see you."

Samantha gave the woman her name and sat in one of the big leather chairs, thinking about the first time she'd come to this office, accused of a crime she hadn't committed and hoping that David could help her. Now, she found herself in the middle of another messy situation, but this time she wanted to keep David out of it.

Within moments, David walked out of his corner office and walked toward her, appearing confused. "Sam! What are you doing here?"

The receptionist seemed smug, offering Samantha a look that said she'd warned her that David was busy.

Samantha stood up. "I'm sorry to barge in, but I wanted to talk for a minute. Here's a peace offering." She held up the wrapped bundle and offered him a tentative smile.

He raised his eyebrows and waved at her to follow him. "Come back to my office. I've got a few minutes before my next appointment."

Samantha followed him and took a seat in yet another overstuffed leather armchair, still clutching the bundle to her chest.

"Is everything all right? I was worried last night after you left so quickly." David's expression conveyed warmth, but also concern.

Samantha's heart sank, realizing she had hurt him. She winced, handing him the bundle. "I'm fine—I just wanted to apologize for racing off last night. I'm really sorry I worried you."

David's green eyes radiated warmth with a tinge of hesitancy. "You've got a lot going on right now, but I wish you would share it with me. I want to help. So, you saw your . . . friend last night?"

Samantha hated the awkwardness. "Yes, my friend Martin. The one you met the other day? He found a few interesting details at the funeral. He thought it might be important to the case."

David raised an eyebrow. "And was it? Important?"

"It helped us narrow in on a couple of suspects. We need more information to pass on to Patty's lawyer." Samantha brushed lint off her pants as she stood up to leave. "I didn't come to take up more of your time with my speculation. I really wanted to apologize for leaving so abruptly yesterday."

David smiled. "It's fine. But before you leave, sit down for another minute."

Perplexed, Samantha took her seat again. "What?"

He riffled through a stack of papers on his desk, unearthing a yellow legal pad. "Now, please don't be mad. You sounded so upset about the money that I called that Adam Muller guy this morning and asked, as your lawyer, about the funds they owe your business."

Samantha's mouth flew open. "Why did you do that?"

David leaned back in his chair. "I wanted to scare him. You've been working so hard, and late payments can sink a business. I didn't want that to happen to you."

Samantha's smile slipped. "While your intentions were good, I wish you hadn't done that."

David's cheeks flushed. "I'm sorry. I was trying to help."

"But I'd been planning on talking to him myself, and now I'm not sure if I'll be able to." Samantha pinched the bridge of her nose, contemplating how to salvage the situation and still question Muller.

David, his face red, laid a hand on top of Samantha's. "I'm sorry. I didn't think about that. I should have listened to you rather than jumping in to solve your problem. But if it helps, he said you could stop by the lodge office today and pick up a new check. If you call him in advance, he said he'd meet you there. He had quite the story."

Intrigued, Samantha wanted to hear more. "What did he say? I'd love to hear his excuse."

"Muller said he has been working to straighten out the lodge's finances for several years now, but that the tennis club project has made the finances even messier. Though the accounting should be completely separate for the two entities, there has been some comingling of lodge and tennis club funds to pay for joint projects. Muller claimed that Ms. Clawson, the dead woman, had signatory powers for the lodge account so she could pay contractors as bills came due. She wasn't supposed to sign anything that hadn't been expressly approved by the board, but apparently, she had nearly drained the construction fund by paying for overages for various upgrades she'd been adding to the project."

Samantha tilted her head. "I don't understand. How does that relate to the festival money?"

"They deposited the festival funds into the lodge account so checks could be cut for the vendors. But with all the overages, money was paid out faster than it came in, and the festival money got caught up in the mess. The upshot is that Muller said they'll be able to cover the vendor payments out of an emergency fund and that you can pick yours up today."

The story made little sense to Samantha. She wanted answers from Muller but was eager to get paid.

She stood up to leave David's office. "Thanks, I guess."

David reached for her hand and squeezed gently. "I'm really sorry about calling Muller. It was out of bounds. Please believe I was only trying to make things easier for you."

She squeezed his hand back. "I know. I'll see you later, okay?"

Samantha left the office and rode the elevator down, more determined than ever to get answers from Muller. As she walked to her car, she replayed their conversation and kept coming back to the idea that Angela had been taking money from the lodge. Though still intrigued by Angela's sister, Mary, Samantha decided the missing lodge funds revelation could move Mr. Muller back to the top of the suspect list.

When she arrived at the kitchen incubator, Lillian and Beth were deep in the throes of cobbler making. Samantha laughed at the flour that coated her mother's shirt. "Mom, didn't you get enough baking last night?"

Lillian looked up in surprise. "Hi, honey. Beth is showing me her trick to getting the dough nice and fluffy. Cobbler is your dad's favorite. I want to learn her secret and make one for his birthday in a few weeks. Anyway, where have you been?"

Samantha plucked her apron off the hook near the door and tied it around her waist. "Just an errand." She sliced up peaches for the cocktail she had planned for tonight's dinner party. As she worked, her mind kept turning back again to what she'd learned from David, trying to decide how best to use it to get more information out of Muller when she went to confront him this afternoon. *He's wrong if he thinks I'm just going to waltz in there to accept payment, with no further complaint. But there's got to be a way for me to leverage that information into making him reveal more.*

The women worked together, preparing the vanilla ice cream and the cognac cream sauce. They prepped the carrots for roasting and marinated the tenderloin. Samantha squeezed the lemon juice, organized the other ingredients for the sidecars, and wrote out a recipe for the spicy bourbon peach cocktail for Beth to make with dessert.

Beth stacked the items in the refrigerator and freezer. "We've finished as much as possible for now. I'll finish the rest of the dinner at the couple's house. Thanks for the help this morning, Lillian."

Lillian smiled. "It was my pleasure. Samantha's dad is going to love that cobbler."

Samantha and Lillian waved to Beth and walked back out to Samantha's car, discussing lunch possibilities. Since they were already downtown, they opted for a local deli that had become a city institution. The low-slung brick building was dwarfed by the skyscrapers in the distance. On the front wall, near the door, a small green outline of Italy, with a red spur near the boot heel, served as a reminder of the owner's Texan and Italian roots. The line out the door was filled with a mix of office workers eager for a quick bite, and blue-collar workers, needing to refuel and enjoy some air-conditioning before heading back out into the blistering heat.

Samantha squinted, trying to read the chalkboard by the front counter. The deli served home-style Italian at its finest, and Samantha loved to check out the specials to get ideas for different recipes. She watched as customers carried away plates of steaming eggplant parmesan, and mounds of glistening meatballs swimming in a deep red sauce, accompanied by the requisite basket of buttery garlic bread. The delicious aroma made her stomach rumble.

"What's good here?" Lillian asked, glancing through the extensive menu.

"Everything." Samantha grinned. "But if you want something a little lighter, their turkey muffuletta is delicious."

Lillian followed her daughter's lead and ordered the oversized sandwiches stuffed with turkey, provolone, and the signature briny olive-vegetable spread.

After collecting their muffulettas, the two women chose a corner booth with the classic red-and-white-checked tablecloth and dug into their sandwiches.

"So, what was your errand this morning?" Lillian's voice was casual, but her eyes were penetrating. "I saw you wrap up one of my strudels. Who was the lucky recipient?"

Samantha nearly choked on a bite of sandwich. She swallowed some iced tea before answering. "I took it to David. I wanted to apologize to him for running out on him last night. He offered his compliments to the chef."

Lillian bit into her sandwich. "So, is it serious with him?"

Samantha chewed for a moment before answering. "I don't know. I really like him, but I'm not sure I'm ready to settle down with someone so quickly. I've never been one to play the field, so to speak, but I also don't want him to be the rebound guy."

"If you don't want to play the field, what's holding you back? From what you've said, he's a nice guy." Lillian gazed earnestly at her daughter.

"He is a nice guy. Such a nice guy. But what if I'm not ready, or it's the wrong time? Or what if he's more like Greg than I think?" Samantha grimaced just saying her ex-fiancée's name. He'd broken up with her about a month before their wedding, and then tried to insert himself back in her life during a particularly vulnerable period last month. Though Samantha wished him well in his new life as a high-powered attorney in New York City, she was thankful not to have him around any longer, making her second-guess herself.

"Like Greg? How?" Lillian seemed surprised.

Samantha relayed the story of David's call to Adam Muller. "It reminded me of Greg. He always tried to solve problems for me, as if I couldn't handle them on my own. I'm getting to a place where I can trust my own instincts again, and I don't want to go back."

"It sounds as though he was acting from a place of kindness. He wanted to help you out. But what matters is how you feel. My only advice is for you to make him understand that while you appreciate his advice, you want to handle things on your own." Lillian squeezed more lemon into her iced tea and stirred it, looking thoughtful.

The discussion reminded her of what David had learned from Adam about Angela's cleaning out the lodge's funds.

Lillian's eyes grew wide at Samantha's retelling. "Now, that is very interesting. I wonder if the rest of the board is aware of the missing money."

"I don't know, but I'm supposed to pick up my check from the lodge this afternoon. I want to see what Adam will say to me." Samantha finished her sandwich and drank the last of her iced tea.

"Is that wise? From what you said, Adam was pretty angry at Angela. Please just don't go confront him by yourself." Lillian pushed away the rest of her sandwich, apparently unable to continue eating.

"It shouldn't be dangerous. He knows that David is aware I am going over there. But to ease your mind, you can come with me." Samantha stood and, clutching her purse, signaled for her mom to follow her out the door.

* * *

Back at Samantha's apartment, the women strategized about the afternoon. Samantha called Adam Muller and arranged to pick up her new check at around two PM.

With an hour to spare, Samantha changed out of her cooking clothes and into a fresh pair of gray slacks and a teal blouse for her meeting with Muller. She wanted to project an air of professionalism. "Mom, you can come with me inside the building, but I'll meet with Muller alone."

Lillian agreed. "Alright, but I won't stray far. I want to be around in case anything happens."

At the lodge grounds, the women walked past construction crews, who had resumed working. Samantha gazed around, amazed at how quickly progress was being made, as crews cleared space for the new floodwater retention pond. "They're not wasting any time here, are they?"

The police tape near the site where Angela was found had been removed, and heavy machinery was clearing the dirt to build the championship court. Samantha paused to take in the scene, amazed at how quickly everyone had moved on since Angela's death.

The women walked toward the existing lodge building, which would soon be demolished to make way for the combination clubhouse and lodge space if the board approved the new plans, as expected tonight. Lillian opened the front door and held it open for her daughter before trailing her inside.

Samantha followed the corridor outside the lodge's meeting hall, around a corner, where she spotted the lodge office. She and Lillian headed in that direction to find Adam Muller, who was inside the office, sitting at a desk, his head bent over a laptop computer.

As she reached the door of the office, Samantha turned to her mother and spoke loudly to make sure Muller had heard her. "Mom, I'll be a few minutes. Just wait for me outside."

Muller looked up, and Samantha walked into the office, closing the door behind her. "Hello, Mr. Muller."

Adam Muller's face blanched as he stood up to face Samantha. "I want to apologize again. As I explained to Mr. Dwyer, we are working to rectify the situation for everyone as soon as possible. The board has approved emergency funds to cut new checks. Here's a cashier's check made out to you, so there should be no further problems."

Samantha reached for the check and inspected it. "I appreciate that, but I want to understand how this happened. As you've acknowledged, it is difficult to run a business when your clients don't pay their bills, and this situation put us into a bind. Mr. Dwyer said the money was mishandled? I think I'm owed an explanation."

Muller ran his hand through his hair and sighed. "As I told Mr. Dwyer, I discovered after the earlier checks had been distributed that someone had made unauthorized transfers of money from our account to pay for overages related to the tennis center construction."

Samantha found it interesting that Muller hadn't mentioned Clawson. She wanted to see how far she could press him to explain further. "I still don't understand. Are you saying someone stole the money? Are you pressing charges?"

Muller bent his chin low and massaged the back of his neck with his left hand. "It wasn't stolen, exactly. It was just an unauthorized transfer. And the person who did it is no longer with us."

Samantha studied Muller, trying to read his expression. "Mr. Dwyer said Ms. Clawson was responsible? But you didn't learn that until she had died? I heard you'd argued with her that evening."

Muller's eyes grew wide. "Our disagreement was about the failed inspection. I had no idea that she'd moved money from our general fund to the construction fund until a few days later, when the first of the vendor checks bounced. And now it's awkward because she's dead and we have this big scholarship about to be named after her."

Samantha raised her eyebrows. "Scholarship?"

Muller sighed. "Oh, haven't you heard the news? The tennis club ladies are organizing a scholarship fund in Angela's honor to help pay for additional at-risk youth to join the club. They've already started raising money, and it's pouring in. So, we don't want to sully her name now."

The story was getting even more interesting. A rich woman diverting lodge money for her own pet project under Muller's nose after he had vouched for her and encouraged his membership to go along with her tennis club plans. If he'd been angry enough, he might have killed Angela in a fit of rage. Samantha wanted to keep him talking.

Though the police had disregarded it, Samantha still wondered about the damage to Angela's car and why the camera in that parking lot had not been functioning. Adam was in the best position to explain what had happened.

"Oh, I had something else I wanted to ask you. One of my workers parked in the lot behind the construction site on Friday, and someone let the air out of her tires. We thought we saw cameras around the parking lot. Can you let us watch the footage? She thinks an ex-boyfriend did it, but we want proof."

Adam Muller stared at a point on the wall just behind Samantha's head. "Unfortunately, the cameras in that lot were not functioning on Friday. There was a problem with the system."

"What kind of problem?"

Adam coughed and his lips curled. "I forgot to turn it on that night. It fell through the cracks."

He stood up and walked to the door to open it. "I apologize for the delayed payment, Ms. Warren. Now, I must say goodbye. I have a few issues I must attend to." Though his words were polite, his tone was frigid enough to chill warm bourbon.

Chapter Nineteen

Samantha stepped back into the corridor, and Muller let his office door shut with a bang.

After rounding the corner, Samantha searched for her mother. A quick glance at her phone told her twenty minutes had passed, leading her to wonder how far her mother had gotten during such a short period of time.

A sound coming from the large meeting hall caught her attention, and she opened the wide double doors. Two women huddled together at a table on stage. One gazed up at Samantha. "Excuse me. We're about to start a closed session of the board. I'm afraid you'll need to leave."

Samantha bowed her head and backed out of the room. "I'm sorry—I'm trying to find someone."

As she turned back toward the hallway, she noticed the curtains rustle near the back of the room. A brief glimpse at the floor revealed her mother's blue flats, which almost blended in with the blue velvet curtains lining the back wall.

Mom will never escape without being noticed. Samantha pretended to trip on a chair and tumbled to the floor, crying out.

"Oh, dear, are you all right?" One woman raced down the aisle to help Samantha to her feet.

"I'm so sorry. I must have tripped, and I'm afraid I can't get up. Can you two help me to my car?"

The women hoisted her to her feet, and Samantha leaned into the larger of the two women and limped gingerly out the double doors and into the corridor.

"Are you sure you'll be all right, dear?" The smaller woman held the door to the outside open as the larger woman continued to support Samantha as she hobbled to her car.

"I'll be fine now. Thank you so much for your help. I'll get home and put ice on it." Samantha fumbled to get the car open and sank into the driver's seat, waving the two women off. She watched the ladies disappear into the lodge building, and breathed a sigh of relief as she saw her mother slip out the front door and walk toward the car.

"Thank goodness, Mom. I didn't think you could get out of there unnoticed. What was your plan if I hadn't come in?" Samantha pulled out of the lodge parking lot, wanting to put distance between herself and the two board members in case they became suspicious.

"I planned to sneak out when the room filled up. I wish you'd given me more time in there. It was just getting interesting." Lillian smoothed her hair, which had become mussed in her hurry to leave the building.

"What did you hear?" Samantha tried to keep the impatience out of her voice, knowing her mother did not like to be rushed in her storytelling.

"Those women were complaining about Angela's spending. They said her death was the only thing that saved the lodge from going bankrupt." Lillian's expression seemed to dare her daughter to top that revelation.

"I know, Mom. Muller admitted the same to me. She'd been moving money from the general fund to pay for overages in the construction account." Samantha rubbed the back of her neck, wishing her mother had found out something new.

"It wasn't only the construction overruns. Apparently, she kept increasing the operating budget as well. Her last expenditure was to hire a costly tennis pro from California over the local guy she'd agreed to hire. Anyway, the skinny woman said Adam Muller threw a beer stein against a wall and broke it when he discovered the overruns. That sounds like the kind of passion it takes to kill someone with a shovel." Lillian arched her eyebrows as if challenging Samantha to minimize her story.

"He claimed that he wasn't aware of the missing funds until after Angela's death, when the first of the vendor checks bounced. But even if that were true, several people witnessed him arguing with Angela before her death. He certainly wasn't happy with my questions." Samantha rubbed her chin as she tried to reason how the tidbits they'd learned fit into the broader puzzle.

Lillian leaned back in her seat. "I was so excited about that Mary Hawkins news this morning, but now I'm moving Adam Muller to the top of our suspect list."

* * *

After depositing the check at the bank, Samantha and her mother drove back to Samantha's apartment to plot out their next move. Sitting on the couch, Samantha relayed the rest of what she had learned from Adam, including the news about the scholarship to be named for Angela Clawson.

"I can't believe they want to honor her after her deception!" Lillian sounded scandalized.

"Well, she raised most of the money for the tennis club. And she died rather unfortunately. I can hardly blame them for wanting to capitalize on her name and her reputation one more time after what she pulled."

Samantha's phone vibrated, and she noticed she'd missed a text message from Marisa, who'd asked her to call her.

Marisa answered on the second ring. "Hey, Sam. Perfect timing. I just finished up class and was walking to my car. I've got some big news."

Samantha felt her pulse race, hoping Marisa's news would help to fill in some of the missing puzzle pieces. "Great. Did you learn anything good?"

"I found her, Sam. I called around to a bunch of the hospitals. Mary is at the Cancer Center. I'm free now—want to go to the medical center and see if we can talk to her?"

The news hit Samantha by surprise. "The Cancer Center? But how can we see her?"

"We'll think of something. Maybe we say we're reporters and want to talk to her about her sister." Marisa's voice betrayed her excitement. "Visiting hours are from three to six, so we can make it in time."

Deciding to go before she could convince herself of the hundred reasons why it was a bad idea, Samantha agreed. "Let's do it."

"Great. I'll pick you up in fifteen minutes." Marisa ended the call.

Lillian's eyes widened as Samantha lowered the phone from her ear. "What is it? What's going on?"

"Marisa found Mary. We're going to go see if we can talk to her." Samantha moved to her desk, where she searched for a fresh notebook.

"I'm coming with you." Lillian picked up her purse.

"No, Mom. It's not a good idea. We need to handle this carefully. The woman is staying at the hospital for cancer treatment. I don't want to gang up on her."

Lillian huffed. "I'm coming to the hospital. I don't have to go in the room with you. But I want to be there. I'll go crazy sitting here."

Samantha sighed. "Fine. But you're waiting in the lobby." She hoisted her purse onto her shoulder and held the door open for her mother to follow her down the stairs to meet Marisa.

* * *

A half hour later, the three women parked in one of the labyrinth garages at the medical center and followed the signs to the entrance of the Cancer Center. The antiseptic cheerfulness of the waiting room, with its muted pastels and abstract geometric patterns, depressed Samantha. She knew the decor was supposed to have a calming influence, but she'd visited enough waiting rooms as a reporter to know that no amount of artfully arranged flowers would be enough to soothe the minds of visitors anxious about their loved ones.

Lillian, gazing around the room, appeared to feel the same way. "You should pick up some flowers in the gift shop. Maybe brighten the woman's room up a little bit."

It wasn't a bad idea. Samantha and Marisa left Lillian in the waiting room and bought a small bouquet before asking for Mary Hawkins's room.

On the way up the elevator, Samantha pondered what to say to her, but any thoughts were swept away when she walked into the room and spotted Mary, sitting up in the bed. The woman was painfully thin, almost gaunt. Samantha's eyes focused fleetingly on the bright floral scarf wrapped around the woman's head before she lowered her gaze to Mary's face. "Mrs. Hawkins?"

Mary nodded, signaling with her head that Samantha should place the flowers on the bedside table. "Who are you?" Her voice was raspy and soft.

Marisa began to speak, but Samantha put her hand on her arm to stop her. The thought of lying to this woman felt wrong. "Hi, I'm Samantha, and this is my friend, Marisa. Do you mind if we sit down and talk to you for a minute?"

"Are you church people? Could you hand me that cup of water?"

Marisa got the water and offered it to the woman, who took a long swig.

"No, it's nothing like that. We're here about your sister, Angela. I wanted to ask you some questions." Samantha took a seat in the chair by the bedside and motioned for Marisa to take the seat opposite her.

The water had lubricated the woman's voice, so it came out slightly stronger. "My sister? She's dead."

"We know. We're friends with the woman accused of killing her—but she didn't do it." Samantha rushed through the sentence, wanting to make Patty's innocence known.

Mary laughed, setting off a coughing fit. She sipped water again. "Well, if you've come to accuse me, you're barking up the wrong tree."

"No, of course not. But I did have some questions about her son. I understand his company recently paid a significant quantity of money for a drilling lease on your property." Samantha paused, noting the confusion in the woman's eyes.

"Her son? What are you talking about? I haven't talked to that woman or her family in thirty years." Mary's eyes displayed surprise.

To Samantha, the surprise appeared genuine. "His company, R&C Group, a few months ago, paid you close to a hundred thousand dollars for the rights to drill on your land. It was strange because, according to a friend of mine who is familiar with the area, your part of the county has been drilled out for years."

Mary kept quiet while she considered. "Mama and Daddy never let anyone drill on our land during the last oil boom. They didn't want the hassle or the disruption to the ranch. I had some folks drill some test wells years ago, and they came up with nothing, but I've heard they've got new ways to find the oil now, and I thought there might be some chance the earlier guys missed something."

Samantha and Marisa exchanged a look. "Who approached you this time?"

"Just some woman. Came out with a business suit, looking very official. Said she was with R&C and wanted to offer me one hundred thousand dollars to lease my land and mineral rights to drill for oil or natural gas. Said if they found anything, there'd be more money." Mary rubbed her hands. "I should have known. When that offer came through, it was like manna from heaven. I'd just learned my cancer had spread, and the medical bills were already piling up. I was accepted into this clinical trial, but I wasn't sure how I was going to pay to come here for the treatment. We were afraid we were going to lose our land."

Mary massaged her hand and fell silent again, considering. "But I don't understand . . . why would he? Angela hates me. We haven't spoken for years."

Marisa spoke softly. "Why hadn't you been in contact with your sister? What caused the rift in the first place? I've got a sister too, and she drives me crazy, but I can't imagine not talking to her for thirty years."

"We were stubborn old cusses. I guess, now that she's dead, I should regret it, but I don't have a lot of time for regrets." Mary grimaced at the IV tube connected to her bruised arm. "We never really got along, but we tolerated each other when we were kids. In high school, we let a man come between us. Jack was my boyfriend first, and she stole him from me."

Marisa's eyes widened. "That must have been awful. You must have loved him a lot."

Mary waved her hand as if swatting a fly. "Oh, not really. We had some fun, but he and I were never well suited. But he was the golden ticket out of town and onto bigger and better things, and she took it, leaving me behind to take care of Mama and the ranch."

Samantha was still confused. "But you married later, and had a child, right? Why did the feud last so long?"

Mary sighed. "Yes, I met my Frank and we had our Kate. I would have let bygones be bygones for the sake of the family. But then there was the matter of the will."

Samantha's ears perked up. "Will? What will?"

Mary grimaced, repositioning herself in her bed. "Our mother's will. While Angela was busy playing society wife in Houston, I was the one nursing Mama, following a series of strokes. Mama left me the house and land because it was my home, and she knew that Angela was already set for life with

Jack. Angela believed I convinced Mama to cut her out of the will, but it wasn't my decision."

Marisa stared at Samantha and raised her eyebrows before turning back to Mary. "It's such a shame when money comes between family like that."

Mary inspected her cuticles. "Maybe it wasn't totally fair, but Mama didn't believe fair was necessarily even steven. She always said fair was making sure that both of her girls had a way to take care of themselves." Mary took another drink of water from her cup. "Angela never got past it. I sent her Mama's jewelry and some other mementos. It's not like she got nothing. But she hasn't spoken with me since then, which is why I don't understand why her son's company would have paid us that money."

Mary appeared genuinely perplexed. Samantha wasn't sure it would be worthwhile to prod the woman any more on the topic of the oil leases. But she did have other questions, so she changed the subject. "Kate's your daughter? Did she come to Houston with you?"

Mary's eyes lit up. "Yes. I don't know what I would have done without her. She drove me up to Houston on Sunday. She's staying in town with me until this Sunday, when she has to get back to Kermit."

"So you didn't leave West Texas until Sunday? When did you find out about your sister? That must have come as a big shock." Marisa offered a consoling smile.

"We found out on Saturday when it made the paper. We had a little Fourth of July get-together at the ranch on Saturday—sort of my last hurrah before my treatment—and one of my cousins brought me a copy of the afternoon paper. The local rag ran the story out of Houston, I guess because Angela was a Winkler County girl."

Mary paused for a long moment. "It was a shock, and I did feel sad." She looked back and forth between Marisa and Samantha. "I'm not a monster. But after so many years of not speaking, it's hard to feel more."

"That's understandable." Samantha offered a half smile. "You have more than enough to worry about on your own right now. I'm sorry to have bothered you."

Mary coughed and swallowed some more water. "It's no bother. It's nice to have visitors who aren't asking me how I feel all the time. I'd rather talk about my sister than go over my laundry list of ailments again. But now it's your turn. Tell me about this lady who's accused of killing my sister."

Samantha told her about Patty and offered a brief rundown of the conflict between Angela and the other lodge members.

"That sounds like Angela, all right. Don't get in her way, or she'll mow you down. But I guess somebody got fed up with her. So, if it wasn't your friend, who's your best suspect?" Mary coughed again before settling back against the pillows.

Samantha didn't want to give too much away, but she felt she owed something to the woman. "To be honest, I don't know. Maybe the lodge president, maybe some other angry lodge member?" She didn't want to get into Christina's suspicions about Matt.

The woman appeared slightly disappointed, as if she'd hoped for more of a story. "Well, I hope you'll be able to figure it all out. And now, I'm sorry, but I'm getting a little tired."

Samantha stood up. "Of course. I'm sorry to have taken up so much of your time. Thank you for talking to us, and best of luck with . . . everything." She reached out and squeezed the woman's hand before walking out the door.

In the elevator, on the way back to the lobby, Marisa gazed up at Samantha. "So, what did you make of all that? Do you believe she didn't know anything about Matt Clawson giving her that money?"

Samantha nodded. "I do. She seemed sincere . . . and sort of like she's past the point of lying."

Marisa sighed. "That was my impression as well. I'm not sure how much any of that helped you. If she was telling the truth about her family get-together on Saturday, that seems to eliminate her and her daughter from the suspect list."

When they reached the lobby, they found Lillian waiting in a chair by the elevator, looking very much like the cat that ate the canary.

Chapter Twenty

"I talked to the daughter, Kate." Lillian's words rushed out as Samantha stepped out of the elevator.

"Back up—you talked to the daughter? When? How?" Samantha signaled that they should start heading toward the garage.

"I ran into her in the cafeteria. She was having a cup of coffee and looked like she could use some company, so I joined her." Lillian smiled.

"And she started spilling her secrets to you?" Marisa stared incredulously at Lillian,

"Everyone trusts a librarian!" Lillian grinned. "But really, she needed someone to talk to, and I was in the right place at the right time."

They reached Marisa's car and climbed inside. Lillian continued her story. "I asked her if she was visiting a loved one, and everything just tumbled out. Her mom has liver cancer, and it has spread to her bones. They came in town on Sunday to check her in for a clinical trial. She's worried that her mother isn't responding to treatment. Poor girl was a wreck."

If nothing else, Lillian's talk with Kate provided some confirmation that she and her mother were not in town the night of the murder. "Did you learn anything else?"

"Well, I wasn't sure if I should mention it, because I didn't know how she would react, but I told her she looked familiar and asked if she had gone to a funeral on Thursday. She seemed to be a little shocked and asked how I knew her Aunt Angela. I told her I didn't, but that my daughter had done some work for her and asked me to go along so she didn't feel awkward attending alone. She seemed to accept that and unloaded about Angela as well."

Marisa turned back to Lillian, clearly impressed. "Don't sleep on the librarian! What did she say?"

"She said she'd never met Angela, but she felt terrible for her cousin, Matt, particularly after he had done so much to help her own mother!" Lillian paused.

"Go on—how did Matt help her mother?" Samantha once again found herself trying to rush her mother through her story. It was probably the librarian in her mom, used to pausing for dramatic effect during story time with kids.

"She said her family was afraid they were going to lose the ranch because of all of the medical bills, and they had no more money to pay to send Mary to Houston for the cancer trial. She had corresponded a few times with Matt over Facebook, and knew his family was well-off, so she asked him for help, and he agreed." Lillian paused again.

"Here's the kicker—he told her he was coming into some money soon, so he was happy to help. What do you think about that? What kind of money? And from where?" Lillian glanced back and forth between Samantha and Marisa.

Samantha raised her eyebrows. "Interesting. But why go through the ruse of buying worthless mineral rights? Why not pay the money outright?"

Lillian's voice registered her excitement. "Well, she said in order to borrow the money, he needed to create a business purpose for it, and since buying mineral rights is what he does, they decided to go with that. Kate also said that her mother would never have accepted the money if she thought it had come from her sister or her sister's family."

Samantha didn't know what to make of the story. "Matt sounds pretty generous in that telling. Could he have had some other motivation? And what could he have meant by 'coming into money soon'?"

Marisa chimed in. "Well, we know how he's coming into money now . . . his mother is dead and he's inheriting the house! I think you've got some good evidence to get the police involved here."

Lillian nodded, echoing Marisa. "I agree. It's very suspicious. The police should check it out."

Samantha wasn't so sure they should run straight to the police. "But what if it turns out to be another false lead? Then we run the risk of making things worse for Patty. I think we need to find out more. At a minimum, I want to talk to Matt's sister, Christina, and see what she thinks of all of this."

Marisa pulled into Samantha's driveway. "I guess it doesn't hurt to dig a little further, but promise you won't do anything dangerous." She gave Samantha a look that said she hadn't forgotten her last brush with danger. "I need to get back to campus to study, but let me know what you learn."

As Lillian and Samantha climbed the steps to Samantha's apartment, Lillian appeared to warm to the idea of a chat with Christina. "Reach out to her and see what she has to say about everything. I'm curious if this will cement her suspicions."

Back in the apartment, Lillian rummaged through her purse for her phone, then excused herself to call Patty. "I want to fill her in on what we've learned today."

As Lillian talked to Patty, Samantha pondered how best to approach Christina. The last time Samantha had seen her, the woman had been propped up in bed with a sore knee. She'd been fairly friendly, if a bit drunk at the time. Samantha had already been to her place. *Maybe it wouldn't be too weird if I pop by her house with a "hope you're feeling better" strudel.*

When her mom got off the phone, Samantha ran the idea by her. Lillian agreed to give away the remaining apple strudel from last night's baking session for the cause. "But I'm going with you." Lillian wrapped the pastry into an extra layer of cling wrap.

"No, Mom. She just lost her mother. I should go by myself." Samantha glanced at her phone and noted it was after four thirty. She could make it to Christina's condo before rush hour. "I'll head over there and meet you here later. I shouldn't be gone too long."

On the way to Christina's condo, Samantha practiced what to say to avoid sounding too nosy. But during the ten-minute drive, her mind drew a blank.

I'll have to wing it. She climbed the steps to the front door of Christina's condo.

After pressing the buzzer a few times with no response, Samantha peered through the side window to note any movement inside the condo. *Darn, I hadn't really considered what I'd do if she wasn't home.*

Samantha fumbled through her purse for the notepad and pen she always kept on hand and wrote a note.

Hi Christina. It's Samantha from the catering company. I just wanted to check in on you after your fall yesterday, and bring you a homemade apple strudel. I hope you're feeling okay. If you want to talk, call me.

Samantha wrote down her phone number and tucked the sheet of paper underneath the nicely wrapped strudel, hoping her note wouldn't blow away, before walking back down the stairs to her car.

Just as Samantha climbed into the driver's seat, the condo door opened, and Christina called out. "Hello? Did you leave this for me?"

Samantha turned around and looked up. "Oh, hi, Christina. I didn't think you were home." She walked back up the stairs to the condo. "It's Samantha, from the catering company."

Christina glanced from Samantha to the strudel. "Of course, but what are you doing here? Why did you bring me this?" She picked up the wrapped pastry, staring at it as if it were a moon rock.

"It's homemade apple strudel. I know yesterday was rough, and I wanted to check on you after your fall."

Christina grimaced before opening her door wider. "I'm so embarrassed about yesterday, but this was nice of you. Do you want to come in?"

Samantha wanted nothing more, but she didn't want to seem too eager. "Sure, I've got a few minutes. How's your knee?"

Christina still had a slight limp as she led the way into her living room, leaving the strudel on the coffee table and falling backward onto the couch. "Still feels pretty bad. I was napping when you knocked, and it took me a while to get downstairs."

She threw one of the couch cushions onto the coffee table and elevated her leg on top. "So, strudel? I thought you were the cocktail maker."

Samantha smiled. "My mom made this. She and her friend get into these baking jags, and we end up with more than we can eat. Like I said, I wanted to check on you and thought you might enjoy a treat."

The woman looked like she was ready to cry, and then she did, wet tears glistening on her long lashes. "I'm sorry. I'm not sure why I'm being so emotional. It's been a long few days." Christina brushed a few tears from her cheek.

Samantha scooted closer to her on the couch and patted her back, as if she were soothing a toddler. "You miss your mom. Of course you're emotional. And then, the stuff with your family . . ."

Christina's breath hitched as she tried to control her breathing. "Yes. My wonderful family." Her emphasis on the word *wonderful* made it clear she believed they were anything but wonderful.

Samantha considered how to proceed. She wanted to ask Christina about Matt and his business dealings with Angela, but she wasn't sure how to broach it. She made a calculated decision and went for it. "Christina, I have some questions about your mother's death."

Christina pulled back from Samantha, registering alarm. "What do you mean?"

Worried by the woman's reaction, Samantha rushed to explain. "The woman who is accused of the murder is my mom's best friend. She says she didn't kill your mother, and I believe her. I'm not saying Olivia or Matt did it either, but somebody did, and I'm trying to figure it out."

Christina's face blanched. "So what? You catered my mother's funeral so you could snoop on all of us?"

Samantha hastened to reassure Christina. "No, of course not. I catered the funeral because I just started a new business and can't afford to turn down any job. I'd worked with your mother, and I wanted to honor her memory with my cocktails."

Christina eyed her warily but made no move to throw her out. Samantha plowed ahead before Christina changed her mind. "I wanted to ask you a few questions after doing a little research myself.

"Are you some sort of detective or something?" Christina shifted in her seat on the couch.

"No. But I used to be a reporter, and I know how to do research and investigate things, so I've been trying to help my mom's friend out." Samantha hoped she appeared nonthreatening.

Christina seemed appeased for the time being. "Okay, so what do you want to know?"

Samantha mentioned Mary Hawkins. "You told me she wasn't in touch with your family any longer. What can you tell me about her?"

Christina seemed confused by the question but answered anyway. "Mama had basically written Aunt Mary out of her life when I was a girl. I never even met her that I remember. They had a big fight after my grandmother died. Mama said Aunt Mary convinced grandma to write Mama out of the will."

So far, the stories about the will matched, but Samantha was curious what explanation Christina had been given to explain the rift. "Why?"

"Mary had nursed my grandmother for several years, and I guess she decided Grandma owed her more than my mama. But the ranch was more valuable than the trinkets my mother received. Anyway, I doubt she could be involved. It's a pretty gigantic leap to imagine she plotted from West Texas to kill my mama at a festival." Christina wrinkled her nose, dismissing the idea.

Samantha dropped the bombshell about Matt's company purchasing mineral rights from Mary, curious how Christina would react. "At least one member of your family was in contact with her. Your brother recently paid her nearly one hundred thousand dollars for the mineral rights on her ranch land." Samantha pulled up the spreadsheet she'd received from her reporter friend in her email and showed it to Christina. "It's probably the money Matt borrowed from your mother."

The color drained from Christina's face. "Why would he do that? If Mama found out, she would have been furious! One time, I remember he suggested she make up with her sister before it was too late, and Mama said she would see Mary in hell before she spoke with her again."

"Yikes!" Samantha had witnessed plenty of family drama in her day, but Angela and Mary's relationship sounded toxic.

She decided it was time to tell Christina about her aunt in the hospital, curious about her take on the story from Kate about Matt's generosity. "Christina, I met your aunt today. She's at the cancer ward in the medical center, undergoing a clinical trial for liver cancer that has metastasized to her bones."

Christina's jaw dropped open. "You met her? She's here?"

Samantha filled Christina in on her visit with Mary and about what Kate had told Lillian.

"I don't know how to make sense of any of this. Matt didn't have that kind of money to throw away. And if Mama knew what he was doing with it, she would have blown up . . ."

Christina's eyes grew wide. "What if that's why she was so mad the night she died? Maybe that's why she told him she was writing him out of the will."

Samantha watched Christina as she wrung her hands in her lap. She looked like a caged tiger, ready to unleash her energy, but because of the sore knee, she was unable to move.

Samantha hesitated to relay the last piece of information because the atmosphere was already charged, but she needed to see Christina's reaction. "There's one other thing: Kate told my mother that Matt agreed to help because he was going to 'come into some money soon.' Do you have any idea what that might mean?"

Christina covered her mouth with her palm. "They did it. They really did it. I can't believe it. There's no other explanation." She dropped her leg from the coffee table and stood up, before wincing in pain. She fell back on the couch again.

"We can't know for sure." Samantha wanted to be certain that Christina was thinking rationally. "Maybe he had some other investment he was expecting to come through in a big way. He had dozens of oil leases—maybe they found oil on one of those properties."

Christina grimaced as she rubbed her knee. "Then why would he borrow so much from Mama? No, I don't see any other explanation. Either he did it himself, or Olivia did it for him. Don't forget what I overheard Olivia tell Matt about everything being okay after next Friday. That's when we're discussing the will with Mom's lawyer."

The whole situation seemed off to Samantha, and though they had no proof of any wrongdoing, it was definitely suspicious. "You mentioned that Angela had a fight with Olivia the night she died. Do you know what happened?"

Christina nodded. "They were fighting about where Mama thought they should send Charles, their oldest boy to school. Olivia told Mama that she was done with her meddling. And let me tell you, Mama was pissed. She took it out on me, yelling at me about my outfit." Christina crossed her arms, as if trying to ward off the memory.

"Thinking back on it, do you really believe Olivia or Matt could have killed your mother?" Samantha was tired of the beating around the bush. She wanted a straight, gut reaction.

"I don't want to believe it, but I'm really starting to think it's possible." Christina tilted her head, seeming like she was trying to remember. "Matt was with my nephews, playing carnival games, when Mama died. I suppose he could have snuck away at some point and killed her, but my money is on Olivia. She straight up disappeared on Friday night. She was supposed to have been watching the pie contest, but she wasn't there. After her fight with Mama, nobody saw her again until we finally reached her about half an hour after Mama was found."

The reference to the pie contest reminded Samantha of how close it was to the scene of the murder. "You were at the pie contest the whole time? Did you see anything unusual? If Olivia was the murderer, you or someone else might have seen her head toward the construction site. It was very close to you."

Christina appeared to think for a few seconds before shaking her head. "I'm sorry, I don't remember anything unusual. It got a little hectic with the contest, and then Mama's friend Calista somehow knocked over a pie display, which took a few minutes to clean up. But I definitely didn't see Olivia anywhere nearby."

Christina picked up a glass of water on the table and took a long drink, peering over the rim at Samantha and waiting for a reaction. Samantha considered Christina's theories. They were conceivable, but there was no smoking gun—or shovel, so to speak.

Chapter Twenty-One

Samantha weighed her thoughts before responding. "If you think Olivia is guilty, do you have any idea how to prove it?"

Christina's face crumpled. "No."

"We need some evidence to take to the police to get them interested." Samantha offered a questioning look to Christina. "Would you feel comfortable confronting Olivia?"

Christina's face went pale. "By myself? If she's a murderer, no way. She'd come after me!"

"What if I came with you? I could hide nearby while you confront her. I know the detective who initially responded to the case. If we brought him proof, he'd listen to us." Samantha watched as Christina drank the rest of her water.

Christina sat in silence as she contemplated the suggestion. After several minutes, her face hardened, appearing more resolute. "It's risky, but it would be worth it to keep Olivia from benefitting from my mother's death. What's your plan?"

An idea came to Samantha. "Ask her to meet you at your mom's house tomorrow morning. Make her assume you know more than you do. Say you were going through your mother's papers and had questions about Angela's latest loan to Matt. I'll hide in the next room, with a tape recorder."

Christina seemed frightened. "But what if she attacks me?"

"We'll have the police on speed dial. If she pulls something, I'll have the element of surprise." Samantha needed Christina to be confident in the plan, or they wouldn't be able to pull it off.

Christina paused momentarily before nodding her head. "I think we can make it work. I'll call Olivia and see if I can arrange things. I'll text you tonight when I hear from her."

The women exchanged phone numbers, and Samantha bid Christina a good evening.

* * *

As she walked to her car, Samantha glanced at her phone and saw it was after five forty-five PM. Traffic was still a little heavy on the way home, but she made it back just after six PM.

Lillian sat on the couch in Samantha's living room, working a crossword puzzle, when Samantha walked in the door. "How'd it go? Did you learn anything new?"

Samantha threw her purse down and nodded. "Nothing new, really, but after everything we heard from Kate and Mary, Christina is now convinced that Olivia killed her mother."

Lillian frowned. "While you were gone, I was thinking about it some more. I know that comment about Matt coming into money sounded awfully suspicious, but I still think Muller is the likeliest culprit."

Samantha threw up her hands. "I'm not sure what to think. We have to narrow the list. Christina and I are working on a plan to confront Olivia tomorrow morning."

Lillian jumped up. "Oh, Samantha, you can't do that. If she's guilty, that's too dangerous. We need to call the police."

Samantha shook her head. "Christina's talked to the police. They haven't been interested so far. We've got a plan to make it safe."

"Well, I'm coming with you. No ifs, ands, or buts." Lillian's face grew serious.

"I'll consider it. We haven't nailed anything down yet. Christina's supposed to text me later today to confirm." Samantha stooped to pick up Ruby, who was weaving around her legs.

Lillian sighed and changed the subject. "Meanwhile, do you mind going to Patty's for dinner? I talked with her, and she's pretty depressed. She needs company."

"Sure. We can buy a couple of pizzas." Sam sat down with her computer, pulled up the website for her favorite pizza place, and made an online order for a sausage and red pepper pizza and a supreme pizza, both of which would be ready in half an hour.

While she was online, she logged into the catering business emails. She and Beth tried to check the email account at least once a day. They received most of their business from phone calls, but occasionally, potential clients submitted queries by email. After deleting the obvious spam, Samantha noticed an email from someone whose address was myob488@gmail.com. Curious, she clicked it open.

Stop your so-called "investigation," before you or someone you love gets hurt.

Samantha's eyes opened wide in surprise. The email was clearly from a fake account, so Samantha saw no point in responding or trying to identify the author. But it made her curious. *Who knows about my "so-called investigation"?*

Samantha summoned her mom, who was in the bedroom, changing to go to Patty's house.

When Lillian read the email, the blood drained from her face. "This changes things. We need to call the police now, Samantha. Someone is threatening you."

"There's nothing the police can do, other than tell me to stop investigating."

Lillian bit her lower lip. "We can't ignore it. Whoever sent this might be the killer."

Samantha shivered, recalling her recent run-in with a different killer in her own home. She'd promised herself she wouldn't put herself in danger again, but it seemed that now trouble was lurking nearby. "If it is the killer, we've got them worried. It must mean we are close to figuring something out. But what?"

Her mother frowned. "I don't know, but I don't like it. We should get in touch with the police." She reached for her phone, but Samantha pushed her hand down.

"Mom, don't. At best, they'd ignore us. At worst, involving the police could cause more trouble for Patty. They might think we are trying to muddy the waters again, after Karl's fiasco." Samantha bit her lip. "We'll just have to be extra vigilant."

Lillian looked unconvinced, but Samantha put on her bravest face. She closed her laptop, hoping to put the unsettling thoughts behind her for now. "It's time to pick up the pizzas."

* * *

A half an hour later, sitting around the kitchen table in Patty's house, Samantha and Lillian filled Patty and Martin in on the latest updates.

"Samantha, you have to take that threat seriously." Patty took tiny bites of her pizza, appearing too nervous to eat much.

"I am taking it seriously, but there's nothing for me to do about it, other than watch my back." Samantha regretted sharing the threatening email with her mother. Lillian and Patty were reacting exactly as Samantha had guessed. She snuck a peek at Martin, curious about his reaction.

He caught her gaze, his expression serious. "I agree with Mom. You need to be extra careful, because you're on someone's radar now. It's not safe for you and Christina to confront her sister-in-law alone. That's why I'm coming with you."

Samantha's eyes widened in surprise. "You're coming with me? No way. Christina is already freaked out enough."

"I'll stay hidden on the property and keep my eyes and ears open. Leave a door unlocked for me. At the first hint of trouble, I'll come running into the house." Martin held Samantha's gaze for an instant, before Patty spoke, interrupting their connection.

"I don't like it. We should inform the police and let the chips fall where they may. I don't want anyone putting themselves in danger on my account."

Samantha switched gears. "What about Adam, Patty? Did you ask your lodge friends whether they saw him on Friday during the time the murder was committed?"

Patty took another mouse-sized nibble from the pizza. "I talked to three friends who were on the festival committee with Adam, and none of them recall seeing him between seven thirty and eight PM. One of them says she was looking for him because she had just gotten wind of the detention pond rumors, but she never found him."

Lillian chimed in. "I still think he's our best suspect, especially after those ladies described him throwing a beer stein against the wall. It sounds as though he had a very violent reaction to the news."

Samantha finished chewing a bite of pizza as she considered her mother's words. "I agree he's hiding something, given how cagey he was with his responses. But we're never going to get anywhere if we don't start narrowing down our suspects. One way is to verify their alibis. Christina and I are going to try that with Olivia."

Patty drank from a glass of water and gazed in the distance. "Are you sure that's a good idea? I don't want to drag any of you further into danger."

Samantha's phone buzzed. With the others focused on their pizza, she tried to glance surreptitiously at the screen. There was a text message from Christina: *Come to Mama's place around 8 A.M. Olivia is coming by at 9 to talk, after dropping her son off at a friend's house.*

Samantha's pulse quickened. Shoving the phone back into her pocket, she stood up and collected her plate and utensils to take them to the sink, hoping to respond to Christina without the others noticing. *Great news. I'll see you then.* She didn't want to hear any more wavering from Patty or her mother, and she really didn't want Martin showing up tomorrow.

As she pressed "Send," Martin walked into the kitchen. "Who are you texting?"

Though they'd been working together on the investigation, Samantha didn't think Christina would appreciate Martin tagging along tomorrow. She said the first thing she thought of. "Oh, just David. I'm supposed to meet up with him later for drinks."

The minute she said it, she decided it was a good idea. She wanted to make up for abandoning David at the restaurant, and a cocktail sounded nice. She noticed Martin's downcast expression and pitied him. Before she could reconsider, she invited him to join her. "Want to come with us?"

Martin's face instantly brightened. "I'd love to. I've been away from the city for so long, I have no idea what's cool anymore."

Samantha squirmed, realizing she'd just offered an invitation to a nonexistent event. She needed to message David and ask him if he'd be willing to go out with her and Martin.

"Why don't you go make our excuses to our mothers while I finalize details with David?" Samantha turned away and stepped into the hallway to make her phone call.

David picked up after the first ring. "Sam. Hey. How are you?"

"Hi, David. Are you free for drinks tonight?" Samantha glanced behind her to make sure nobody had overheard. She saw Martin talking to their mothers in the dining room.

"I just finished up a deposition half an hour ago, and I was going to get some dinner. Can we pick a place with drinks and food? Do you want me to pick you up?"

Samantha paused, worried about how he would take the news of the third wheel joining them. "There's one catch. Martin is still in town, and he hasn't seen much nightlife since he's been here. Do you mind if he joins us? We've already eaten dinner, but we can have a drink while you eat."

David paused before answering. "That's not exactly what I had in mind, but sure. I guess we can meet somewhere. How about the Fig and Fern in half an hour?"

The restaurant/bar was a good choice. On the first floor, a small café served pub-style food. The second floor was more of a lounge, with classic cocktails and occasional jazz acts.

"Perfect, David. I'll see you there."

She ended the call and walked back through the kitchen to the dining room, where her mother and Patty were still chatting. "Where are you guys going?"

Lillian smiled. "Martin told us you two are leaving us on our own, so we are going to check out bunko night with some of the lodge members to see if we can learn any more about Adam Muller's activities last weekend."

Samantha considered objecting, but figured bunko night wouldn't be too dangerous, plus Patty needed a distraction. "Okay, but be safe." She turned to Martin, who had changed into a pair of jeans and a button-up shirt. "Are you ready? I need to stop by my place to change before we meet David."

They walked outside with their mothers before heading out for their own adventure for the night.

* * *

Back at Samantha's apartment, Martin patted Ruby in the living room while Samantha changed, opting for a purple sundress with a chunky necklace. She slipped on a pair of silver sandals, selected a small handbag, and was ready to go.

Martin gazed appreciatively when she walked out of her bedroom. "You look great!"

Samantha blushed, hurrying toward the door. "Thanks. Let's head out. I don't want to be late."

On the way to the Fig and the Fern, Samantha kept the conversation light, pointing out her favorite restaurants and stores along the way to the Museum District, where the lounge was located. But despite her calm exterior, Samantha's palms sweated as she wondered how drinks with David and Martin would go. Though David now knew about her involvement in the investigation, she hoped Martin wouldn't talk too much about the case. She didn't want David to worry any more than he already did.

They found David in the pub, seated in a corner booth with low lighting and pictures of English hunting dogs lining walls covered in damask-print wallpaper. The pub reminded Samantha of the best parts of pubs she'd frequented in London during her brief study-abroad semester there, small and cozy, filled with dark corners lit by wall sconces, with comfy booths covered in faded fabric. The crowd was light, with only a few smaller groups clustered around tables, or singles drinking proper English pints at the long wooden bar. David stood up when Samantha and Martin walked in and leaned over to offer Samantha a hug as she slid into the booth next to him. Martin sat opposite them and scrutinized a menu. "This doesn't really seem like your kind of place, Sam."

Samantha smiled. "Why not? I like a good pub. But if it's cocktails you want, they're upstairs. Nothing too fancy, but well-made, and with good music to accompany them."

David chimed in. "Oh, on that front, we're in luck. A samba singer from Brazil is starting her set in half an hour. I reserved us seats upstairs. You've eaten, right? If you guys don't mind, I'm going to order dinner first. I'm starving."

David ordered the fish and chips, while Martin ordered a beer and Samantha stuck with water, since she was driving. Samantha filled David in on her meeting with Adam Muller earlier that afternoon and confirmed that she'd received the check Adam had promised David. Though still annoyed by his interference with Adam, now was not the time to mention it, especially with Martin sitting across the table.

As he drank his beer, Martin peppered David with questions regarding his law practice, his clients' net worth, and whether he enjoyed helping rich people get off for crimes when so many poor people didn't have adequate representation.

"We're lucky that we have a family connection and that my mom can afford good representation, but don't you think there is something inherently wrong with a legal system where so many innocent people can't afford a decent defense?" Martin's eyes glinted, like he'd just scored a point in a tough tennis match.

"I don't disagree that there are problems, but we have to do what we can to work within the system. That's why my firm tries to do as much pro bono work as possible." David took a swig from his beer.

"But that's the problem, those pro bono cases never take precedence over your paying clients, which means poor people always get the short end of the stick," Martin took a breath and appeared as if he was about to launch into another diatribe.

Samantha took the opportunity to try to ease the tension. "Well, I don't think we are going to solve the wealth-equality problem tonight . . . Did I tell you, David, that Martin has started his own woodworking business? And Martin, David is a painter."

She talked up David's recent gallery show, hoping the two could connect artistically. But it was obvious the conversation was strained.

After an uncomfortable twenty minutes, Samantha was relieved to head upstairs, where samba tunes might break up the awkwardness. A hostess led them to a small table near the front of the stage. The atmosphere in the club was more intimate than the pub downstairs, with almost a speakeasy vibe. Flickering candles topped small, round tables, casting their warm glow onto the stage, where a dark-haired woman in a long red dress stood behind a microphone. Samantha detoured to the long bar to order a round of cocktails, hoping a good drink might help ease the tension. She dropped off two brandy sidecars at the table before returning for her tonic water and lime, and seating herself between the two men.

While the singer crooned about someone tall and tan and young and lovely, Samantha tried to settle into the moment, allowing herself to imagine strolling through the sand on a Brazilian beach. She pictured David holding her hand as they felt warm water lap against their ankles. Lost in her daydream, she was startled to find Martin watching her. Samantha's face grew warm as she turned her focus to the singer on stage.

All remained quiet until intermission, when Martin referenced their evening together the previous night.

"It's nice to get out and hear music tonight, though the drinks were better at your place last night, Sam." Martin nudged Samantha with his elbow. "Yesterday was busy with the funeral, so I enjoyed our Netflix and chill night."

David raised his eyebrows as his gaze moved back and forth between Samantha and Martin, the atmosphere at their table shifting. "Am I missing something here?"

Samantha shot daggers at Martin as she responded to David. "No, nothing important."

She clenched her fists to refrain from shouting at Martin, taking a few calming breaths before she stood up. "Martin, I hope you don't mind taking an Uber home tonight. I should probably head out now. I've got an early start tomorrow morning. David, do you mind walking me out?"

Martin's face paled, and he opened his mouth as if to speak, but Samantha turned, not willing to give him the chance to respond. She only hoped she could find the words to rectify the situation with David. As she walked out the front door, a blast of heat and humidity collided with the cold air-conditioning, leaving her skin feeling clammy. Afraid of his reaction, she turned to look at David, who had followed her outside. "I'm so sorry about that, David. I don't know why he behaved that way."

David's brows knit together. "Did you spend the night with him last night?"

Samantha's stomach dropped with the realization of what she might lose if she couldn't get David to understand. "He fell asleep on my couch after watching a movie. Our brains were fried after the funeral and trying to investigate his mom's case. Nothing happened."

She reached for his hand and squeezed it. "I'm sorry about all of this."

David stared intently into Samantha's eyes for a short spell. "I'm an adult and can handle it. I've told you; I don't intend to pressure you. But I also don't want to waste my time. Clearly, you've got a lot of history with that guy."

Samantha scoffed. "Yeah, a lot of not great history. We hadn't spoken for nearly two decades before this week. I thought we had put the past behind us and could be friends again, but maybe I was wrong. I wanted to be with you tonight. I only invited Martin because I felt sorry for him. There's no excuse for his actions."

David brushed a stray hair off her forehead. "What now? Do you really have an early morning?"

Samantha sighed, remembering her meeting with Christina tomorrow. "Unfortunately, I do. I hate to leave things like this, but I should head home." She stood on her tiptoes and kissed him lightly on the lips. "Let's plan some alone time soon."

"I'll be counting the minutes." David walked her to her car and watched as she pulled out of the parking lot and drove away.

* * *

When she got home, it was midnight, and her mother was fast asleep in her bedroom. Samantha was relieved, not wanting to tell her mother about Martin.

What was up with him tonight? Though Martin's eyes on her at the bar left Samantha with a sneaking suspicion that she knew exactly what was up. *Could Mom be right? Is he interested in me?*

Though she was still angry at him, a tiny part of her wondered what it would be like to test out those emotions. Feeling disloyal to David, she tried to shut the idea out of her mind and turned her attention to other matters.

As she prepared for bed, she wondered whether her mother or Patty had learned anything useful at bunko night. She nestled into the couch, with Ruby purring softly at her feet.

Chapter Twenty-Two

In the morning, Samantha woke to the smell of fresh coffee and the sound of her mother bustling in the kitchen. As she stumbled in to make tea, her mother greeted her. "Good morning, sleepyhead. Did you enjoy yourself last night?

Samantha, not ready to join the world without her caffeine, shook her head. "No, and I don't want to talk about it. Instead, why don't you tell me about your evening? Did you learn anything new?"

Lillian's expression offered concern, but there was also a hint of excitement. "We might have. I don't want to say too much yet, but I need to do a little more research this morning."

"You've got to give me a hint, at least." Samantha stared at her mother.

Lillian bounced on the balls of her feet. "It's better left unsaid for now. But if it pans out, I'll let you know."

"Where will you do this research?" Samantha wondered what her mom was planning.

"I'd rather not say just yet. I'm going to pick Patty up this morning. We should be able to find what we need quickly. Maybe we can meet again at lunch."

Samantha didn't like the idea of her mother and Patty going off to do "research" on their own, but she also wanted to keep her meeting with Christina a secret for now so that Martin didn't show up and ruin everything. "All right, Mom. We'll meet back here. I've got a few things to take care of myself."

* * *

Samantha waved as her mother drove away, partially wondering how Lillian was going to manage Houston Saturday morning traffic, but deciding her mom could make it to Patty's place with little trouble. After her mother's car disappeared around the corner, Samantha picked up her purse, hopped in her own car, and headed to Angela's.

When she arrived, Christina appeared fidgety. "What if she attacks me?" She paced up and down the front hallway.

"I'll be in the next room. If she tries something, it will be two against one." Samantha sat down on the sofa. "Now, let's go over your script."

The women discussed their plan of attack. Since the plan was to confront Olivia in the study, they decided Samantha would hide in the adjoining library, connected by French doors between the two rooms. Before Olivia arrived, Christina would call Samantha and leave her phone on speakerphone, hidden somewhere close by in the study, where it could pick up the conversation. Samantha would listen in and record what was being said from the next room. If there was any hint of trouble, Samantha would rush in to help overpower Olivia.

Christina was still nervous and insisted that Samantha hold the fireplace poker and be prepared to use it against Olivia in case she attacked. Samantha hoped it wouldn't come to that, but agreed to arm herself, anyway.

Twenty minutes later, positioned in place, hidden behind curtains in the library, Samantha heard the door chime as it opened. Olivia's voice rang out, calling for Christina.

"In the study, Olivia." Christina's voice sounded firm, not betraying a hint of the nervousness she'd exhibited earlier. Samantha hoped Christina kept her composure as Olivia's heels clicked closer.

"So, Christina, why was it so urgent for me to meet you here this morning?"

Samantha listened in, trying to detect any hint of suspicion in Olivia's voice. She braced herself for Christina's next line.

"I wanted to discuss this with you." According to the plan, Christina should show Olivia the loan documents for the one-hundred-thousand-dollar loan Angela had given to her son.

"What about it? You already knew Angela loaned Matt money. We discussed it earlier. The money will be repaid to Angela's estate. You don't need to worry." Olivia sounded annoyed.

"Why did Matt borrow money to pay to Mama's sister, whom she hated? That seems pretty sketchy, Olivia." Christina's voice did not waver.

There was a pause that left Samantha wondering if she needed to race into the next room. But Olivia spoke before she could move. "That's something you need to discuss with Matt. I told him he needed to talk to you about it, but that's between you and him. So if that's all . . ."

Christina spoke hurriedly, before Olivia could leave the room. "I have a few other questions. Where were you between seven thirty and eight PM on the night that Mama died? I saw you arguing with Mama earlier, and then you were supposed to come to the pie contest, but you disappeared until Matt called you around eight thirty, after we found Mama."

Samantha clutched the fireplace poker harder as she anticipated Olivia's reaction to Christina's question.

"What do you mean? I was at the festival."

"But no one saw you. I asked around, and nobody saw you anywhere." Christina's voice grew stronger.

"If you must know, I had an important phone call that night. I was probably on that call. What are you getting at?" Olivia sounded annoyed.

"Did you kill my mama?" Christina practically shouted the question.

Olivia's voice turned shrill. "Are you out of your mind? Why on earth would you think that?"

Samantha listened carefully for any sound of a scuffle, but Christina's voice remained steady. "Let's see. Number one, you never liked Mama. You always said she was too nosy. Two, you had a fight with Mama that night. Three, Matt also fought with her on Friday night, and she threatened to write him out of the will. Four, you disappeared around the time she was murdered. Five, Matt apparently told our cousin he was coming into money soon. And lastly, I heard you tell Matt that everything would be okay by next Friday, which we all know is when we are meeting with Mama's lawyer to discuss her will."

"How can you even think that I'd kill Angela?" Olivia's voice sounded confused and hurt. "You know me, Chrissie."

Following a beat of silence, Christina cried out. "Don't touch me!"

Samantha gripped the poker as she threw open the French doors and ran into the study, expecting to find Olivia attacking Christina. "Get off her!"

Olivia, who had reached her hand out toward Christina's arm, looked up in confusion. "Samantha? What on earth are you doing here?"

Samantha's gaze moved between Olivia and Christina. The atmosphere of the room was charged, not with danger, but with hurt and misunderstanding. Suddenly, Samantha felt as though she had made a huge miscalculation. "I'm just helping Christina. She didn't want to confront you alone."

Olivia turned from Samantha to Christina. "I'm not even going to get into the lunacy of you bringing a caterer armed with a fire poker as backup. We'll leave that for now. But, Christina, do you really believe I hurt your mother? Yes, we had our disagreements, but she's my husband's mother and my kids' grandmother. Plus, I'm not a murderer!"

Christina backed away from her sister-in-law. "You're not refuting any of what I've said."

Olivia blinked rapidly. "This is pure insanity. You're really asking me for my alibi?"

Christina stared hard at Olivia. Her face betrayed doubt, but she maintained eye contact and nodded.

Olivia sat down in one of the blue wingback chairs in front of Angela's desk and slumped forward. "All right. From around seven fifteen to eight thirty that night, I was on a very important phone call."

Christina scoffed and attempted to break in, but Olivia cut her off. "Before you interrupt, I had a witness. A notary public was with me the entire time until Matt called me with the news about your mother."

"What kind of phone call? And how about the money and the fight . . . and the promise that everything would be good by next Friday?"

Olivia sighed. "It's supposed to be a secret. I can't tell anyone because it might jeopardize the deal."

Christina's eyes glinted with suspicion. "What deal?"

"You'll find out the details next Friday, when the story comes out in the *Wall Street Journal*, but for now you'll have to content yourself with my promise that I had nothing to do with your mother's death." Olivia pulled out her phone and scrolled through her contact list.

"What kind of deal? What about the *Wall Street Journal*?" Christina's face was ashen with shock.

Olivia appeared to wrestle with something for a moment before she responded. "Sorry, I can't give you any of the details. But I developed some software, which a major brand owner is buying for a significant amount of money . . . The deal is being announced on Friday with an exclusive story in the *Wall Street Journal*. That's why I told Matt everything would be fine on Friday."

Christina still appeared to be skeptical. "Why should I believe any of this?"

Olivia pressed a button on her phone. "If you don't believe me, I'll call the notary right now. She can confirm the timing of the call."

Christina nodded her head, refusing to back down from her suspicions. Samantha had the sinking feeling that her reputation was falling every minute she stayed in the room. Suddenly, her phone beeped, reminding the other two women of her presence in the room. She turned off the speakerphone and answered the call from her mom. "Mayday! Mayday! Please come help. Adam Muller just got home, and Patty and I are stuck hiding in his closet!"

Samantha's jaw dropped open. *What in the heck are they doing? And more importantly, how can I get them out?*

"Christina, are you okay now? Because I've got to go. I have a bit of an emergency to deal with."

Christina offered the briefest of nods before Samantha raced out of the house and into her car, plugging in the address her mother had texted her into Google Maps. On her way, she tried to invent an excuse to distract Adam until her mom and Patty escaped from his house.

* * *

With no plan formulated, Samantha had to wing it when she arrived at Adam Muller's front door ten minutes later. Fortunately, there was no fence surrounding the property, so if Lillian and Patty could get out the back door, they'd be home free. She texted her mom that she was outside the house and was about to ring the doorbell to talk to Adam. If they wanted to make their move, it would need to be fast.

She pressed the button and waited, wondering what to say when he answered the door. When the door swung open less than a minute later, Adam met her with a scowl. "Ms. Warren. To what do I owe this pleasure?"

Samantha took a deep breath. "To be honest, I have questions about the night Angela died."

Spots of color formed in his cheeks. "I thought we'd covered this already. I don't like your insinuations, and I won't listen to them."

Samantha sensed he was about to shut the door in her face, but she needed to give her mom and Patty time to leave out the back door. "Well then, how about I listen to you? Tell me where you were between seven thirty and eight PM on Friday night. Several witnesses said you were nowhere to be found at the festival."

Adam's face bloomed red. "If you must know, I was here. I had to run home for something."

The answer surprised Samantha. "In the middle of the opening day of the lodge's most important event of the year? What could you have needed at home that was more important?"

His expression was still flustered. "It was a personal matter. Now, I have things to attend to, and I must ask you to leave." He closed the door on her.

Samantha hoped the brief conversation had given her mom and Patty enough time to exit out the back, because she hadn't been able to hold him any longer, and the look he'd been giving her had made her realize that trying to do so might be dangerous.

She turned away from the house and walked back to her car, where she texted her mother. *Where are you guys?*

Instantly, she saw the three dots indicating that her mother was typing a message. *We made it out. I'm taking Patty home, but you stay at a safe distance, where you can watch the house. If Adam leaves, you've got to tell the police which way he went. We found evidence. He killed Angela.*

Samantha's head nearly exploded with the shock. She began to type a response but then instead dialed her mother. This was no time for text messaging.

"Mom, care to explain to me what in the heck you're talking about? What evidence? And why am I waiting here?"

Lillian's voice sounded jumpy. "We just dialed 911 and told the police there is evidence in Adam Muller's house regarding the murder of Angela Clawson. We found his T-shirt, and just as Patty's friend said, it was splattered with blood."

Samantha couldn't believe what she was hearing. "What? What shirt? How do you know it's blood or, even if it is, that it's Angela's blood?"

"There's no time, Sam. We found it, but we didn't want to take it with us because we didn't want to disturb the chain of evidence. The police are on their way. Just watch the house." Lillian hung up the phone.

Samantha hoped her mother was right. Another wild goose chase for the police would not do Patty any favors.

It didn't take long for the blue lights and sirens to appear. Samantha sat in her car, still parked a few houses down from Adam's house, and observed the activity. She watched as Adam held up his hands while two police officers stood outside his door.

Samantha was thankful that her mother had remembered the chain of evidence, but unfortunately, the police couldn't enter Adam's house unless he invited them in or they had a search warrant. Surprised, she watched as he opened the door and allowed the officers to enter.

Why would he do that? Does he assume the officers won't find whatever evidence Mom found? Samantha sat in her car, waiting to see what happened next.

Twenty minutes later, after a few rounds of Spider Solitaire and incessant email checks, Samantha heard a knock on her window. Startled, she looked up and caught the eye of Detective Jason Sanders. Heat rose in her cheeks as he motioned for her to roll down her window.

"Ms. Warren. Fancy meeting you here. You're not interfering in another of my cases, are you? I thought we'd come to a mutual understanding."

Samantha swallowed hard. "No, Detective, I'm not interfering." She figured the less said, the better for her.

"Then why exactly are you sitting two houses down from a house where an anonymous caller suggested there might be evidence relating to the Angela Clawson case?" Sanders's expression was stern.

"I didn't make the call—my mother did. She just wanted me to find out what happened, so I agreed to watch from a completely noninterfering distance." She wondered which part of her statement he would react to first.

"Your mother? You mean there are two nosy wanna-be detectives in your family? And pray tell, why is she interested in this case?" Sanders's tone matched his serious expression.

Samantha quickly filled him in on her mother's relationship with Patty and how they both knew that Patty was incapable of murder.

Sanders's expression softened. "Listen, I know you made some good discoveries last time, but I trust you also remember the consequences? This is serious business, and I don't want you getting involved."

"But—"

"No buts. I assure you, we will keep an open mind. Now, do us both a favor and drive home before someone else spots you here." Sanders raised his eyebrow, as if daring her to argue with him.

Samantha took heart in his promise that he would keep an open mind, and agreed to leave.

Sanders walked up the street to Adam's house but turned back to make sure that she kept her promise. She put the car in gear and drove slowly away. As she passed the house, she saw officers walking out of the house with white evidence bags.

Was it possible that Patty's luck was about to change?

Chapter Twenty-Three

It was noon when Samantha arrived at Patty's house. She wasn't relishing the idea of seeing Martin, but she had to fill in her mom and Patty on her talk with Detective Sanders, as well as what she'd learned that morning with Christina. Patty answered the door and led Samantha into her dining room, where Martin and Lillian were eating sandwiches.

"So, it's been an eventful morning for everyone." Samantha spotted Martin sending her apologetic glances, but she ignored them.

First, she caught everyone up to date on her conversation with Detective Sanders, and included the fact that she'd seen the police exit Adam Muller's house with evidence bags.

"Well, that's a positive sign, right? It means they found what we found." Lillian's eyes looked hopeful.

"And what exactly did you find? In all the hullabaloo, I never heard the story behind your search of Adam's house this morning."

Lillian seemed pleased with herself as she relayed what they'd picked up at their bunko meeting the night before. They had run into a woman named Nancy, from the lodge, whom Adam had hired to clean for him. "She told us that when she was over at his house earlier this week doing laundry, she found his festival shirt at the bottom of his laundry pile with two bright reddish or purplish stains on them. The bad news is that she washed the shirt, but the good news is that the stains didn't come out. She'd put Spray 'N Wash on the shirt and left it in the basket to run through next time she came."

Samantha's expression was skeptical. "The woman just offered you that information?"

Lillian shot an annoyed look at her daughter. "No, of course not. We were discussing the case and asking people if they had noticed anyone behaving strangely, including Adam Muller. One woman said she saw that he wasn't wearing his event shirt at the end of the evening, which she thought was odd."

Samantha raised her eyebrows, and Lillian continued. "So, after that, Nancy, the housekeeper, mentioned the stain."

"Nobody thought to tell the police about it?" Samantha wondered how much heartache could have been avoided had that information come to light earlier.

"Nancy didn't make the connection until we started talking last night." Patty spoke for the first time. Her mood was lighter than Samantha had seen for days. "Lillian and I went to check to see if the stained shirt was still there."

"How did you get into Adam's place? And how did you know he wouldn't be at home?" Samantha kept her eyes trained on her mother and Patty, still avoiding Martin's gaze.

Lillian blushed. "Well, we borrowed the house keys from Nancy and had Karl call Adam with an emergency at the lodge."

Though impressed with their ingenuity, Samantha still chastised her mother for the risk she had taken. "What if I hadn't been able to distract him? Do you know how risky that was?"

Lillian scowled. "It was worth it if there's a chance of getting Patty off. The police can't ignore hard evidence."

Samantha's expression softened. "Hopefully not. I think Detective Sanders will do a thorough investigation."

She filled them in on her less than fruitful morning with Christina and Olivia, only leaving out Olivia's soon-to-be announced deal. Samantha was glad they had eliminated Olivia as a suspect. She had liked her, though she realized her appearance this morning had likely ended any hopes of getting any repeat business from the Clawson family.

"Anyway, you had a more productive morning than I did." Samantha finished eating her sandwich. "I hate to eat and run, but I've got to go meet up with Beth to help prep for a brunch we're catering tomorrow morning."

Samantha stood up, followed by Lillian, who walked her to the door.

"I think I'll stick around here with Patty this afternoon. I have to head back to Corpus tomorrow afternoon, so I want to spend more time with her. But call me when you're done, and we can go have dinner, just the two of us."

Samantha smiled and hugged her mom. "Thanks, Mom. I'll see you later."

As she walked down the sidewalk to her car, Martin called after her. "Sam, wait a minute, please."

Samantha groaned to herself. *I'd rather not.* But she turned to face him anyway.

"Sam, I'm sorry about last night. I know I was acting like a jerk . . ."

No argument there! Samantha said nothing.

"It's just, the other night was like old times." Martin reached out to touch her arm, seeking a connection, before letting his fingers fall away. "We missed out on so many years, and the other night made me realize I don't want to miss any more. We could be good together. And I watched you with David last night, and I guess I wondered, why him? And why not me?"

Samantha winced as she felt a dull ache at the back of her throat. Part of her wished she could reach for his hand and travel with him back to the past, when they could have had their moment if he'd been more assertive and she'd been less stubborn and full of pride. But the last thing she wanted to do was lead him on or offer a promise of something she didn't know if she could deliver.

"Martin, I know we have a connection. But you don't even know me anymore. I don't even know myself fully yet. But I'm trying to learn. I owe myself that. And you owe yourself something better than that." She reached out and gave his hand a squeeze before turning toward her car.

She felt a lump in her throat as she turned on the car, but she swallowed it. *We can't ever seem to get our timing right.*

* * *

As she drove to the kitchen incubator to help Beth, Samantha pushed her thoughts about Martin and David out of her mind. She decided she should call Christina. After running out on her so quickly that morning, she wanted to explain why she'd left. Plus, she was eager to share the news about Adam, knowing that Christina would want to be kept in the loop on anything else she'd learned.

Christina didn't answer, so Samantha left her a voicemail, filling her in on what her mother and Patty had found and the fact that the police were now questioning Adam Muller about Angela's murder.

In the kitchen, Samantha found Beth busy mixing up blueberry muffin batter when she walked in the door. "That looks delicious. What else is on the menu?"

Beth's gaze rose from her stirring. "Hey, Sam! I'm glad to see you. I'm just getting started with the assorted muffins and pastries, but we've also got to make mini quiches, fresh fruit, egg strata—and, of course, your elevated mimosas. Jump in wherever you think it makes sense."

Samantha took out a fresh bowl to make a pan of Beth's homemade orange cinnamon rolls—the one pastry she'd mastered over the last month under Beth's tutelage. As she worked, she filled Beth in on the latest on the Angela Clawson case as well as the fact that her mother may have helped to catch the true culprit.

"That's great news! Oh, that reminds me, we had a call from someone from that lodge this morning who wanted to hire us for a fundraiser or something." Beth filled the muffin pans almost to the brim with the batter.

Samantha recalled Adam Muller's mention of a new scholarship to be named in Angela Clawson's honor. "Oh, I just heard about a new scholarship being planned yesterday. Who called? What are they wanting us to do?"

Beth placed the muffin pans into the preheated oven. "It was a woman named Calista. I told her she could stop by this afternoon while we were working, and give us the details about a tennis-themed fundraising luncheon."

Samantha wondered how the possibility of the lodge president being arrested for murder might impact the planned luncheon, but she figured it wouldn't hurt to meet with Calista anyway, if only to stay in the good graces of the wealthy tennis club set. "That's great! As weird as it has been, we've gotten a lot of word-of-mouth business from participating in the festival."

Beth nodded as she began chopping vegetables for the mini quiches. Together they resumed their complicated ballet of prepping, baking, and mixing everything for the book club brunch in the morning.

As Samantha pureed the strawberries and mangos for the mimosas, she spotted a woman with the recognizable blown-out blonde hairstyle heading down the hallway toward their section of the kitchen.

"Oh, I hope I'm not interrupting anything." Calista stepped into the room, and Samantha stopped the blender, walking over to shake the woman's hand.

"It's no problem. We're grateful that you thought of us for the luncheon. Come have a seat." Samantha pointed the woman toward a set of barstools next to a kitchen island.

"I loved your cocktails at the festival . . . and, of course, at the funeral. We'll need something equally unique for this luncheon. It absolutely must be the highest quality. After all, the scholarship will be Angela's legacy." Calista picked up one of the cooling muffins and sniffed in the aroma. "Oh, this smells heavenly. Do you mind if I sample one?"

Beth offered Samantha a sideways glance but nodded her assent. "Help yourself. Now when is this luncheon, and what do you have in mind for it?"

Calista bit into the blueberry muffin and moaned with appreciation. "We're hoping to create an endowed scholarship in Angela's honor, to make sure that ten area youths will have full privileges at the club each year. It was a cause very dear to Angela's heart. We want the luncheon to be held outside. Since none of the new courts are ready yet, I thought the lodge's old tennis court would work. But the food must rival the best in the city if we are to make the guests feel generous."

Beth walked over with a notepad and took notes. "How many guests are you thinking about? And how many courses for the luncheon? Is there a particular theme?"

Calista continued munching on the muffin. "It should be a traditional four-course luncheon, with appetizer, salad, main course, and dessert. We're targeting around a hundred ladies. In terms of theme, nothing specific—just elegant."

Samantha had a brainstorm. "What if we had a unifying element that tied everything together? Something that represented Angela? Like a flower, or—oh, I don't know . . . a pearl? I still remember your beautiful eulogy and your reference to her pearl necklace. We could incorporate pearls in each course somehow, like maybe oysters for the first course. And Beth could make her special sorbet served as a pearl inside two oyster-shaped cookies."

Beth nodded. "I like that idea. I can work with that. And Sam, you could make a pearl-themed cocktail."

Samantha nodded but didn't speak. She and Beth sometimes got carried away, and she wanted to give Calista an opportunity to offer feedback. When she glanced over, Calista had a faraway look on her face, but when she noticed Samantha's gaze, she perked up and nodded. "That sounds wonderful. I knew you'd come up with something perfect."

Beth made a few more notes and then closed her book. "We'll brainstorm and let you know what else we've come up with tomorrow afternoon, when we come to visit the site."

Samantha offered a worried glance at her partner. "Tomorrow afternoon? What about the brunch in the morning?"

Beth nodded. "We should be finished by then. If we're not, you can leave early and meet Ms. Beech there first."

Calista finished the last bite of muffin and picked up her purse. "Excellent. I'll see you at the lodge tomorrow." She walked back down the corridor toward the exit.

Once Calista was gone, Beth locked eyes with Samantha. "Well, that went pretty well, right? A formal luncheon for one hundred? That will be a nice fee and good advertising for our business. That pearl idea was genius, though I'm not sure what to suggest as a main entrée. How'd you come up with that so fast?"

Samantha shrugged. "I don't know. It just came to me."

She picked up a pineapple and sliced the fruit. As she cut, she pondered what impact there would be on the event if the police arrested the lodge president for Angela's murder. She wanted the arrest for her mother and Patty's sake, but she hoped there wouldn't be any interruption in the luncheon planning. She and Beth could use another big event to tide their business over for a while.

They finished up their preparations and made plans to meet back at the kitchen early the next morning, to finish cooking and get everything ready for the book club brunch.

* * *

When Samantha arrived home, Lillian jumped up from the living room couch to greet her. "I just heard from Patty. According to her friend's son, who works at the police station, Adam is still being interviewed. He hasn't been arrested yet, but it's got to be good news, right?"

Samantha breathed a sigh of relief. A part of her had trouble believing that her mother and Patty had cracked the case, but now the police were focusing their attention on a new suspect. "Let's celebrate. Change your clothes. For your last night in town, we'll do it right."

Samantha changed into a lavender wrap dress and pulled her hair up in a French twist. When her mother walked out of the bathroom in a black maxi dress, Samantha fed Ruby, got her bag, and walked out the door.

The two women drove from the Highlands neighborhood, where Samantha lived, over to the Montrose area to Hugo's, one of the city's best restaurants, known for showcasing the different regional flavors of Mexico.

They took a seat in the elegant dining room at a table overlooking Westheimer. Though the street stretched across much of Houston, the section winding through Montrose was Houston's funkiest, filled with restaurants and bars, boutiques, antique stores, tattoo parlors, and vintage clothing stores. Samantha loved the hustle and bustle.

They shared a bowl of homemade guacamole and sipped hand-shaken margaritas before Samantha ordered the carne asada and Lillian ordered the barbacoa. With the police now focusing on someone other than Patty, their chatter turned to more casual topics. They discussed Samantha's business and Lillian's work back home.

"I can't believe I've been away for an entire week. It will be nice to see your father and get back to the library." Lillian told her daughter in greater detail about a new children's program she was planning to start up at her branch.

As they shared a plate of dulce de leche–stuffed churros and ice cream for dessert, Lillian's phone beeped.

As Lillian looked down to read the screen, Samantha watched as her mother dropped her spoon. "What is it, Mom?"

Lillian gasped. "The police let Adam go. They say he's no longer a person of interest."

"But how can that be? What about the shirt and the blood stains? What about his lack of an alibi?" Samantha had been certain they had landed on the only person left who could have committed the crime.

Lillian continued to read a series of text messages from Patty that were filling her screen. "Her friend's son, who works at the police department, says apparently it wasn't blood. The red stain was cabbage juice that he spilled on himself while trying to hide sauerkraut in Angela's car. That was his big plan for revenge. He was going to make her car stink."

Samantha recalled an earlier reference to food being spilled in Angela's car, but shrugged. "Okay, so it was cabbage juice. That doesn't mean he didn't kill Angela. Maybe she caught him in the act."

"No, according to Patty's friend, he drove home to change. He talked to his neighbor and helped him jump his car at around 7:25 and didn't head back to the festival until after eight PM. His alibi is solid. He couldn't have done it." Lillian pushed the phone away from her as if trying to escape the bad news.

"Who else could it be? What happens next?" Samantha glanced out the window, wishing the answer was somewhere out there.

Lillian sighed. "We're back to square one, and Patty is back as the prime suspect."

Chapter Twenty-Four

As they drove back to Samantha's apartment, Lillian wrung her hands. "I wish I could stay, but I just can't. It's been a week, and I've got to get back to your dad and my job."

Samantha patted her mother's leg. "Patty understands that. There's nothing more you can do anyway. I'm here, and if something comes up, I'll help check it out. The heavy lifting will have to be done by Patty's lawyer now."

* * *

Back at Samantha's apartment, full from dinner but depressed about Patty's situation, they sat down to brainstorm other alternatives. In one day, they'd eliminated their two best suspects.

Samantha pulled out her notepad, where she'd outlined the potential suspects. She crossed off Adam and Olivia. Since it was now clear that Adam and Suspect X—the suspicious man seen near Angela's car just before her murder—were one and the same, she crossed him off the list as well. Now, her list was empty apart from Karl, whom she didn't see as a murderer.

"What we need are more facts." Samantha walked to the kitchen to brew some ginger tea. It was too late for caffeine, but she hoped the spicy flavor would help keep her and her mother awake long enough to make some headway.

Lillian placed tea bags into two mugs, ready to steep in the hot water. "How about that threatening email you received? Let's assume for now that the killer sent it. In that case, it would have to have been someone you had contact with or, at a minimum, someone who heard about your snooping."

Samantha carried her mug back into the living room and sat on the couch. "I'm not sure that narrows it down much. Hundreds of people attended the funeral."

Lillian fiddled with the tea bag, bobbing it up and down in the hot water. "Let's leave the funeral aside for now. The email came after you spoke to Christina, right? What about her? Did she mention your investigation to anyone?"

Samantha considered the question. She supposed it was possible. Glancing at her watch, she saw it was only eight PM. "You know what? Let me call her. I need to update her on Adam, anyway."

Lillian sipped her tea while Samantha dialed the number. Christina picked up after two rings. "Hey Samantha. Sorry I didn't call you back this afternoon. I was with Matt. We talked for a while."

"You guys alright now?" Samantha hoped the siblings had been able to patch things up.

"Yes. He told me he doesn't want anything to come between us like it did between our mama and her sister. Oh, and that reminds me—I'm finally going to meet my aunt and cousin. We're going to the hospital tomorrow for a visit." Christina sounded genuinely happy.

"That's great!" Samantha was glad that the two sides of the family could reunite, even if it had occurred after Angela's death. "How's Olivia doing?" She winced at the memory of her last encounter with the woman.

"After she got over the initial shock of my accusation, we cleared the air. We won't be besties soon or anything, but the entire experience might bring us closer together. She understood my reasoning for considering her a suspect, and I understand her secrecy."

Relieved that Olivia bore no ill will against her sister-in-law, Samantha still worried about how Olivia viewed her actions. She had hoped to get additional referrals from Olivia and her family, but now was not the time to focus on that. Samantha filled Christina in on the news about Adam.

"So who's left? If you're sure your friend Patty didn't do it, who killed my mama?" Christina's voice shook, and Samantha felt terrible for stirring up the woman's pain again.

"I'm hoping you might remember something else from that night." Gently, Samantha prodded Christina to repeat what she remembered from the night her mother had died.

Christina sighed. "I've gone over it a million times. I can't remember anything unusual. Mama was mad about Matt and Olivia, but other than that, she was acting pretty normal, chastising me for my outfit. She told me I was young and needed to be bolder with my fashion choices. She even made me swap necklaces with her so that I had a signature piece."

"You didn't see anything out of the ordinary? Where was your mom going after she left you?" Samantha hoped to jog Christina's memory, thinking there had to be something she was missing.

"She didn't say. I left to make it to the pie contest on time, and she headed in the opposite direction, toward the construction site."

Samantha tried to frame the question she wanted to ask next. "Remember the day I brought the strudel to your house? After I got home that night, someone sent me a threatening message. Did you tell anyone else that you'd talked to me?"

Christina paused, considering. "No. I don't think so. I didn't talk to anyone else that night."

This felt like another dead end. Samantha asked Christina to call her if she remembered anything else and hung up the phone.

She turned to her mother's expectant face and shook her head. "She says she didn't talk to anyone and can't remember anything else. I'm sorry, Mom." Samantha sat next to her mom. "I can't think of anything else to do."

Lillian nodded and stood up, heading to Samantha's room to pack her things for her return trip to Corpus Christi the next morning. After twenty minutes, she reentered the living room, dressed in her pajamas and looking determined. "I know we've missed something. I don't like giving up if there is a chance we can help Patty."

Samantha, who had been noodling around with ideas for cocktails and other food for her meeting the next day, glanced at her mom. "I'm all ears. What do you want to do?"

Lillian reached for Samantha's computer. "Mind if I use this? If we looked at photos from Friday night, we might find a clue, or something might jog our memories."

Samantha turned the laptop on and logged in, handing the slim computer back to her mother. "Be my guest."

Lillian pulled up news stories and searched Twitter and Instagram for photos from the festival. It didn't take long before they found a video of the fight between Patty and Angela, which someone had live tweeted under the hashtags #highlandsindependencefest and #catfight.

The video's vantage point was far away, but it clearly showed Patty pushing Angela down and Angela pulling herself up and dusting herself off. Samantha imagined a jury watching the video and shuddered out of concern for Patty.

She searched through other photos on social media, using the #highlandsindependencefest hashtag, but they were mostly photos of musical groups, fireworks, and kids eating funnel cake, or pictures from the pet parade. Nothing stood out as important.

Something kept Samantha from connecting with a stray thought. With eyes tired from staring at the screen, Samantha glanced at the time and realized she needed to wake early the next morning to help Beth with the brunch. She looked up at her mom, who continued to stare at the video. "Mom, I'm sorry, but I really have to go to bed now. I've got an early start tomorrow. I wish we'd found something to help Patty."

Lillian smiled sorrowfully. "I know, honey. You did more than anyone could have asked. I'm sorry this investigation has consumed our visit, but I've enjoyed spending time with you."

Samantha hugged her mom and went to get ready for bed. Lillian took the borrowed laptop into the bedroom, to continue her searching.

Chapter Twenty-Five

In the morning, Samantha awoke early to the smell of French toast and found her mother humming at the stove and making her favorite breakfast for lazy Sundays. The scene reminded her of countless mornings as a student when her mom woke early to make a nutritious breakfast before a test or presentation, insisting that breakfast was the most important meal of the day.

"Mom, what are you doing up so early?" Samantha poured steaming water into an awaiting mug, savoring the scent of cinnamon and cloves from the toast combining with the spices from her chai tea.

Lillian lifted the hot toast from the pan onto a plate and handed it to her daughter. "I wanted you to at least have a good breakfast before I have to leave. You've got a big day ahead. And since I won't see you, this is my way of saying thank you for putting up with me this past week."

Samantha took a bite of the lightly browned, eggy toast and smiled at the memories it evoked of unrushed Sundays of her childhood, when fighting her dad for the first crack at the Sunday comics was her biggest worry. "You didn't have to do this, but it's delicious."

Samantha searched for the words to reassure her mother, but those words didn't exist. She finished up her breakfast and hopped in the shower, getting dressed quickly so she could make it to the kitchen in time to meet Beth.

Preparing to leave, she gave her mom a big hug, telling her to try not to worry too much about Patty. "Easier said than done, I know. Hopefully her lawyer comes up with something."

"I hope so." Lillian hugged her daughter back. "I love you. Take care of yourself."

"Back at you, Mom." Samantha waved to her mom as she walked down the steps to her car.

* * *

For once, Samantha beat Beth to the kitchen incubator and got started on the remaining preparations for the brunch. She cracked eggs and diced ham and fresh tomatoes for the mini quiches, leaving the tiny pastries for Beth to finish when she arrived. She shredded a blend of cheddar and pepper jack cheeses from a local dairy and stirred it in to complete the dish. As she worked, she brainstormed more pearl-themed ideas for the luncheon, coming up with a sea scallop entrée and a drink called the French Pearl, with gin, lime juice, and Pernod, which would take on the cloudy luster of a pearl in each glass when the anise-flavored liquor hit the other liquid. She was thrilled at the prospect of another well-paying luncheon. Though they'd had a busy few days, business needed to stay that way, and the only way to ensure a steady stream of income was to have a steady stream of satisfied customers.

Her reverie broke when Beth started moving pans around, diving into the rest of the brunch preparations.

"I'm not sure why I'm so sluggish this morning. I'm going to make a coffee. Want one?" Beth scooped coffee grinds into a stovetop espresso maker and heated it.

Samantha declined the coffee, as she was already feeling wired from her creativity kicking in.

"Did your mom get off okay this morning?" Beth poured a cup of the strong coffee and blew on it to cool it.

"She's going to visit Patty one more time before she leaves this afternoon." Samantha filled her friend in on the latest in the case. "It's awful. We've run out of suspects, and there's not much hope of finding new information." Samantha finished packing up her supplies and got ready to carry them out to the rental van.

Beth patted Samantha on the back. "Something will come up."

The two women worked to pack the van and made plans to meet at the palatial Highlands home to prepare for the brunch.

The home was one of the few historic homes remaining on the block. It seemed to have jumped right off the pages of a *Better Homes & Gardens* spread on garden parties. There were fresh-cut flowers in crystal vases spread throughout the formal living room, where the meeting was to be held.

Beth and Samantha arranged their stations in the room's corner, away from the circle of chairs designated for the members, but close enough for those members to help themselves to food whenever they were hungry. Samantha pulled out her blend of strawberries and mangoes to mix with the champagne for the elevated mimosas. She set a pitcher to chill in ice, ready to pour into the waiting champagne flutes.

Before long, ladies arrived, each carrying a copy of the latest in the Coffee Lovers Mystery Series, ready to discuss a new vexing murder that had rattled the fictional seaside town.

"It smells delightful in here. I should start with coffee, but I can't resist one of those." A middle-aged woman with twinkling eyes lifted one of the champagne flutes from a tray and took a sip. "You always come up with the most unusual cocktail recipes. I told Nora she ought to hire you ladies for book club."

Samantha smiled at the woman. "Have we met before?"

The woman took another taste. "Not *met* exactly, but I tasted your delightful sparkler drink at the festival and then had that divine blackberry drink at Angela's funeral."

The mention of Angela's funeral piqued Samantha's interest. Everywhere she looked, there was a connection to Angela or the festival or the funeral. She said as much to the woman. "We've gotten lots of good referrals since the festival. We're trying to get the word out to as many people as possible, so we appreciate anyone willing to recommend us."

The woman popped a mini quiche into her mouth and uttered a moan of delight. "With such high-quality food and drinks, you should have no trouble making it."

The woman had a friendly smile. As she grazed, selecting more food, Samantha kept the conversation going. "I'm going to meet another tennis club member after this to discuss plans for a scholarship fundraising dinner to honor Angela. Calista Beech is heading it. Do you know her?"

"Oh, a bit. I've served on a few committees with her and Angela." The woman bit into a cinnamon roll and sighed in ecstasy. "I'm frankly surprised to hear she's organizing something to honor Angela after the fight they had over Calista's nephew."

This was the first word Samantha had heard regarding a fight. She pressed the woman to reveal more. "What about her nephew?"

"Calista had all but promised him the tennis pro job at the club. She'd even gotten approval from Angela. But then Sarah O'Grady mentioned this hotshot tennis star from California was available, and Angela dropped Calista's nephew. Calista is not one to cause a scene, but you could tell she wanted to strangle Angela." The chairs on the other side of the room were filling up. "I should head over there. We're ready to start. Thanks again for the cocktail."

The story sent Samantha's brain into overdrive. *Could Calista have done it?* She thought back to her earliest encounters with the woman and did recall Calista's intense discussion with Angela at the VIP tent. But it seemed so unlikely. She had spoken so highly of Angela in the newspaper and at the funeral. Nothing about the competent and collected woman suggested murderer. Plus, she had an alibi. Christina had confirmed seeing her at the pie contest before the body was found. Samantha didn't want to jump to any more conclusions after the disastrous day of false accusations yesterday.

Still, she wanted to understand the dynamics between Calista and Angela. During a quiet interlude, Samantha texted Christina, asking her when exactly she'd seen Calista at the pie contest and whether she'd been there the whole time.

She saw the dots on her phone, signifying that Christina was responding. *She knocked the pies over a few minutes before the police found Mama. I assumed she'd been there the whole time, but I don't know for sure. Why?*

Though she didn't have much time, Samantha responded back. *She and your mother apparently argued that night. What can you find out about your mother's recent interactions with her?*

Christina's response was brief. *I'll check with some of Mama's friends and get back with you.*

Samantha put her phone in her pocket and turned back to the bar. While the book club ladies discussed red herrings in their mystery, Beth refreshed the pastry and fruit trays. Samantha was making a new batch of mimosas when her phone dinged with an incoming text message. Christina had responded.

Mama's friend said Mama sometimes took advantage of Calista. She'd talk up Calista's ideas as if they were her own. But she said Calista didn't seem bothered by it. She says no way is Calista a killer.

Samantha wasn't sure what to think. Two people had noticed a tense relationship between the two women. The second person had expressed doubt that Calista was a killer, but was it possible Angela had pushed her too far? People could snap. Samantha had seen it happen. She wondered whether she should cancel her meeting with Calista, not wanting to risk another confrontation with a dangerous killer. But she didn't want to lose out on a lucrative job, particularly with no evidence that Calista was guilty.

After another half hour of book discussion, the book club ladies came back to the food and drink stations to reload for their social hour. Beth and Samantha spent a busy twenty minutes refilling food plates, making coffee and tea, and mixing up more mimosas.

Most of the women left by the end of the hour, leaving Samantha and Beth to clean up. With the food put away and everything spit-spot, it was nearly time to head out.

"Beth, why don't you let me handle this next meeting with Calista on my own? You handled that dinner party the other day, so I can handle this one. I've got your notes. There's no reason for us both to waste our time." Samantha didn't want to scare Beth with her concerns regarding Calista, but she also didn't want to put her friend in any danger.

"Are you sure? If you don't mind, that's great. I'm beat today. Oh, but I had one other idea for a pearl-themed entrée." As Beth dug through her bag to find her notes, Samantha had the sudden sense that she was on the cusp of figuring out something important.

Beth pulled out a piece of paper and handed it over to Samantha. "It's similar to a paella with shrimp and chorizo, but made with pearl couscous rather than rice."

"Pearl couscous. That's a great idea, Beth! I'm sure Calista will love it." Samantha reached for her purse and headed out to her car, feeling something just below her consciousness struggling to come to the surface.

As she opened her car door, the thought hit her like a lightning bolt. *Pearls. Pearl necklace.*

She searched Twitter for the video she and her mom had watched last night. She slowed it down, searching it frame by frame until she found what she was searching for—a flash of red at the nape of Angela's neck. Angela hadn't been wearing a pearl necklace on the night she had died, at least not at first.

Samantha started her car and called Christina on the way. The woman answered after the second ring. "Christina, what kind of necklace did you give to your mother on Friday?"

Christina laughed. "It was a pearl necklace. Mom told me I needed to wear her ruby necklace because the pearls were too old-fashioned. Why?"

It clicked now. Calista couldn't have seen Angela wearing her pearl necklace on Friday, as she had said in her eulogy, unless she saw it right after Christina gave it to her mom, which was right before Angela died. "I think Calista killed your mom.

There's no time to explain now. I'm meeting her at the lodge in a few minutes."

Samantha hung up, her pulse thrumming in her ears as she got closer to the lodge and her meeting with the person she now knew in her heart was a killer. Should she abandon the meeting? The last thing she wanted to do was to face another crazed killer. But Samantha rationalized that Calista wasn't aware that Samantha had figured out what she had done. Plus, there should be plenty of people around, what with the construction workers and people at the lodge office. It would be difficult for Calista to try something around so many people.

Still, Samantha decided it wouldn't hurt to tell people she was meeting Calista and what she suspected. Four miles from the lodge, she pulled over to the side of the road and sent three texts, one to Martin, one to David, and one to Detective Jason Sanders, hoping that at least one responded.

No time to explain, but I am on my way to meet Calista Beech at the old tennis court at the lodge grounds. I think she killed Angela Clawson.

Her hands shaking, Samantha started the car again and drove slowly toward the lodge. Arriving at the grounds, Samantha's stomach sank when she noticed the empty parking lot. During each of her past visits, the site had been full of construction activity and general hustle and bustle at the lodge building. The absence of activity today was noticeable and alarming. Samantha considered whether she should leave. Her meeting with Calista, which had seemed fine when she expected other people to be nearby, now seemed like a terrible idea.

As she sat in her car, she picked up her phone and saw it was blowing up with text messages from Christina, David, Martin, and Detective Sanders. As she pressed the button to open the first message, a hard rap sounded on her window. Startled, she glanced over. Her fingers went cold and numb as she met Calista's gaze on the other side of the glass.

"There you are, Samantha. I wasn't sure if you were going to show." Calista waited expectantly outside the car door.

I guess this is happening now. It's too late to turn back. Samantha held up a finger, signaling to Calista to wait. She indicated that she needed to finish up a message on her phone, and quickly sent a text to Martin, the last text message open on her phone.

Heading to the tennis court with Calista. Nobody else here. Worried. Please help.

She pressed "Send" and prayed that Martin would react quickly. Before she stashed her phone in her purse, she pressed the memo function to record and opened the door to follow Calista.

"It's quiet out here today. Where is everybody?" Samantha followed a few steps behind Calista on their way to the tennis court. The quiet was disconcerting. She'd never been to the lodge without her senses being accosted by dozens of sights and sounds.

"Somebody reported a gas leak this morning, so construction was halted until the gas company can send someone to check it out. Since this is a Sunday, it's going to take a little extra time. Anyway, I thought the quiet would be good for our meeting." Calista smiled back at Samantha, whose stomach knotted. Was Samantha imagining a hint of malice in the smile? She couldn't decide if it was fear or instinct controlling her thoughts. She kept the conversation light for now, hoping to give whatever cavalry might come to her rescue more time to make it.

As they walked down the hillside toward the tennis court, Samantha spotted three tables laid out with sample linens and china on the left side of the court, the white and cream-colored linens blotting out a quarter of the faded green surface. Directly adjacent to the tables was a red and white machine that resembled a mini push mower, filled with fuzzy green tennis balls, which Samantha recognized from her middle school tennis years as an automatic ball feeder. It must have been left out following a recent practice.

Samantha kept up the small talk for now, hoping to put Calista at ease. "Beth couldn't make it today. We got caught late at another event this morning. A brunch at a local book club. But she came up with great ideas for the luncheon."

Calista pointed toward a chair. "Have a seat, please. I wanted to hear the rest of your ideas for the menu."

Samantha took a seat just out of Calista's reach. She fiddled with the edge of the cream-colored tablecloth draped over the table in front of her. Her nerves ratcheted up, but she didn't want to signal any fear to Calista. "Sure. So we ran with the pearl theme we discussed yesterday." She motioned toward her notebook.

After spending several minutes outlining all of the proposed recipes, hoping to buy herself some time, Samantha began to worry that the police would arrive, and she'd have no way to prove Calista was guilty. She decided to risk pressing a few buttons just to see how Calista reacted.. "It's so nice that you're heading up this luncheon. I was talking to someone just this morning who was surprised. She said she thought you were too angry about your nephew."

Calista looked up sharply, her face pink. "Oh, that. A simple misunderstanding, really. I certainly wouldn't let something as minor as that keep me from honoring an exceptional woman." Calista stared intently at the notebook and appeared to regain her composure.

Samantha stood up under the pretext of checking out table service samples on one of the other tables, farthest from where

Calista still sat. "I understand most of her great ideas were actually your ideas." She lifted up a silver-plated butter knife, appearing to examine the scalloped design on its handle.

Samantha glanced up to meet Calista's gaze, which had turned steely. Samantha eased off the pressure. "The more I discuss Angela, the more apparent it is how few people actually liked her. I'm not complaining, because it's brought me good business, but I don't get why everyone is spending time and money to honor someone with so few redeeming qualities."

Calista's face softened, her expression almost wistful. "She rubbed many people the wrong way, but she also raised a lot of money for important projects . . . and to be fair, while I had good ideas, Angela was right that I didn't execute them. She made things happen."

Though frightened, Samantha needed to keep pressing Calista. "You know, with all of this talk about pearls, I looked for a photo of Angela wearing those trademark pearls you mentioned in her eulogy, but in all the photos I saw of her on the day she died, she's wearing a bright red ruby necklace."

Calista's expression showed puzzlement briefly, but she shook it off. "I must have misremembered. Most of the time she wore pearls."

Gravel crunched under a tire in the nearby parking lot. Had the cavalry arrived? So far, Samantha didn't have Calista saying anything remotely suspicious, and certainly not enough to get the police interested. Samantha would have to press Calista to the breaking point before she ran out of time.

"What was the final straw, Calista? Why did you kill Angela?" Samantha locked eyes with Calista, silently urging her to rise to the bait.

"What are you talking about? I didn't kill Angela! I had an alibi, remember? A dozen ladies, including Angela's daughter, saw me at the pie contest." Calista remained defiant.

Samantha decided it was time to show her hand. "But you don't really have an alibi. You managed to stir up so much confusion by knocking those pies over, that people remembered you being at the contest for longer than you were. When I asked people again today, nobody remembered you being there for longer than five minutes before the police showed up. That gave you plenty of time to commit the murder and get to the pie booth."

Calista's eyes grew dark as she reached for something in her bag. "I didn't want to hurt her any more than I want to hurt you, but you've left me no choice. Take a seat, Samantha."

Samantha backed into a seat, her pulse racing. "What are you going to do?"

Calista held a silver revolver in her hand, aimed directly at Samantha's chest. "Stop talking. None of this had to happen. If you'd left well enough alone, we wouldn't be here right now. You should have backed off when I sent that email."

"What about Patty? She doesn't deserve to go to prison for something you did." Samantha regretted speaking out, thinking anger was not the right tack for someone like Calista.

"It's unfortunate that her fingerprints were on the weapon and that she was seen fighting with Angela. It wasn't my intention for her to be accused of the crime. But that's what lawyers are for. A good lawyer could have gotten her off." Calista aimed the gun at Samantha.

To Samantha, it appeared that Calista was having trouble holding the gun straight for long, as her hand began shaking. Calista didn't strike her as the kind of person who typically carried a weapon, and Samantha hoped she could use that to her advantage. For now, she needed to keep Calista talking. "People will understand you didn't mean to kill Angela. It was obviously an accident."

"It wasn't an accident. She didn't ever shut up. I was so sick of her, and I had to get her to stop talking somehow. The shovel was right there, so I picked it up and used it." Calista's eyes cast down for a moment, but when she looked up, they had turned wild, like those of an animal caught in a trap. "Now, your turn to tell me something. How many people know about this?"

Samantha felt her pulse quicken. "Everybody. Or at least everybody who counts. And multiple people are aware I'm meeting you. You won't get away with killing me."

Calista's eyes narrowed. She kept the gun trained on Samantha with one hand while she reached out with the other. "Hand me your phone. I want to see what was on that last text."

Just as Samantha dug around in her purse, hoping to find something to defend herself with, a shout rang out in the distance. "Stop! Let her go!"

In the instant that Calista's attention wavered, Samantha lunged forward, pushing the table over before racing to the ball machine. She flicked a switch, causing tennis balls to shoot out at high velocity, and aimed it at Calista, who instinctively ducked.

Samantha dropped and rolled out of the way just as two police officers headed down the hillside toward the tennis court, their weapons aimed at Calista.

When Samantha looked up, she was being pulled to her feet by familiar warm hands. "Mom! Where did you come from?"

"Are you all right, honey? I'm so glad she didn't hurt you." Lillian pulled her daughter into a tight embrace.

As she separated from her mom, more familiar faces appeared before her.

"David! Martin! Thank God you got my messages!"

David pulled her toward him in another hug before releasing her and giving her a once-over. "Yes, I got your message and called the police while I headed here."

"And I called your mom." Martin squeezed her shoulder. "How did you figure this out? And why on earth did you face Calista alone?"

Samantha watched as police officers handcuffed Calista. "I didn't figure it out until I was on my way here. She came to my car door after I made it to the parking lot. I didn't have time to think, so I followed her."

More police officers arrived. One approached the group and pulled them aside individually, to take their statements. Amid the discussions, Beth ran toward her. "I raced here as fast as I could. Is everything okay?"

Samantha hugged her and assured her everything was fine, when Detective Jason Sanders pulled her aside. "Ms. Warren. Didn't I warn you not to show up to any more crime scenes?"

Samantha met his gaze. "I didn't know it was going to be a crime scene. I was supposed to be meeting her to discuss a catering event."

He stared at the now overturned tables on the tennis court. "At least you had the foresight to message me with your suspicions. I'm glad you're alright, but I hope this is the last time we meet under these circumstances."

Samantha nodded. "Me too. Does this mean you'll be dropping the charges against Patty?" She offered him the recording of her conversation with Calista on her phone.

"We've still got work to do in our investigation, but your mother's friend is no longer our top suspect." The detective thanked her for the recording and walked away to join other officers gathered on the opposite side of the tennis court.

She turned back toward her growing entourage. Her body slumped as the adrenaline lost its effect.

Lillian stepped forward and grabbed Samantha by the arm. "Let me take you home now. I'm sure you need to decompress for a bit."

"But what about your trip? You're supposed to be on your way home now." Samantha looked at her watch. "Even if you left now, you'd be getting home pretty late."

"I'll take another day off and leave tomorrow, if that's okay with you. I don't think I can handle a long drive after these last few hours." Lillian rolled her shoulders, as if attempting to release the tension that had lodged behind her neck.

"Plus, Mom is going to want to host a party tonight. Everyone is welcome." Martin nodded specifically at David, signifying that the invitation included him. "Let's say Mom's place around six PM? We'll have a real German celebration!"

Samantha nodded. "We wouldn't miss it." She made eye contact with David, who nodded his head in assent that he would attend.

With that settled, she allowed her mom to lead her to the parking lot. She left her car parked there and climbed into Lillian's front passenger seat for the short ride home.

"You are really lucky, Samantha." Lillian's expression had turned grave again, as she considered an alternate ending to the morning.

"I know." Samantha leaned her head back and closed her eyes.

* * *

Later, at Patty's, the party was in full swing when Samantha and Lillian arrived. Festive brass music played from a sound system outside. The air was redolent with the smell of pork schnitzel in the kitchen and grilling brats, sizzling in the backyard. The space was filled with people Samantha recognized from the lodge.

Patty raced over and wrapped Samantha tightly in a hug. "I can't thank you enough for what you've done. I was afraid that I would never get out of this, but thanks to you . . ." She broke off and hugged her tightly again before turning toward Karl, who was waiting to drag her out to the backyard for a turn on a makeshift dance floor.

Lillian waved to the ladies she had met at the bunko game earlier in the week, but then Martin approached. "Can I borrow Samantha for a minute?"

Samantha nodded her assent to her mother, who joined the bunko ladies.

Martin led her away from the other dancers to a more secluded part of the porch, where it was quieter. "I want to thank you for everything you did for my mom. You risked your life to help her, and I don't know how to repay you."

Samantha felt heat rise in her cheeks and interrupted, but Martin touched her lightly on the shoulder. "I also know that I behaved like a total jerk yesterday, and I'm sorry. I don't want to mess anything up with you and your . . . David. Truly. I want you to be happy."

Samantha smiled. "Thanks, Martin. Now that your mom is safe, I'm happy." Their gaze fell on the dancers, and they watched Karl and Patty start another dance together. It had been a long day, and Samantha didn't want to analyze her feelings any longer. She wanted to enjoy the evening with her friends and family. She leaned over and playfully punched Martin on the shoulder. "Looks like I'm not the only one who's happy. If Karl were any happier, he might explode."

Martin smiled at the couple as they danced. "They may be just what the other one needs."

The friends stood to the side, watching the rest of the party, and then spotted Lillian walking back toward them. "Samantha, I've been talking you up to the ladies from the bunko meeting. They want to meet you."

As they crossed the yard, Lillian reached for her daughter's hand and took it in her own. "I'm proud of everything you've done here, from solving a murder to building a business, to surrounding yourself with great friends. I can't wait to see what's next for you."

Samantha reached over to squeeze her mom into a side hug. "Thanks, Mom."

They chatted for a few minutes with the bunko crowd, then Lillian turned to her daughter. "You know what this celebration needs? One of your cocktails. I want one last cocktail before I have to hit the road tomorrow."

Samantha headed into the kitchen in search of ingredients. Patty's bar was limited, but there was champagne, bourbon, and bitters, so she got to work. Just as she'd sprinkled the last bitters into the cocktail shaker, Marisa and Beth walked into the kitchen.

"If that's what I think it is, make one for us too!" Marisa squeezed Beth's hand and smiled. "We all have a lot to celebrate today."

Smiling, Samantha mixed two more drinks and led her friends out to where her mom waited in the yard. "Look who I found."

"Ladies, it's great to see you." Lillian hugged both of the women before reaching over to snag her drink. "I propose a toast to Samantha."

The ladies raised their glasses, but Samantha interjected before they could raise their glasses to their lips. "And to friends and family who've always got your back."

As they clinked glasses and Samantha savored the champagne, its bubbles popping just under her nose, she looked around her, amazed by the new life she'd managed to build for herself. Her business was growing, her friendships were solid, and she had the love and support of her family.

There wasn't much more that she could ask for . . . still, she found herself scanning the crowd, her eyes searching for something, or someone. She spotted Martin first and smiled as she watched him pull Patty out onto the dance floor. But her gaze didn't rest there for long before she found herself searching again. Finally, from across the patio, her eyes locked on David's warm green eyes.

He strode quickly across the yard until he was by her side. He held out his beer bottle and clinked it with her champagne flute. "I see, you're holding out on the good stuff." His voice was teasing, but Samantha's face warmed. "Oh, I'm happy to make you something if you'd like."

As she turned back toward the kitchen, David grabbed her hand and twirled her back around to face him. "Don't. I've got everything I want right here."

Butterflies flitted around in Samantha's stomach as she met his gaze and smiled, squeezing his hand in her own, suddenly certain of what she wanted. "Me too."

Recipes

Blackberry-Glazed Salmon

1 cup water
12 oz blackberries
1 oz lemon juice
¼ cup sugar
2 T fresh thyme
1-inch piece of ginger, peeled and sliced
1 large salmon filet (2–3 lbs)
1 T olive oil
Salt and freshly ground black pepper

Preheat oven to 350°

In small saucepan over medium heat, combine water, blackberries, lemon juice, ginger, and thyme. Bring to a boil, then reduce to a simmer, allowing the mixture to cook until the berries begin to turn red and break down, about 5–8 minutes.

Remove from heat and strain mixture into a bowl, removing the blackberry seeds.

Add mixture back to the saucepan, add sugar, and bring to a boil. Simmer until mixture thickens and is reduced, about 20–25 minutes. Remove from heat and let cool.

Divide sauce in half.

Place salmon, skin side down, on an aluminum foil–topped baking sheet. Lightly oil the foil, and lightly oil the top of the salmon filets. Season with salt and pepper.

Brush cooled glaze onto the salmon and bake until salmon is cooked through, about 20–25 minutes. Remove from oven and brush more glaze on top. Turn the oven to broil, and broil for 2–3 minutes.

Serve salmon with additional glaze on the side.

Samantha's Grandmother's Fig Cake

2 cups sugar
1 cup vegetable oil
2 eggs
1 tsp baking soda in 1 cup of buttermilk
8 oz of dried figs, chopped
½ tsp salt
½ tsp cloves
½ tsp nutmeg
1 tsp cinnamon
2 cups flour
1 cup pecans chopped
1 tsp vanilla

Preheat oven to 350°

Cream together sugar, oil, and eggs.

Add other ingredients, one by one, mixing well after each addition.

Pour into a greased 9 x 13-inch cake pan. Bake for 1 hour and 15 minutes.

Fig Cake Frosting

2 T butter
2 T fig juice (if fig juice is unavailable, soak dried figs in water for 24 hours, and use 2 T of that water)
1 T lemon juice
½ tsp salt
½ tsp cinnamon
2 cups powdered sugar

Cream the butter.

In small bowl, mix fig juice, salt, lemon juice, and cinnamon.

Add powdered sugar to the butter mixture, alternately with the fig juice mixture, beating after each addition.

When cake is cooled, frost the top.

Samantha's Sparkler Cocktail

2 oz aged white rum
½ oz blue Curaçao
Handful of mint leaves
1 oz lime juice
¼ oz simple syrup
5 dashes Angostura bitters
5 dashes Peychaud's bitters
Crushed ice

Add blue Curaçao to the bottom of a tall, skinny Collins glass.

Fill glass with crushed ice.

In shaker filled with ice, shake together rum, lime juice, mint leaves, and simple syrup until well blended.

Gently pour mixture over the crushed ice, being careful to avoid mixing layers.

Dash 5 dashes of each Angostura and Peychaud's bitters on top.

Garnish with a mint sprig.

Angela's Blackberry Blush

1.5 oz gin
¾ oz blackberry shrub
¾ oz lime juice
Champagne or sparkling wine

In shaker filled with ice, shake gin, blackberry shrub, and lime juice until well mixed and cold.

Pour mixture into coupe glass. Top with champagne or sparkling wine.

Garnish with a blackberry.

Blackberry Shrub

1 cup sugar
1 cup water
2 cups blackberries
2 tsp fresh thyme
1 cup apple cider vinegar

Over medium-high heat, prepare a simple syrup by boiling the water and sugar until the sugar is dissolved. Add blackberries and thyme, and bring mixture to a boil. Simmer it for 10–15 minutes. Add vinegar and allow to simmer for another 10–15 minutes. Strain out and discard the fruit, and pour shrub into a jar. Store in the refrigerator. It will keep for about a month. The shrub can also be mixed with seltzer water or lemonade for a delicious mocktail.

Acknowledgments

While writing may be a solitary endeavor, book publishing most certainly is not. I owe a debt of gratitude to dozens of people who helped to make this book possible.

First and foremost, thank you to my editor, Melissa Rechter, who encouraged me to breathe more life into my characters. Thank you also to the rest of the Crooked Lane team, from the amazing cover designer to the copy editors who caught my worst mistakes.

I want to thank my agent, Dawn Dowdle, and the rest of the Blue Ridge Literary Agency, for the encouragement and support.

My friend, Lis Angus, took time from her busy writing schedule to beta read this book for me. She caught countless inconsistencies and clunky language in my first awful draft and offered wonderful suggestions to get me back on track again. (She's also released an amazing book of her own—*Not Your Child*!)

Thank you to my mom for being a perceptive reader, a constant booster, and my number-one fan. I'm grateful for your love and support always.

To my husband, Edward, thank you for listening patiently, reassuring constantly, and always being willing to test out a crazy cocktail idea. I can't imagine doing any of this without you.

To my daughter, Evaline, who is always ready to brainstorm a recipe idea or a plot point—you bring so much joy to our world. Thank you for making life fun.

For all of my friends and extended family, near and far, who have supported me on this journey, I am so grateful. Lastly, to my readers, thank you for taking the time to read my stories.